PRAIS

BEST-SELLING ROMANCE NOVELS

"A breathtaking tale...I absolutely loved it!"–Romance Junkies on Dark Craving, Dark Kings Series

"The author has created a fantastic and mesmerizing fantasy world with intriguing twists, surprises and unique elements that keeps the reader turning the pages to the very end." –Night Owl Reviews on Dark Heat, Dark Kings Series

"Evie and Malcolm is a couple that makes it impossible not to love them."–The Jeep Diva, Dark Warriors Series

"Grant's smoldering seventh Dark Warrior outing will grip readers from the first page, immersing them in her wounded, lonely couple's journey of redemption...each scene is filled with Grant's clever, complex characters and trademark sizzle."–Romantic Times Magazine (RT Book Reviews), Dark Warriors Series

Don't miss these other spellbinding novels by
NYT & USA Today bestselling author DONNA GRANT

CONTEMPORARY PARANORMAL

REAPER SERIES

DARK KINGS SERIES

Smoke and Fire

Dragon Fever

Firestorm

Blaze

Dragon Burn

Constantine: A History, Part 1

Heat

Constantine: A History, Part 2

Torched

Constantine: A History, Part 3

Dragon Night

Dragonfire

Dragon Claimed

Ignite

Fever

Dragon Lost

Flame

Inferno

The Dragon King Coloring Book

Dragon King Special Edition Character Coloring Book: Rhi

DARK WARRIORS SERIES

Midnight's Master

Midnight's Lover

Midnight's Seduction

Midnight's Warrior

Midnight's Kiss

Midnight's Captive

Midnight's Temptation

Midnight's Promise

Midnight's Surrender

CHIASSON SERIES

Wild Fever

Wild Dream

Wild Need

Wild Flame

Wild Rapture

LARUE SERIES

Moon Kissed

Moon Thrall

Moon Struck

Moon Bound

~

<u>HISTORICAL PARANORMAL</u>

THE KINDRED SERIES

Everkin

Eversong

Everwylde

Everbound

Evernight

Everspell

DARK SWORD SERIES

Dangerous Highlander

Forbidden Highlander

Wicked Highlander

Untamed Highlander

Shadow Highlander

Darkest Highlander

ROGUES OF SCOTLAND SERIES

The Craving

The Hunger

The Tempted

The Seduced

Box Set

THE SHIELDS SERIES

A Dark Guardian

A Kind of Magic

A Dark Seduction

A Forbidden Temptation

A Warrior's Heart

Mystic Trinity (A series connecting novel)

DRUIDS GLEN SERIES

Highland Mist

Highland Nights

Highland Dawn

Highland Fires

Highland Magic

Mystic Trinity (A series connecting novel)

SISTERS OF MAGIC TRILOGY

Shadow Magic

Echoes of Magic

Dangerous Magic

Box Set

THE ROYAL CHRONICLES NOVELLA SERIES

Prince of Desire

Prince of Seduction

Prince of Love

Prince of Passion

Mystic Trinity (A series connecting novel)

Box Set

∽

MILITARY ROMANCE / ROMANTIC SUSPENSE

SONS OF TEXAS SERIES

The Hero

The Protector

The Legend

The Defender

The Guardian

∽

COWBOY / CONTEMPORARY

HEART OF TEXAS SERIES

The Christmas Cowboy Hero

Cowboy, Cross My Heart

My Favorite Cowboy

A Cowboy Like You

Looking for a Cowboy

A Cowboy Kind of Love

Check out Donna Grant's Online Store for autographed books, character themed goodies, and more!

www.DonnaGrant.com/shop

ROGUES OF SCOTLAND BOX SET

BOOKS ONE, TWO, THREE, & FOUR

DONNA GRANT

THE CRAVING

THE HUNGER

THE TEMPTED

THE SEDUCED

ISBN 10: 1942017219

ISBN 13: 978-1942017219

Available in ebook and print editions from DonnaGrant.com

THE CRAVING

ROGUES OF SCOTLAND - BOOK ONE

DONNA GRANT

NYT BEST SELLING AUTHOR OF *THE DARK KINGS SERIES*

PROLOGUE

Highlands of Scotland:
Summer, 1427

Ronan Galt brought his mount to a halt at the top of the mountain, his gaze taking in the majestic view of the wild Highlands. His gaze lowered to the valley below, and a smile broke over his face when he spotted his three friends in the valley.

A small nudge from his knee, and his horse was racing down the mountain, deftly missing the rocks protruding from the ground.

"About time," Stefan grumbled crossly once Ronan reached them.

Ronan raised his brow as he looked into Stefan's hazel gaze. "You might want to reign in that tempter, my friend. We're going to be around beautiful women this night. Women require smiles and sweet words. No' furrowed brows."

There was laughter from everyone but Stefan, who gave Ronan a droll look.

"Aye, we've heard enough about this Ana," Daman said as he turned his mount alongside Ronan's. "Take me to this gypsy beauty so I can see her for myself."

Ronan regarded his friend sternly. "You think to take her from me?"

Daman's confident smile grew as his eyes twinkled in merriment. "Is she that beautiful?"

"Just you try," Ronan dared Daman, only half jesting.

Morcant shoved his long, sandy blond hair out of his eyes with his hand. "Be cautious, Ronan. You wrong a gypsy, and they'll curse you. No' so sure we should be meddling with such people."

Ronan laughed and reined in his jittery mount. "Ah, but with such a willing body, how am I to refuse Ana? Come, my friends, and let us enjoy the bounty that awaits."

He gave a short whistle and his horse surged forward in a run. Ronan didn't wait for his three comrades, because he knew they would follow – no matter what.

It began a decade earlier when they chanced upon one another during the Highland games between their four clans. After that, they made sure to meet regularly until they were as inseparable as brothers. The four formed a friendship that grew tighter with each year that passed.

Ronan looked over his shoulder to find the other three racing each other trying to catch him. He spurred his stallion faster, the wind brushing his face, and the ground a blur beneath his horse's hooves.

One by one, the three caught him. Ronan pulled up, easing his stallion into a canter until they rode their horses four abreast. A glance showed that even Stefan's face had eased into something that could almost be considered a smile.

Ronan grunted when he spotted two riders atop a hill. Even from the distance he recognized the plaid of his clan. It came as no surprise that his laird would have him watched. He was, after all, Ronan's uncle.

He and his friends rode from one glen to another until Ronan finally slowed his horse to a walk. With his friends beside him, they stopped atop the next hill and looked down at the circle of gypsy wagons hidden in the wooded glen below.

"I've a bad feeling," Daman said as he shifted uncomfortably atop his mount. "We shouldna be here."

Morcant's horse flung up his head, but he easily brought his mount under control with soft words. "I've a need to sink my rod betwixt willing thighs. If you doona wish to partake, Daman, then doona, but you willna be stopping me."

"Nor me," Ronan said. Normally he would have listened to Daman, but he had been to the gypsy camp for four days straight and left without any difficulties.

Stefan was silent for several moments before he gave Ronan a nod of agreement.

Ronan was the first to ride down the hill to the camp. A young beauty with long black hair came running out to greet him in her brightly colored skirts. He pulled his horse to a halt and jumped off with a smile as Ana launched herself into his arms.

He caught her and brought his lips down to hers. Ah, but she had the most alluring lips. They could bring him to the point of ecstasy.

"I've missed you," she said in her thick Romanian accent.

"Is that so?" he asked with a wink. He turned her to the others who had ridden up behind him. "Ana, these are my friends, Daman, Morcant, and Stefan," he said, pointing to each of them in turn.

Her smile was wide as she held out her arm. "Welcome to our camp."

Morcant was the first to dismount. He dropped the reins

to allow his horse to graze and walked between two wagons into the center of the camp.

It didn't take Stefan long to follow. Ronan saw the indecision on Daman's face. It was long moments until Daman slid from his horse and gathered the reins of all four mounts to tether them together.

"I'll keep watch," Daman said as he sat outside the camp near a tree.

Ronan wrapped an arm around Ana, briefly wondering why Daman was suddenly wary of the gypsies. Then Ana rubbed her bountiful breasts against him, and Ronan forgot everything but his aching cock.

He didn't give any of his friends a second thought as Ana took him to her wagon. Ronan wasted no time in quickly undressing her. His body was starved, and the gypsy was an enthusiastic and willing accomplice.

Ronan yawned, his body fully sated after hours in Ana's arms. Damn, but the little gypsy knew how to wring pleasure from him. He was lucky to have found her. He closed his eyes and was lulled by the haunting melody of the violins being played around the camp's fire.

He was drifting off to sleep when Ana snuggled against him, one leg thrown over his. She was tenacious about lying against him.

"When will we marry?" she asked.

His drowsy mind was yanked from the fringes of sleep. "Hmm?" Surely he hadn't heard her mention marriage. Theirs was just a mutual meeting of pleasure.

He'd made sure to give her multiple orgasms. Wasn't that enough? Marriage – or any long-term commitment – had never been uttered. He knew that for a fact.

"Marriage, Ronan," she said, rolling the R in his name.

Now he was wide awake, a vise around his chest. His heart thumped, his blood pounded in his ears. Marriage was a word he never wanted associated with him, much less mentioned. It was something he intended never to partake in.

Ever.

He pretended to be asleep hoping Ana would drop the matter. It took great effort for him to remain where he was, and not jump up and ride far, far away.

All he had to do was convince her marriage was a bad idea. Then he would wait until she slept and leave. Never to return.

Perhaps he should have listened to Daman and not visited Ana this night.

She nudged him with a slight laugh. "Wake up, Ronan. You've come to see me for five nights now. You've shared my bed. You've eaten the food I've cooked. It's time to speak with my family about what you plan to do."

Do? What he planned to do was get up and leave. Aye. Fast. How had he gotten into this mess? He thought he'd be safe from any mention of the word marriage by dallying with the gypsies. Apparently he'd been wrong.

"Ronan," she said louder.

He cracked open an eye, feigning sleep. "Aye?"

"Will we leave in the morning to meet your family?"

"Nay, sweet Ana," he said and closed his eyes with a fake yawn. She had given him such enjoyment the last few days, he would let her down gently, and then pleasure her again before he left. Maybe a lie would be best. Yes, a lie. Something where he didn't have to explain his family or his past – or his abhorrence to marriage.

"I'm promised to another."

The bed moved as she flopped on her back and then sat

up. Had he gotten out of the marriage business with just that small lie? Ronan sure hoped so.

He heard her moving about the small wagon. A brief look showed she was gathering her clothes. He'd remain until she was out of the wagon, and then he would sneak out. At least that was his plan until she sank onto the edge of the narrow bed after dressing and began to cry.

How he hated when women used tears. His mother and sister did it often enough, and he was immune to such machinations because of it. His desire for Ana waned to nothing and then quickly turned to revulsion.

Once more a female had tried to use him.

She had succeeded in snaring him with her body, but not marriage. When that hadn't worked, she resorted to tears as they all did.

"I love you, Ronan," Ana murmured.

He squeezed his eyes shut. A part of him, a cruel, vicious part, wanted to tell her that there was no such thing as love. Love was a tool used by women to entrap men. His father had fallen into such a trap, as had his brother-in-law.

Ronan had tried to tell his brother-in-law, but the besotted fool had actually thought Ronan's sister loved him. What she loved was the money her husband had.

A memory from when Ronan was just a lad filled his mind. He witnessed a fight between his parents where his father vowed his love, and his mother laughed in his face. Then and there Ronan knew that love was just a word. There was no meaning, no emotion that poets wrote about or minstrels sang about.

He blew out a harsh breath and rose from the bed as he grabbed his kilt. "I think it's time I left."

"No marriage?" Ana asked, tears pouring heedlessly down her face.

Ronan gave a quick jerk of his head side to side and

fastened his kilt. Ana cried even harder as she rushed from the wagon. He let out a deep breath and pulled on his boots. After his sword was belted into place he found his saffron shirt.

Just as he was reaching for it he heard an anguished scream, a soul-deep, fathomless cry that was drug from the depths of someone's soul.

Ronan forgot about the shirt as he leapt from the wagon, his hand on the hilt of his sword, ready to battle whatever had disrupted the camp.

He looked one way and then the other for the threat, but found only Daman standing outside the wagons. He was staring past Ronan with a resigned expression on his face. Ronan turned and found the old woman, Ilinca, who was often with Ana, looking down at something in the grass.

Ronan took a step toward her and instantly came to a halt when he spotted Ana's bright pink and blue skirts. Even in the fading light of evening there was no mistaking the dark stain upon the grass as anything but blood.

"What the hell," Morcant said as he exited a wagon still fastening his kilt.

The night of pleasure and laughter Ronan had envisioned with his friends seemed as far away as the stars in the sky. He wanted to go to Ana, but with the dagger sticking out of her stomach – and her hand still around it – the last place he needed to be was the gypsy camp.

They would blame her suicide on him, all because he refused to take her as his wife.

"Ronan," Stefan called urgently as he stood amid a group of gypsies.

There would be no walking away. If Ronan wanted to leave with his life, he and his friends were going to have to fight their way through the group of gypsies who stood with various weapons.

Before he could pull out his sword, Ilinca let loose a shriek and pointed her gnarled finger at him. Ronan was frozen, unable to move or even speak.

Words tumbled from Ilinca's mouth, her wrinkled face a mask of grief and fury. He may not comprehend the words, but he knew they could be nothing good. Especially since she was somehow holding him immobile.

Morcant, however, wasn't in such a bind. He rushed to Ilinca with his sword raised, but in a heartbeat, the old woman had him frozen in his tracks as well.

A bellow of anger rose up in Ronan, but he couldn't let it loose. He was only able to shift his eyes. He tried desperately to silently tell Stefan and Daman to run, but he should've known his friends wouldn't leave.

The ever-present rage exploded in Stefan and he let out a battle cry worthy of his clan as he leapt over the fire toward Ilinca. But once more, the old gypsy used her magic to halt him.

Her gaze shifted, and Ronan found his own on Daman. Daman glanced at the ground and inhaled deeply. Then, with purposeful strides, crossed some unseen barrier into the camp.

Instantly, Ronan's head exploded with pain. He squeezed his eyes shut, but there was no blocking it out. It seemed to go on for eternity.

As quickly as it came, it was gone. When he opened his eyes, there was nothing but blackness. There was no sound, no movement.

"This is for my Ana," Ilinca's disembodied voice in her thick Romanian accent suddenly declared around him. "You killed her as surely as if you held the blade yourself. For that I curse you, Ronan Galt. Forever will you be locked in here until such time as you earn your freedom."

Ronan turned one way and then the other. He ran until

he couldn't run any more, and then went another direction and ran for miles. And still it was always the same.

Blackness.

Where were Daman, Morcant, and Stefan? How was he supposed to earn his freedom? He hated the stillness, hated the silence. But more than anything, he hated being alone.

CHAPTER 1

Ravensclyde Castle:
Northern Scotland 1609

"Nay!" Meg Alpin screamed as two wolfhounds bounded around her. They knocked her off her feet to land in a tangle of skirts, though they did nothing to cushion her fall. "You great big oafs!"

No amount of scolding could rein in the dogs now that they were inside the room. The white sheets draped over the furniture were only something for them to pull off and play tug-of-war with.

Meg shook her head and climbed to her feet as she dusted herself off. She then put her hands on her hips and rolled her eyes. As if she didn't already have enough on her hands. As mad as she wanted to be at the wolfhounds, she couldn't quite manage it.

She understood what it was to be left behind. The dogs had been all but forgotten until she arrived three months earlier. She had lavished them with affection and attention. In return, they had become the animals they should have been – loyal, protective, clever. And with their antics, they were obviously making up for lost time.

"Enough!" she called and clapped her hands together.

The two wolfhounds immediately dropped the sheet they had been tugging between them and loped over to her. She gave them a rub on their heads and pointed out the door.

"Go chase some rabbits."

With their tongues lolling out of their mouths, the wolfhounds took off at a dead run, skittering around a corner before disappearing – loudly – down the stairs. There was a distant shriek, letting Meg know the dogs had scared one of the maids again.

She was smiling even as she shook her head. The wolfhounds might think she was their savior, but the dogs had helped her as well. Most nights she had one on each side of her in the bed. Somehow, they always knew when she would give in to her tears. They would leave their spots before the fire and jump up on the bed to lay with her, as if protecting her from the memories that wouldn't let go.

Meg squared her shoulders and took a look around the large room, her eyes flitting over each covered piece. Her great-aunt had offered her refuge at Ravensclyde. In doing so, Aunt Tilly had given her leave to rearrange the castle as Meg saw fit.

After nearly a month of sitting and staring off into nothing with a book in her lap, reliving the last half year of her life, she finally realized that if she didn't do something she would waste away to nothing.

Since she needed to occupy her days – and her mind - going through the old furniture that was stored in the top floor of the tower seemed a great place to start.

Meg pulled the first sheet off what turned out to be a large wardrobe and promptly began coughing from all the dust. She waved away the particles she could see in the sunlight that filtered through the windows.

She turned her head before pulling the sheet off the second item, a side table. One by one, Meg exposed the long-forgotten furniture, her smile growing by the minute.

For a brief space of time, she was able to think of Ravensclyde as hers. All the worries, all the heartache of the past year could be pushed away – and hopefully forgotten. Even if it wasn't, Ravensclyde was giving Meg the time she needed to right her crumbling world.

She took the noon meal in the tower room so she could continue looking over her findings. Some were crumbling into dust, and others were too chipped or faded to put out. Already Meg knew where she would put the wardrobe, three side tables, a landscape painting, two tapestries, and a bench.

There was a settee with three matching chairs she was considering having recovered to put in the parlor to brighten up the room.

With the last bite in her mouth, Meg dusted off her hands and stood to wander around the pieces. She had hoped to find more – and Aunt Tilly had led her to believe there was much more – but she would make do with the few items she had found.

She would have repairs started on the others immediately. There was history in all of the pieces, and she wanted to see all of it every day.

Meg walked around a buffet table that needed to be sanded down and repainted. She took a step back to get a better view of the side, and ran into the wall.

And heard the click of a door latch.

She immediately turned to see that a door had come open. A door she had been too busy looking at furniture to notice.

Meg pushed open the door and leaned her head inside. A

slow smile spread over her face when she saw another room, twice the size of the one she was just in, and filled with more covered furniture.

Immediately she began to move from piece to piece uncovering them. It wasn't until she neared the far left corner that she spotted a tall covered piece set aside, as if separated from the rest.

Curious, Meg walked toward it. With each step, a prickling stole over her skin that was a peculiar and exciting mixture of foreboding and anticipation.

When she lifted her hand to grasp the sheet, she found it shaking.

Suddenly, the tower was too quiet, the room too still. She forced a laugh, hoping the sound of her own voice would help calm her.

It didn't.

"How silly I'm being," she said aloud and swallowed. "I wanted to be here by myself."

Meg took a deep breath once she realized how foolish she was being. And with a yank, pulled down the sheet.

To find a huge mirror.

It might look like a mirror, but it couldn't be because it didn't reflect her or her surroundings. There was nothing but darkness in the glass. It gaped around her, seeming to suck all the light from the room.

Meg shivered and hastily threw the sheet back over the mirror before she ran out of the tower as if flames were licking at her heels.

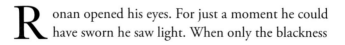

R onan opened his eyes. For just a moment he could have sworn he saw light. When only the blackness met his gaze, he realized he must have been dreaming of sunshine.

Again.

How much time had passed? There was no way to tell, and he probably didn't want to know. It seemed lifetimes ago that he had stood with his friends in a gypsy camp eager to ease the ache of his cock between Ana's beautiful thighs.

Twice before he had been let out of the mirror. The first time he had been so shocked he hadn't realized what was going on. The woman had been startled by his sudden appearance and ran screaming from the room.

Ronan had taken his chance and climbed out the window, scaled the wall of the castle, and started running across the countryside.

He got away. Or so he thought. Two days later, he woke up back in that room with the female staring down at him angrily. Next to her was an old woman who had the dark eyes of a gypsy.

Ronan had reached out his hand, in the middle of begging them to let him stay, when the mirror sucked him back in.

The second time, he was more prepared. As soon as he was thrown out of the mirror, he gave the young lass a charming smile.

She was a rather plain female, but the seduction that had always come easy to him failed, as she hastily sent him back. That's how he discovered it was a mirror he was in. And that the mirror belonged to the Alpin family.

Both times he had been in Scotland, but a quick glance at the women's clothes told him that a considerable space of time had passed in both incidences.

Ronan let out a loud sigh and closed his eyes again. He wondered where his friends were, what they were doing, and how they had lived their lives.

Were they dead? Had they found wives? Did they have children?

Had they tried to find him?

He knew the answer to his last question. Of course they had. Morcant, Daman, and Stefan were his brothers. Not once had any of them not been there for the others.

Ronan wished he could let them know he was all right. Maybe they could figure out how to free him. Magic might have put him here, but the old gypsy had told him there was a way to earn his freedom.

He didn't realize until it was too late how he had taken everything for granted. The sunlight, the taste of food, staring at the moon, swimming the cold waters of the loch, making love to a pretty lass, the excitement of battle, or just sharing a dram of whisky with his friends.

The darkness he was bound to had brought to light one thing – he should have handled Ana better.

So many times he had gone over that night in his head and said something different, done something different. His abhorrence to wanting a wife was not Ana's fault. She might have blindsided him with her question of marriage, but he shouldn't have been so callous.

It never entered his mind that she would kill herself. She was young and beautiful, holding an allure only a gypsy could.

She claimed to love him, and once he had said no to marriage, she took her life. All his dealings with love had proven it wasn't worth pursuing.

Another lesson learned, and one he'd known before Ana. His mother and sister had taught him all too well.

Ronan rubbed a hand down his face. At least in the cursed mirror he didn't have to worry about shaving, eating, or growing old. It was like all of that had been muted.

The one thing that wasn't muted? His need.

It was agonizing, excruciating to be in such a constant state of arousal with nothing to relieve him. He had tried many times, unsuccessfully, to ease himself. Always he was left wanting, needy.

He didn't know what was worse – the loneliness, or the ever-present craving to ease his heated flesh.

If he ever got the chance to get outside the mirror again, he would do everything in his power to remain and get free of the damn mirror once and for all.

Ronan stilled. Was that...could it be...

He opened his eyes and gasped when he saw the light shining through the mirror. He sat up and stood, the light beckoning him. Ronan was powerless to ignore it, not that he would.

His one thought, one goal was to get out of the mirror once and for all. The old gypsy had gotten her wish. He had atoned for what happened to Ana. Now it was time to live his life.

When Ronan reached the light, he tried to step through the mirror, but he couldn't. He didn't know what had to happen to pull him out. All he knew was that it wasn't happening now.

He was getting a peek at the light and a room he didn't recognize. There was no one in sight, no Alpin woman who had summoned him.

At least that's what he assumed took place. Then again, he knew next to nothing about what was going on with the mirror or how it was connected to him.

Ronan put his hand against the invisible barrier that kept him in his dark prison. The light touched his skin, the heat of it sinking into his pores and racing along his hand to his arm and then over his body.

How he longed to bask in the sun, to stand beneath the moon, to feel the rain upon his skin.

A soft, very feminine sigh broke him from his thoughts. Ronan's breath caught in his lungs. He silently prayed and begged to any deity who would listen to let him out of the mirror.

He searched for the woman to no avail. He couldn't see her, but she was near. Whatever was covering the mirror had slid part-ways off.

"I can't," said a female voice laced with a Scottish brogue. "I can't look in that mirror again."

The barrier holding Ronan evaporated, sending him face-first against the wooden boards of a floor. His arms caught himself before his face could hit. He stood, scrambling away from the mirror and looking around.

He immediately went to the window. Ronan took in a deep breath and closed his eyes as the sunlight hit his face.

Free at last.

And he was going to make damn sure he stayed that way.

CHAPTER 2

Meg stared in silent wonder at the man standing before the window, soaking in the sun as if he had never felt its heat before.

His hair was long, falling just past his shoulders, and the color was a deep brown bordering on black. Even from his profile she could see the hard line of his jaw. Her eyes drifted lower and her heart slammed into her ribcage. The man wore no shirt with his kilt, displaying an abundance of thick, corded muscles.

Meg pulled her eyes away, but in an instant she was back to staring. His arms hung casually at his sides, but there was nothing cavalier about the man. He was a warrior, a man who went after whatever he wanted – and got it.

She saw the scars covering his torso, proving he had seen his share of battles. Yet they did nothing to detract from his allure. In fact, his prowess inflamed her blood.

Meg didn't recognize the woman responding so...flagrantly to the stranger. No man had ever made her stomach flutter or her skin dew just thinking about him. Her blood was pounding in her ears, her heart beating fast and furious as her hands itched to run over his body and learn every contour.

Suddenly the man's eyes opened. For several heartbeats he stared out the window. Then, slowly, he turned his head to her.

Meg's breath locked in her lungs and her knees threatened to buckle. If she thought the stranger was appealing before, she was wholly unprepared for when he faced her.

He was Adonis, so blindingly handsome that she couldn't fathom what he was doing in her tower. He was the kind of man women fought over – and killed over. He was the kind of man who looked at anyone but Meg.

And yet, his beautiful pale green eyes were focused directly on her. The dark brown eyebrows slashed fiercely over his eyes, and his nose was slightly crooked from having been broken a time or two. His square jaw and chin only heightened his sexiness. However, it was his wide lips - with the bottom fuller than the top - that made her blood race in her veins.

He embodied virility and masculinity, almost as if he had created the two simply by being born.

"Hello, lass."

The sound of such a smooth, deep voice did something strange and glorious to Meg. Was there nothing about the man she didn't like?

"Who are you?" she managed to ask around her thumping heart.

The stranger gave a slight bow of his head, his gaze never leaving hers. "Ronan Galt, at your service. And you are?"

And she was what? It took a moment for Meg to realize he was asking her name. Could she make a bigger fool of herself? "I'm Meg. Meg Alpin."

"Meg." He said her name slowly, letting it fall from his lips as if a prayer.

At this rate, she would be a puddle of nothing. God help her if he came toward her.

Ronan couldn't take his eyes off the fetching Meg. It could have been because he spent so much time alone in his dark prison, but he found her...refreshing. Her auburn hair, having come loose of its pins, was falling about her face in tempting waves.

He wanted to know how long her hair was. And he wanted to feel it slide through his fingers. As much as her hair tempted him, the woman was simply luscious. She had curves to make a saint's mouth water with desire.

Full breasts, a small waist, and flared hips begged for his touch. Her large, expressive gray eyes watched him like an eagle. With her pert nose, wide forehead, and gently arching auburn brows, she would be an invitation for any man.

But it was her high cheekbones and plump, kissable lips that truly made her a temptation no man could pass up.

Meg. The name suited her. Part imp, part seductress. She could have a man on his knees in a matter of moments if she so wanted. But did she know her power?

By the wariness that stole over her gaze, Ronan realized she didn't. That was fortunate for him.

"How did you get in here?" she asked nervously.

He could listen her to soft lilt all day. She was temptation in the most beautiful package, and the constant, aching need he'd had for so long was difficult to control.

All Ronan wanted to do was push her against the wall and kiss her inviting lips while removing her gown so he could look his fill at her womanly curves.

"I'm no' sure you'd believe me if I told you."

She raised an auburn brow, anxiety replaced with strength. "Try me."

Ronan glanced at the hated mirror. Everything hinged on getting this beguiling, beautiful woman to believe him and let him remain in her world. If he couldn't, he would be forced back into the hated mirror once more. He had to gain his freedom.

He slowly released a deep breath and motioned to the mirror with his hand. "From there."

The disbelief on Meg's face was just what he expected. "From the mirror?"

"Did you no' pull the sheet down, lass? There was naught to see, was there? Just blackness, a void that stretched endlessly."

She took a step back, fear and confusion mixing on her lovely face. "I don't understand."

"I didna either for a long time." He'd never had a chance to explain himself before, and he worried he would say the wrong thing. So much had never ridden on so little. "The first Alpin woman who released me sent me back into my prison before I could tell her anything. The second gave me a little more time, but no' much. This is just my third time."

"Alpin?" she asked with a small frown marring her forehead as she looked from him to the mirror and back to him. "My ancestors? That's not possible."

"There is much that is possible with magic."

"Magic?" she repeated, as if testing the word on her lips. For long moments she stared at him as if trying to decide if he was daft or not.

Ronan bit back the words that wanted to tumble from his mouth. He was prepared to fall upon his knees and beg her for at least a full day so he could see the sun and the moon, taste food and ale, and perhaps ease the ache of his cock. Instead, he stood staring at her, silently willing her to give him a chance.

Relief poured through him as she said, "I'm not saying I believe you, but how long have you been in the mirror?"

"What year is it?" he asked, almost afraid to hear the

answer.

"1609."

Disappointment speared Ronan. It was as he feared. He hadn't just spent decades in that awful mirror. He had spent centuries.

"Ronan?"

He met her gaze, surprised to find pity in her stormy depths. "Nearly two hundred years it seems."

Silence filled the room as their gazes locked – hers unsure, his accepting. Ronan didn't know if she was attempting to believe him, but it didn't matter. He was taken aback at the fact that his friends, the men he considered brothers, were long dead. He would never see them again, never share a keg of whisky, never ride into battle together.

The sadness that fell over him was debilitating, devastating. Unbearable.

What was he going to do now?

Meg bit her lip as she studied Ronan's face. He was visibly shaken by the realization that two centuries had passed. She wanted to toss him out on his arse for the liar that he was, but the more she watched him, the more she began to believe him.

No one could fake such alarm. As difficult as that was to watch, it was the sorrow, the grief that filled his light green eyes that broke her heart.

"Did you leave a wife behind?" she asked hesitantly.

Ronan shook his head as he turned to stare out the window once more. "Nay. It's my friends I mourn. We were brothers in every sense of the word."

The desolation in his voice made her throat close up with emotion. What did one say in response? She couldn't think of anything that would help.

Meg looked around, her gaze going to the mirror. It had been nothing but blackness when she looked into it before.

If...magic...had been used, and he had been stuck in that awful thing for two centuries, she couldn't imagine how he was feeling.

She bit back a snort. Nor could she comprehend that she was even considering his words as truth. He might very well be jesting with her, but the simple fact was that one moment he hadn't been there, and then the next he had.

Magic or not, trickery or not, he was a man who was deep in torment. "Are you hungry?"

A small grin flitted over his lips. "I've no' eaten in so long I no longer remember the taste of food."

"That I can remedy," Meg said with a nod. She had a purpose now. To feed Ronan. That she could do easily enough.

She turned and hurried out of the rooms to the stairway. Halfway down she realized she hadn't asked him to stay put. But then again, where would he go? Back into the mirror?

Meg ordered a tray of food to be brought up to the tower and dashed back up as quickly as she could. She was out of breath by the time she walked into the room.

Her gaze immediately went to the window, but Ronan was nowhere to be found. A quick scan showed nothing. Had he really gone back in the mirror?

Just as she was walking to the object in question, Ronan came out from behind the mirror, his attention focused entirely on the large piece.

"How long has this been in your family?"

Meg shrugged and came to a stop when she realized how close to him she had gotten. Seeing him from a distance was difficult enough, but up close he robbed her of her will. "This isn't my home. It's my great-aunt's. I'm staying for a bit."

At her words, Ronan's green gaze shifted to her. "Why are you no' married? I'd have expected some man to have stolen your heart already."

Meg swallowed and turned to the doorway as memories threatened. "The food will be up soon. As a matter of fact, I think I hear Mary on the stairs."

She fled, like the coward she was, from Ronan and his questions. For a little while, she had forgotten what had sent her to Ravensclyde. Those precious few moments had been amazing.

"Put it here, Mary," Meg directed the maid to a small table more suited for teacups than a large tray filled to the brim with food.

"You barely ate your luncheon, my lady," Mary said eyeing the tray.

Meg smiled. "Exactly. I've found my appetite."

"That's good to hear," Mary said with a sigh. "We were most worried about you. You need more meat on that thin frame of yours, milady."

With those words, Mary was gone, leaving Meg alone with Ronan. Meg wasn't sure why she didn't want anyone else to know about Ronan. Maybe because he could just be a figment of her imagination.

Or it could be that she didn't want to explain how he arrived.

Mostly, she realized it was because she didn't want to share him yet.

"Why are they worried over you, sweet Meg?"

His words, spoken so near her, made her stomach flutter. Meg shifted to the side a couple of steps so she could see him. "I was ill."

"Ill? And they let you up here to sort through these rooms alone?" he asked suspiciously, almost angrily.

Meg pulled up a stool that looked capable of holding Ronan and pointed to the tray. "Please. Eat."

Thankfully his attention was diverted to the food. He inhaled deeply, a smile on his face as he sat. He looked at each item in turn before he reached for the mug of ale. In short order he polished off the entire tray. Meg sat and watched him savor each bite as if he would never eat again.

Once he had finished the last chicken leg, she asked, "How did you get in the mirror?"

There was the slightest pause in his movements as he wiped his hands and mouth. "I'm no' sure it's a story you want to know."

"I assure you it is. The more I know, the better I can make my decision."

"And what will you do with me if you doona believe me, sweet Meg?" he asked softly, those stunning eyes of his pinning her to the chair. "Will you send me back just to see if you can?"

"I'm not that cruel."

He looked her over and shook his head. "Nay, I doona believe you are."

"It's all just so hard to believe."

At this he snorted. "Hard to believe there's magic? In Scotland? Lass, you should know the mountains are full of it."

"I've never seen magic," she admitted, hating the tremor in her voice.

His head cocked to the side. "Did you look in my mirror today?"

"Aye."

"Did you see your reflection?"

"I did not."

"That is because magic was used to give you a glimpse into my prison."

"That place scares me."

He sighed and reached for the ale. Just before he brought the mug to his lips he said, "It's good at doing that."

CHAPTER 3

Ronan no more wanted to talk about what had happened that fateful night – two hundred years ago – than he wanted to think about it. But if he was going to be free from the damned mirror, he had to convince Meg never to send him back.

He could try to lie to her, but he had a feeling the woman would know immediately. That only left the truth – as hard as it was to acknowledge.

"I was with my friends, Daman, Morcant, and Stefan," he said. "Though we were all from different clans, we were together more than we were apart. If one of us needed something, the other three would be there."

Meg's lips turned up in a small smile. "That sounds nice. I've never had anything like that."

"I took it for granted, just as I did everything else." Damn. Those words were more truth than he had ever acknowledged, even to himself. "I loved to have fun, and took advantage of every opportunity that presented itself. When a band of gypsies came to the land of Daman's clan, I was the first to visit."

"Why?" Meg asked, her brow knitted in confusion. "Did you want your fortune told?"

Ronan drained the last of the ale from the goblet and gently set it down. "A woman caught my eye. With her black hair and eyes, her dark skin, and the vibrant colors she wore, she was stunning."

"Ah. I see."

"I wasna a man to take a woman's innocence," Ronan stated when he saw the condemnation on Meg's face. "Ana wasna an innocent. I didna force her either."

"Nay, I don't imagine you had to. I'm sure she was as enamored with your good looks as you were with her."

Ronan shrugged. "Regardless, we found pleasure in each other's arms. I would come to her at night, and leave before the dawn. I assumed our relationship was one of mutual pleasure and nothing more."

"But she wanted more," Meg guessed.

"That she did." Ronan set his hands on his legs and sighed. "On that last night, I brought my friends with me to partake in what the gypsies freely offered. It had never entered my mind that Ana would assume I wanted her as my wife."

Meg's face scrunched up, something haunted and broken flashing in her gray eyes. "You broke her heart."

Ronan stood and walked around the room amidst the furniture. "I told her there would be no marriage between us. When that didna stop her words, I thought a small lie would. I told her I was already promised to another. She ran crying from the wagon."

"I take it the gypsies weren't happy?"

"I doona think I'll ever know. I was getting ready to leave the camp when I heard a scream. I jumped out of the wagon ready to defend the gypsies when I saw Ana. She had taken her own life. Because I wouldna marry her."

Meg wiped at a strand of hair tickling her cheek. "The gypsies cursed you, didn't they?"

"The old woman did. I think she might have been Ana's grandmother. She sent me into the black void. I didna realize it was a mirror until the second time I was released."

"Are you cursed to remain in the mirror forever?"

Ronan turned and faced her. "The old woman said I would be in there until I earned my freedom."

"What does that mean?" Meg asked as she leaned forward.

"It means, sweet Meg, that if you doona send me back, I'll be free."

Her back straightened. "Oh. Is that all? Fine. I won't send you back."

Ronan nearly shouted with joy. It hadn't taken nearly as much effort on his part to convince Meg as he thought it might. He'd felt the sun, had a delicious meal, and no longer had the mirror to worry about.

Best of all, he had engaged in conversation with a most enticingly beautiful woman. And he found himself hungry for something else.

"Why are you here, Meg?"

Suddenly twitchy, she rose to her feet and shrugged. "I needed a place to think. Aunt Tilly offered Ravensclyde, and I accepted the invitation. Now, back to you. What are you going to do?"

"Do?" Ronan hadn't thought about that. His attention had been focused on getting free, not what would happen once he did. He expected it to take days - weeks even - to convince Meg to release him.

It had gone frighteningly easy. That sent a niggle of worry down his spine. Nothing that came easy was good.

Ronan pushed that concern to the side for a moment.

With Stefan, Daman, and Morcant dead, there was no one for him to find. And nowhere for him to go.

He was homeless, penniless, and friendless. A hell of a problem to find himself in. Then he looked at Meg again, an idea taking root. "Do you need help around the castle?"

Her mouth twisted as she shook her head. "Not really." She paused as if considering his words. "Then again, you don't know anyone or the times. I'm not sure I should just let you go out on your own."

"I'll be fine, I assure you."

"Things are different than when you knew them."

Ronan smiled. "So you believe my tale, sweet Meg."

"I'm not saying that," she replied saucily. "But I'm leaning in that direction. Too much doesn't add up. Your tartan is an old weave for one."

He closed the distance between them and smiled when he realized he had her backed against the chair with nowhere to run. "Where is your man, sweet Meg?"

Her gaze darted away before coming back to his. He made her nervous, and by the rapid pulse beat at the base of her neck and the way her eyes darkened when she looked at him, her body had a reaction to him.

"I don't have a man," she said in a husky whisper.

Ronan's gaze dropped to her lips. They would taste as sweet as wine. "Their loss."

Meg slipped to the side and backed away from Ronan. He was more than temptation. He was sin, begging her to sample what he offered.

And did she ever want a taste of it.

"If you're in need of a woman, I'm sure you'll find plenty willing to accommodate you throughout the castle."

Ronan's smile was predatory, as if he knew she wanted to give in to the desires heating her body. If he only knew just how much she yearned to do just that.

"How will you explain my appearance?" he asked.

Meg grimaced. "I don't know yet. You can't just come down with me."

"Why no'?"

Why not, indeed? She was in charge of the castle for the moment. Already a story was forming about Ronan, clarifying his position as someone who just arrived seeking work. It wasn't a lie. She just wouldn't tell anyone he came from a mirror.

"You can remain for as long as you need. During that time, you may help around the castle. Follow me, and I'll introduce you to everyone."

She turned on her heel and walked out of the room to the stairs. Ronan was one step behind her. His presence was comforting, even as he put her on edge.

Days turned into weeks, and during that time Ronan thought of Meg, of leaning over her, her soft curves cushioning him before he thrust inside her. There was something very compelling about her. Ronan couldn't pinpoint exactly what it was, but he knew it was more about the woman herself than the fact he had been alone for so long.

He hungered for food and the pleasures of the flesh.

He craved the feel of the rain upon his skin.

He yearned for the sun and the wind.

But Meg's presence dimmed everything else.

There was pain in her gray eyes, but the light within her brightened all. She was tempting, arousing, and fierce without even knowing it.

Ronan had been given odd jobs throughout the castle. The fact there wasn't much for him to do showed how well run the castle truly was.

He would often find himself near Meg, and he used every opportunity to speak with her in the hopes of learning more about her. Each time he made her laugh was a small triumph.

As the days flew by, he found himself searching for her to make sure she was within reach and safe. When he wasn't checking on Meg, he was working outside any chance he got so he could bask in the sun.

It had felt good to use his muscles and his mind. How he used to complain about the menial work his uncle made him perform. Wouldn't his uncle be laughing now if he could see that Ronan was looking for work to occupy him.

A month to the day that he had been freed from his prison, he waited for Meg. Three nights in a row he had woken with a feeling that he needed to go to the mirror, and every night that feeling increased. It unsettled him, because he feared he might not have a choice of remainin and making a life. He could be back in the hated mirror regardless of what Meg said.

He pushed away from the wall and smiled when he spotted her walking from the castle with a basket laden with food. He quickly fell into step beside her. "Need some help?"

He didn't give her time to answer as he took the basket. Her strides were long and purposeful as her gaze darted to the ominous clouds that filled the sky.

"Did you sleep well?" she asked as she nodded in passing to a man tending to the horses.

"I didna sleep." Even in the night he was battered on all sides by the sounds and sights around him. It was so different than the silent blackness he had known for so long. As he soaked it all in, sleep was the farthest thing from his mind.

His chamber – on an opposite side of the castle from Meg's – had a lovely view. Yet, he found himself standing outside her door most nights fighting his desire to taste her lips and skin. He wouldn't go uninvited into her room when she was offering him a roof over his head, food in his stomach, and most especially, freedom from the mirror.

But how he hungered for her.

So much so, that when he had found a willing woman, he had walked away. Him. Walked away! It unheard of. Particularly when his cock ached for relief.

The maid's kisses had been experienced, her body soft, but she hadn't been Meg. Even now he couldn't believe he had left a willing female to instead stand guard outside Meg's door with desire burning through him.

She frowned as she cut her eyes to him. "Aren't you tired?"

"When there is only darkness around you, there's no need to open your eyes. I feel as if I've slept away years. I want to take it all in while I have the chance."

"You still think I'm going to send you back," she said, appalled. "I said I wouldn't."

He shrugged. It wasn't like Ronan could tell her he didn't trust women. He knew them to be manipulative, devious creatures who wanted nothing more than their own pleasures.

Meg came to a halt. It took a moment for Ronan to realize that she had stopped, so he was a couple of paces ahead before he paused and turned to look at her.

Her gray eyes blazed with fury as the wind whipped at the strands of her auburn hair that had come loose of the simple braid. "You think I'm lying. Me!"

Ronan shifted the basket to his other hand and braced himself. First there was anger, and then women cried. He hoped Meg wouldn't shed any tears. It would ruin everything. "Two other women have sent me back."

"I don't know how I called you out of the mirror, so it just goes to show that I don't know how to send you back.

Plus I told you I wouldn't. Obviously, you take a woman's word as nothing."

"It was a woman who put me in the mirror."

Meg's eyes widened in annoyance. "Oh, well then never mind that you refused to wed her granddaughter after bedding her."

"I didna kill Ana," Ronan said in a low voice. He was surprised at the anger that rose up so quickly. He was many things, but he wasn't a murderer.

The ire evaporated from Meg's face instantly. "You're right. You didn't. Ana was weak. Men regularly go back on vows and seduce women with false promises, and we survive. Ana should have as well. Men aren't worth the time, and they certainly aren't worth our souls."

Ronan could only stare after Meg as she walked past him onto the worn road from the castle. There had been something in her voice, a note of regret and desolation that was like a sword through his gut.

He wanted to know what had happened to her, but more than that, he wanted to know who had hurt her. She was a gentle spirit, but he had glimpsed the fire and passion in her gaze. She was a beauty waiting to break through the chains holding her back.

With little effort, Ronan caught up with Meg. They walked in silence for a while. He kept going over what she had said in his mind. There was no doubt some man had forsaken her. Had he stolen her innocence and refused to marry her?

The idea made Ronan grip the handle of the basket so hard that it creaked in protest. Gradually, he loosened his hand until he had his rage under control.

"You doona trust men," he said into the silence. "Why are you trusting me, lass?"

She looked at him with wide gray eyes and smiled tightly. "Oh, I don't."

"I doona understand. Why let me have my freedom then? Why allow me to sleep in the castle, to work and eat there?"

They came to a small rundown cottage, and Meg stopped and reached into the basket. "You didn't hurt me, Ronan, and everyone needs a second chance to build their lives."

"Is that what you're doing? Building your life?"

She laughed, but the sound was forced. "Nay. Mine was over before it ever began."

He could only watch as she knocked on the cottage door and handed cheese and a loaf of bread to a woman so bent with age she couldn't stand straight.

There were no more words as he walked beside her to the next cottage where five small children gathered around her before she could even get to the door.

The pleasure on her face as she interacted with them was evident. Meg was a woman made to be a mother. She nourished and encouraged as if it were second nature. And the children responded to her.

For once, he was looking at a woman as something more than a source of pleasure. He was seeing Meg, really seeing her. It was something new, and it felt as if the earth had been yanked out from beneath him.

Women were all the same. Weren't they?

Weeks ago he would have said yes, but after meeting Meg and coming to know her, he was reevaluating his ideas. She hadn't manipulated him into giving her anything. She hadn't cried or used her body.

She had, however, given him the one thing he wanted above all – freedom. While asking for nothing in return.

Was that why he felt compelled to remain near her? Was that why he desired her as deeply as he did?

She may have acted differently than any other woman he knew, but he wasn't yet convinced that she wouldn't become what he had learned women truly were.

Still...he couldn't stop thinking about Meg.

Ronan propped a hip against the stone wall surrounding the cottage. The roof was in desperate need of repair, and the stack of wood for the fire only had a few logs left. As he catalogued what needed to be done, he took note of how Meg gave a treat to each child that sent them running around the yard with bright smiles and laughter.

By the time Meg rejoined him, a serene smile was in place.

"What?" she asked when she saw him staring.

"You should have children of your own."

She licked her lips and brushed past him to continue on the road without responding.

"Do you deny you want children?" he asked, unsure why it seemed so important to him.

"Nay."

That one word held a wealth of meaning – fear, pain. But more than that, there was resignation.

CHAPTER 4

Meg was surprised Ronan joined her as she visited the sick tenants. She hated the way her body responded to him, loathed how she tried to brush against him in any effort to feel him. She was pathetic in her need to be near him, and yet she refused to send him away.

As if he would do what she wanted. Ronan was stubborn and thick headed. He would do whatever it was he wished. She was thrilled that for the moment she was some kind of fascination for him. It wouldn't last, which was why she would soak it up now.

Her arm heated where she knew his gaze landed. The heat traveled to her neck, and then to her chest. Her breasts swelled and her nipples tightened. Just knowing he was watching her made her heartbeat accelerate.

"Where are the parents from the last cottage we visited?" he asked.

Meg swallowed twice, trying to get moisture back to her mouth. She was grateful for the change of subject. She didn't want to think about her life without a husband or children. All she had ever wanted was a family of her own to cherish.

"Their mother died last winter trying to bring another babe into the world. The babe didn't make it either. The father was desolate after his wife died, which is understandable. He spent his nights drinking away his pain. It caused him to fall and break his ankle when he was trying to bring in some sheep."

"How long until he gets back on his feet?"

Meg gave a little shrug. "A few more weeks. I know there is a young girl from a neighboring cottage that comes over when she can to cook and look after the young ones."

Ronan nodded as he listened, his gaze intent upon the road before them.

She darted her gaze to him. He might be willing to do common work, but there was nothing common about Ronan. He stood straight and powerful, commanding and forceful. It was obvious that he was used to being in control.

"Who were you?" Meg asked. "Before the curse. What did you do?"

He laughed and glanced at her. "I did what any good Highlander does, lass. I fought my enemies and protected my clan."

"But who were you? You walk like a man used to being in charge, a man who made his own rules."

"That's because I did." He gave her a crooked smile to ease the harshness of his words.

Meg was more curious than ever. She didn't recognize the tartan he wore, but clans would subtly change their plaids for reasons like banishments, marriages, and such.

She watched Ronan out of the corner of her eye. There was no denying his confidence, his air of authority. No man, not even a Highlander, got that without being born into it.

"You were no crofter's son," Meg said. "You were son to the laird."

If she hadn't been looking for any reaction, Meg would have missed the slight tightening of his muscles.

"A good guess, but no' quite true."

"It makes sense," she stated.

Ronan pierced her with his pale green eyes. "So it would seem."

"Why do you want to hide that fact?"

"I wasna the laird's son. I was his nephew. And it's a good thing my father wasna laird. My mother had him twisted around her finger so tightly all he could see was her."

Meg swallowed at the hatred she heard in Ronan's voice, though she wasn't sure if it was toward his mother or father. She guessed it was because of his mother. "Is that why you disdain women so much?"

Her question caused him to throw back his head and laugh. "Disdain? Lass, I love women. Why do you think I was cursed?"

Meg took the trail branching off from the road, undeterred by his words. His laugh was too loud, too long. "You despise women. You regard us as a means to ease your body, but you find no other need for us."

She stopped him with a hand on his arm before he could respond. After taking a loaf of bread and meat wrapped in a towel, Meg made her way to the door of the cottage.

This was the only place Aunt Tilly had begged her to visit daily. Not that the old woman who lived there ever said much to Meg, but it was such a small request.

Meg gave a sharp knock, only to have the door open immediately. She smiled, noting how the black eyes of the woman stared at her for long moments before looking over her shoulder to Ronan.

"This will get you through tomorrow, Ina," Meg said as

she handed over the items. "Cook is making soup, and I'll be sure to have some brought over for you."

Ina's gaze came back to her before she promptly closed the door in Meg's face. With a shrug, Meg turned and walked back to Ronan.

"Who is that woman?" he asked.

Meg glanced over her shoulder to the cottage to find Ina peering at them from her window. "I don't really know. She's important to Aunt Tilly. Why?"

"She has the look of a gypsy about her."

They spent the rest of the morning in companionable silence visiting the remaining cottages. By the time the basket was empty, thunder was rumbling at a steady rate.

"I doona think we'll make it back to the castle before it rains."

Meg sighed loudly. "I was hoping we would, but we have at least three miles to walk before we get to the castle."

"Why no' take a horse. It would be quicker."

"It would, but I like to walk."

There was another rumble of thunder before a crack of lightning made Meg jump. Not a heartbeat later it began to rain.

"Is there shelter nearby?" Ronan asked.

Meg knew of only one. The abandoned cottage deep in the woods. "Aye. I'll show you."

She took off at a run. To her surprise, Ronan grabbed her hand as she lifted her sodden skirts and dashed into the forest. She slipped on damp leaves and earth, but Ronan easily kept her on her feet.

A laugh escaped her. For the first time in…years…she felt lighthearted and…free. It was a glorious feeling.

Meg looked up through the trees at the rain falling and never saw the rock. Both legs came out from beneath her. A cry welled up in her throat, and just as suddenly, she was hauled against a rock-hard chest.

She didn't know how much time passed as she stared at Ronan's bare chest. When she did look up into his eyes, there was a fire burning there.

It caused her heart to skip a beat and something seductive and erotic unfurl low in her belly.

But it frightened her too.

The stark desire was there for her to see. Ronan held nothing back. There were no false words, no lies, no empty promises.

There was just him.

His hand settled on her chest above her breasts, and then he slowly caressed up her neck to cup her cheek. All the while his head lowered to hers.

Meg should turn away. She knew it, but her body wouldn't listen. Ronan only wanted to ease his own desires. He cared nothing for her.

What does it matter? Why can't I have such pleasure in my miserable life?

As soon as the thought flitted through her mind, the last vestiges of her restraint vanished. Meg watched the water run down the hard planes of Ronan's face. She parted her lips and let her eyes drift shut. The first brush of his mouth against hers was but a touch. The second was more purposeful, as he pressed his lips to hers.

Meg could feel herself melting against him. Then his tongue slid along the seam of her lips. She gasped, her fingers digging into his shoulders.

It was the moan, the hard, needy moan pulled from deep within him that left her trembling for more. When he turned her slightly in his arms and opened his lips wider, Meg followed suit.

She sighed as their tongues met, tangled. The attraction

between them exploded into hot flames of desire. He deepened the kiss, pulling her against him until she could feel his arousal.

The kiss was searing, scorching. It burned her from the inside out.

And she couldn't get enough.

It was hard for her to hide the disappointment when Ronan ended the kiss and stared down at her. Without a word, he took her hand and walked her to the abandoned cottage.

As soon as he stepped into the structure, he pulled her inside and shut the door. In the next instant, he had her pressed against the door, his mouth on hers again, more ravenous than before.

Meg slid her arms around his neck and sank her fingers into the thick strands of his wet hair. The kiss stirred her already heated blood. She gasped when he rocked against her, his thick rod pressing against her sex.

"Aye," he murmured as he kissed down her neck. "Feel me, sweet Meg."

She felt the cool air on her skin, and realized he was undressing her, but she no longer cared. All she wanted was more of the pleasure Ronan was giving her. She would think about her actions and the consequences later.

Now was all about what she wanted.

It was a new sensation for her. Never had she thought of herself before anyone else, and she found she quite liked it.

Her gown fell around her feet in a flurry of material. Ronan never stopped kissing her the entire time he was getting her naked. When Meg was completely nude, Ronan pulled her against him and looked into her eyes for long moments. She wished she knew what he was thinking, that she had some hint of what went on in his mind.

"I didna lie, sweet Meg. I've never taken an innocent before."

She might have blushed before, but not now. Not when her body ached for him. His large hands were roaming over her, gripping her bottom and teasing the undersides of her breasts.

"You don't bed virgins, remember. What makes you think I'm an innocent?" she asked, her voice shaking when he drew close to her already hard nipple.

"A man like me always knows."

Her lids drifted shut when she ground against him. "I don't need to be seduced. I'm more than willing."

"I should walk away from you, from this."

Meg's eyes flew open to see him staring down at her breasts. He had bent her backward, exposing her breasts. She couldn't imagine him leaving her in such a state of need. Besides, she knew he needed release as well.

"Don't." Meg didn't care that he heard the pleading in her voice. "Please."

He drew his gaze up to hers. "You doona know what you're asking."

But she did. To prove it, she reached between them and wrapped her hand around his cock. "I know."

With her words, Ronan unfastened his kilt and let it drop to the ground. He knelt in front of Meg and cupped her breasts in his hands before he closed his mouth over one turgid peak.

Ronan had never wanted a woman like he wanted Meg. He teased her nipples mercilessly until her hips were rocking against him. Only then did he take the precious few moments to spread his kilt over the dirt floor and lay her down.

That's when he finally got to feast his eyes on Meg in all her glorious splendor. Her nipples were a pale pink, her breasts large and full. She had a narrow waist and full hips. He glanced at her lithe legs, but it was the triangle of auburn curls between them that held him transfixed.

"You are a beauty, sweet Meg."

Her smile was soft, seductive, and it caused a bolt of need to rush through Ronan. She had no idea of her appeal. He knelt between her legs and leaned over her to kiss her again.

Their limbs tangled as they rolled about touching and learning each other while soft sighs and moans filled the cottage.

Ronan couldn't get enough of her. He fondled her breasts before caressing one hand down her stomach to her sex.He groaned when he found her already wet and ready. Sliding one finger inside her, he was rewarded when she moaned and arched against him.

While he continued to thrust his finger in and out of her tight sheath, he rubbed his thumb around her swollen clit. Her moans turned into cries of pleasure. Every time lightning lit up the sky he was shown a vision of pure eroticism.

Ronan felt her body stiffen, and knew she was close to peaking. He continued his assault, adding a second finger to the first. Then, he leaned down and gently bit a nipple before flicking his tongue over it.

She came apart with a scream, the walls of her sex clenching his finger. And it was the most beautiful thing Ronan had ever seen.

CHAPTER 5

Meg didn't know her body could feel so good or be taken so high. She opened her eyes as Ronan pulled his fingers from her body. He was leaning over her, the head of his cock at the entrance to her sex.

She knew why he hesitated, and it made her smile. Meg rested her hands on his sides and urged him to her. His pale green eyes widened in surprise.

And then he was pushing inside her, stretching her, filling her. Meg lifted her legs and was amazed when he slid deeper. He paused, and withdrew until just the tip of him was inside her.

With one thrust, he pushed through her maidenhead, burying himself fully.

Meg stiffened at the pain, but it wasn't long until it diminished. Then something primal, something ancient had her moving against him. As soon as she felt him slide in and out of her, the pleasure, when it returned, was amplified.

She gave herself up to the rhythm Ronan set. The tempo

increased as he went deeper, thrust harder. And each time the pleasure low in her belly tightened.

Her second climax was as fierce as the first, sweeping her away on a ride of ecstasy. She knew in that instant that her body belonged to Ronan. He had marked her without even meaning to.

He threw back his head and gave a shout just as he pulled out of her. Meg held him when he collapsed on top of her, his body jerking. That's when she realized he had poured his seed on her stomach.

Meg smoothed his hair back from his face and closed her eyes as she enjoyed the feel of his weight atop her. No one had ever touched her as deeply as Ronan had.

She wasn't the naïve girl this time. This time she knew exactly what he offered – nothing.

Ronan rose up on an elbow and placed a gentle kiss on her mouth before he stood. He tore a part of her chemise off before tearing that section in two. When he returned, he knelt and wiped her blood from between her legs and then his seed from her belly.

With the storm still raging outside, Ronan lay down beside her and pulled her into his arms. Meg welcomed the respite and nestled against him with her head upon his chest.

"Will you tell me what happened to send you to Ravensclyde, sweet Meg?"

His voice was a whisper, barely heard above the rain. But heard it she had. Her eyes opened and she stared at the wall of the cottage. "Will you tell me why you hate women?"

"I doona think it a tale worth telling, but if you want to know, I will tell you."

She shifted her head until she was looking at him. "I want to know."

"All right," he said with a shrug of one shoulder. He tucked his free hand behind his head and looked at the ceiling. "My father fell madly in love with my mother the first time he saw her. What he didna know is that she was trying to win my uncle's attention. Uncle had already married and wasna interested. My father worked twice as hard to win her favor."

"I gather he did," Meg said.

"Unfortunately. My mother used him. She told him she loved him, but it was only to get him to marry her. She made his life hell. Nothing he ever did was good enough. She turned a proud man into a shell of what he once was."

Meg swallowed, because it all became clear to her. It wasn't that Ronan hated women. He didn't believe in love. Add that to the cunning way his mother tricked his father and ruined his life, and it was no wonder Ronan had balked at marriage to the gypsy.

"My sister learned from our mother," Ronan continued. "She was just as scheming and unscrupulous when she was trying to get what she wanted. I tried to warn her husband, but he was too enamored with her to listen. He learned soon enough. But by then it was too late. He was in the same trap as my father."

Meg laid her head back on his chest. "I'm sorry, Ronan."

"It's in the past."

"But still ruling your life," she pointed out.

She closed her eyes as silence stretched between them only broken by the rain and thunder. Meg was almost asleep when his fingers brushed across her cheek to move away her hair.

"I've shared my story. Where is yours?" he asked in a low, husky voice that sent chills racing over her skin.

Meg drew in a deep breath and slowly released it. "There's nothing really to tell. I was given a promise. The promise was broken, leaving me betrayed and alone."

Ronan knew there was much more to the story. He

might not know Meg's past, but he knew enough of her to know that she was a good, sweet soul. Whoever had hurt her should be hung up by his balls.

Suddenly, Ronan wanted to look into her gray eyes. He rolled her onto her back so that he leaned on one forearm beside her. Her gaze met his without hesitation.

"Tell me," he urged.

She looked away, all emotion draining from her face. "I met a man I thought cared for me. He told me he wanted me to be his. He even asked me to marry him. I was overjoyed. He was very handsome and charming. My family liked him as well. I thought everything was going along fine."

When she fell silent once more, Ronan ran a finger between her breasts to her navel. "What did he do?"

"He left me. Abandoned me on the day of our wedding to run away with someone else. I've never felt such shame."

"You doona have reason to be ashamed, sweet Meg. He was the fool who let you go. You should be happy no' to be shackled to a man like that."

Her gaze swung back to him. "You're right. Had it not happened, Aunt Tilly wouldn't have offered Ravensclyde to me, and I wouldn't have found you."

"You freed me." The impact of what she had done for him, and given him, slammed into his chest like a battering ram.

"And you awakened my body," she said with a sly smile.

If only she knew how wonderful her body was. It might have been a long time since he'd had a woman, but he knew the pleasure he found with Meg was profound.

Enough to make him think about running as far away as he could.

What stopped him was realizing Meg wasn't like his mother or sister. She had been abandoned by a man. She was wounded, her heart sore. And yet she had given him her most precious gift – her innocence.

No other man had touched her, kissed her, loved her as he had. It was a first for Ronan, and he quite liked how it felt.

"What a pair we are," Meg said with a small laugh.

Ronan rolled to his back. "Aye. A pair for sure."

Meg returned to her spot on his chest. "How long will you stay at Ravensclyde?"

"I've no' thought much about it. Why? Do you wish me to leave now?"

"On the contrary. I want you to stay as long as you want."

Ronan idly played with the drying strands of hair that had come loose from her braid. "I doona understand why you gave yourself to me. That man was an arse to be sure, but you will make a good wife and mother."

"I am the second of four daughters. My father gave my intended the dowry before the wedding."

"And the bastard ran off with it."

"Aye. My sisters need to find husbands as well. There's nothing left for me to find another husband with."

Ronan soaked in that bit of news. "What about your aunt? Can she no' help?"

"She did. She allowed me to come here and make it my home. At least I have somewhere to go that isn't the convent."

"So you've resigned yourself to being alone?"

"I have."

Ronan didn't quite understand why the thought of Meg with another man made him want to hit something, but he also knew Meg shouldn't be alone.

Meg wondered if everyone would be able to tell she was no longer a maiden as she and Ronan walked back to the castle once the storm had passed.

When no one looked twice at her, she relaxed. No matter how wrong it was, she couldn't berate herself for what she had done. For those few moments, she had been worshipped, needed, and loved. It went a long way to bolster her failing self-esteem.

Just before they reached the castle, Ronan stopped her with a hand upon her arm. "Is all well?"

"Aye," she said with a smile.

"You're glowing, lass." There was a very male smile pulling at his lips. "I did that to you."

She playfully rolled her eyes. "So you did. I suppose I should thank you."

"Oh, but you did. With a most precious gift," he said in a low whisper.

Meg shivered as she always did when he talked in that husky, seductive voice. "I must go. There are things I need to tend to. Will you be at dinner?"

"Aye."

Ronan watched her walk into the castle before he strode into the stables and gathered the tools he would need. With his arms full, he was about to head out on foot when the stable master stepped in front of him.

"Where are you headed with those?" the man asked.

Ronan nodded in approval of the man. "I'm off to one of the cottages to make some repairs."

The man eyed him for a few moments before he let out a whistle and a white gelding ran up to the fence. "Take a mount. You'll get there faster."

"Thank you."

"How long will you be staying at Ravensclyde?"

Ronan stopped on his way around the man. "I doona know."

"Where did you come from?"

It wasn't like Ronan could get upset with the man. He was looking out for Meg and the castle. "Somewhere far away. Meg has offered for me to rest at the castle for a while. I want to pay her back by helping out where I can."

The old man's blue gaze went to the castle. "She came here several months ago heart sore. I've no' seen a true smile from her before today."

"I've no intention of hurting Meg if that's what you're asking," Ronan said. "She should be protected. It's good that she has someone like you looking out for her."

The stable master gave a nod of his head and disappeared back into the stables. Ronan quickly grabbed a halter and readied the horse. With his tools in hand, he mounted and rode out of the bailey.

For once, he knew exactly what he needed to do.

CHAPTER 6

Meg found herself searching for a glimpse of Ronan throughout the rest of the day. Disappointment filled her when she couldn't find him. And a part of her worried that he had left.

"It's not like he promised he would stay," she told herself.

Ronan had given no promises, nor would he ever. After he told her what happened to him, she knew without a doubt that he would remain for only as long as he wished. Afterward, she would never see him again.

Meg's mind was so full of Ronan that she couldn't concentrate on the chores she needed to get done. Her body still hungered for more of him, but there was something else on her mind, something she was afraid to let linger.

Ronan had made sure not to plant his seed within her. She hadn't thought much about it at the time, but now...now she knew he might be the only way she could have the family she wanted.

Meg ran the back of her hand across her forehead as she helped stir the boiling water for the washing. Her time at Ravensclyde was limited to the remainder of Aunt Tilly's life.

Once she died, the castle would pass to her eldest son. Even though he had his own castle to manage, Meg was sure he wouldn't be too happy with her remaining forever.

Eventually, Meg was going to have to leave, and even if she could convince Ronan to give her a child, there was nowhere for them to go. Meg was fully dependent on her family, and with no dowry, she could very well end up in a convent.

The thought chilled her.

It always had, but now, more than ever, the reality of her future was weighing heavily upon her shoulders. If only she could decide her own fate.

Meg finished with the laundry and went into the castle. She was in her chamber when she glanced out her window and spotted Ronan talking to the stable master. Her heart immediately began to pound at the sight of such a man, a man she knew to have gentle, loving hands that wrung multitudes of pleasure from her.

The conversation done, Ronan turned to a water barrel and dunked his head. He flipped his head back, water flying everywhere, as a huge smile graced his handsome face.

Meg glanced down at her stained and sweaty gown and immediately began to undress. She took her time in cleaning her skin with a cloth and bowl of water. Then she brushed out her long hair until it glistened before she put on a clean gown.

Anticipation of possibly seeing Ronan urged her down the stairs well before the evening meal. But once more, she was disappointed, as he was nowhere in sight.

With nothing else to do, Meg walked into the kitchens to help.

∼

R onan smiled when he saw the saffron shirt laid out on the bed along with another kilt. The Galt tartan was all he had ever worn, but it was filthy. He was no longer in a world he knew. Two centuries had passed, and much had changed in Scotland. Perhaps it was time he did as well.

The only claim he had to the Galt clan was his name, and even that didn't give him the desire to search them out. He had no coin, no home...nothing. He was well and truly on his own. There might have been something to interest him away from Ravensclyde if Stefan, Daman, and Morcant were with him.

Alone, well, that was a completely different story.

Meg had offered for him to remain at Ravensclyde for as long as he wanted. Oddly enough, he didn't feel the desire to leave. Was it Meg holding him? Surely not. He knew better than to let a woman close.

It had to be the fact that he was alone. That was a solid explanation, and the only one he would even consider. Despite the fact his cock was already hardening at the mere thought of Meg.

Ronan removed his kilt and folded the tartan carefully before setting it atop the chest against the wall. He then pulled the saffron shirt over his head and let it settle against his skin. Next, he picked up the Alpin kilt and made quick work of putting it on.

He paused before leaving the chamber to run his fingers through his hair. It wasn't until he scratched his jaw that he felt the whiskers. It had been so long since he had to shave that Ronan had forgotten about it.

It was obvious someone else had thought of it though when he turned and found everything he needed to shave set on a small table near the window.

With a chuckle, Ronan set to work. It took longer than

usual as he got used to holding the blade in his hand once more. At least he didn't cut his face. When he finished, he ran a hand over his jaw pleased not to feel any stubble.

He hurried out of the chamber, and only belatedly realized halfway down the stairs that it was excitement that urged him onward – excitement at seeing Meg again.

He came to a halt in the great hall when his eyes landed on her. She was a vision with her auburn locks flowing around her, the color like a beacon for him. She was talking to the servants when she glanced up and saw him. A soft, welcoming smile tilted her full lips as she stopped mid-sentence.

Ronan started toward her. With a quick word to the servants, Meg met him in the middle of the great hall. She eyed the kilt and gave a nod of approval.

"You look very handsome."

He gave her a wink. "It was a nice way of telling me my kilt needed to be cleaned."

"The Alpin kilt looks good on you."

She gestured to the table. "It's time for our meal."

They had no sooner taken their seats than the hall began to fill with people. Food was then brought out and set on the tables. Ronan looked around the great hall noting the ease in which everyone ate.

There had been too much tension between his parents and his uncle and aunt for there to have been a nice supper – or any meal for that matter.

"What did you do today?" Meg asked.

Ronan swallowed his bite and shrugged. "I began to fix a roof."

Meg paused in her eating to look at him. "You went back to the cottage."

He wasn't sure if she was happy or not since no emotion

showed on her face. Ronan gave a small nod. "I want to earn my keep."

"And the discussion with the stable master?"

"He offered two of his sons to help me tomorrow."

For long moments, she silently stared at him. "Thank you. I've been trying to find the time to help the family, but there are few men to spare."

"That's what I'm for," he said, suddenly happy at the delight in her gray eyes.

"You would've been a good laird, Ronan."

He looked away. "It was never my position to have."

"Aye, but it's in your blood."

Ronan wanted to change the subject. He hated thinking of his past. "And how long will you be here?"

"Who knows," she replied flippantly.

But Ronan instantly knew she was keeping something from him. "I thought you said your aunt gave you leave to remain here."

"She did."

He took a drink of his ale and surveyed the great hall before he turned his head to her. "What are you no' telling me, lass?"

"Nothing," she was quick to assure him.

Ronan let it go. For the moment. It was difficult for him to concentrate with his body aching with desire for her. She was sitting next to him, but he couldn't touch her.

In all his years, not once had he held back from taking whatever he wanted. Why was he stopping now? Especially after already having Meg.

And the answer was the woman herself.

He wanted to protect her, shelter her. He saw the honesty and passion in her eyes. She looked at him as if he were worthy of her, and he found he desperately wanted to be worthy.

When the meal was finished, Ronan relaxed for a while before he scooted back his chair and held out his hand. "Walk with me, sweet Meg."

Her gray eyes darkened from the shared attraction and intimacy. How he wanted to jerk her against him and kiss her in front of everyone. To claim what was his.

With her hand in his, Ronan escorted her up the stairs to the battlements and out into the night.

"There are too many clouds to see the stars," Meg said.

"I didna bring you out here to see the stars. I brought you out here for this," he said as he pulled her against him and covered her mouth with his.

The explosion of desire was instantaneous, urgent.

Blazing.

His hands slid into the cool locks of her hair and held her captive as he ravaged her mouth. She was beauty, innocence, temptation, and strength.

She was his weakness, and his power.

His.

Ronan ended the kiss, his breathing harsh as he tried to control his raging body. Meg rested her head on his chest as they held each other.

"This is like a dream," she whispered into the night.

A dream that was unsettling. Ronan didn't understand the fierce feelings rolling through him. Maybe if he did he could just accept them.

It wasn't just the strange emotions, there was also the burning need to claim her again that pounded through his veins with a constant beat.

He smoothed her hair away from her face and rested his chin atop her head. "If you doona talk of something, I'm going to lift your skirts right here and take you."

"That sounds...exciting."

Ronan closed his eyes and groaned. "Doona tempt me."

"What do I talk about?"

"You can tell me what you didna in the great hall. How long do you plan to remain at the castle?"

He felt her take a deep breath before she said, "Until Aunt Tilly dies, I suspect."

"Is she that aged?"

"She's an old woman. Many are surprised she has lived this long."

"And the castle is hers?"

"In a manner," Meg answered. "It was her brother's who had no heirs. He left the castle and lands to Aunt Tilly's eldest who is laird of his own castle."

Now Ronan understand it all. "You think your cousin will make you leave?"

"I'm sure he will."

"Why? You're taking care of his castle. I see it as a reason for him to want to keep you. If he doesna, he'll have to hire a steward to do it."

Meg's head lifted as she looked at him. "I hadn't thought of that. Do you really think he would consider it?"

"I doona see why you can no' plead your case if you do a good enough job, which it seems you have. Who was here before?"

"Aunt Tilly for several years, but she's taken to visiting family now. Until I came, there was no one."

Ronan chuckled. "It almost sounds like destiny."

"Almost."

Their gazes locked, and the simmering passion flared again. Ronan turned her toward the door to walk her to his chamber when a lone shape in the darkness snared his gaze.

Even from the distance he recognized the gypsy woman from the cottage, and a ripple of unease rippled down his spine.

CHAPTER 7

M eg knew something was wrong by the way
Ronan's body stiffened. She glanced over and
spotted Ina just before the old woman moved
back into the shadows.

"That was odd," Meg said as they entered the castle. "I
can't remember the last time Ina left her cottage."

Ronan said not a word as he escorted her down the corridor. A glance at him showed Meg that anger and worry
simmered just below the surface.

"She won't bother you," Meg told him.

"There will be little you can do to stop the gypsy."

"How do you know she's a gypsy? No one has ever said
anything like that about Ina." Especially Aunt Tilly. In a
short order of time, Meg had begun to think there really was
something like magic in Scotland. And someone had to be
able to use that magic.

"I know what she is," Ronan stated coldly. "It's in her
eyes, and the way she stared at me. A gypsy recognizes one
who has been cursed."

Meg stopped and faced Ronan, forcing him to halt as well. "You earned your freedom."

"Have I? I'm no' so sure. Knowing Ilinca, it wouldna be so easy as to find a woman who said I didna have to return to the mirror. Ilinca would make things much more difficult."

"What could you possibly do to ensure that the mirror would never be your prison again?" The thought of Ronan disappearing left her...cold.

"That wisdom she didna impart, and I suspect on purpose."

Meg might not be in control of her own life, but she could help Ronan. She covered her mouth as she faked a huge yawn. "It's been a long day."

"Aye," he said and frowned at her. "Let me see you to your chamber."

How deeply his mind was entranced with the curse was evident by the way he deposited her at her chamber door with a quiet good-night and turned on his heel to walk in the direction of his chamber.

Meg let out a long sigh. Magic. Gypsies. Mirrors as prisons. It was all laughable, or should be.

If Ina really were a gypsy, then she would be able to answer Meg's questions. Meg hurried down the stairs into the great hall and came to a halt when she saw Aunt Tilly standing in the doorway.

Aunt Tilly was a loud, boisterous sort that even old age couldn't dim. She was laughing at something one of the maids said, her voice easily carrying around the hall while she leaned heavily upon her cane.

Meg smiled as soon as Tilly's direct blue gaze landed on her. Her aunt opened her arms, and Meg walked into them to be enveloped in a fierce hug that was unexpected from the thin, frail looking woman.

"You look more yourself," Aunt Tilly said and then

pulled back. She scrutinized Meg's face with shrewd eyes for several silent moments. "Meg, if I didn't know better, I'd say you found yourself a man."

Meg could feel the color drain from her face. No one was supposed to know. How had her aunt figured it out?

"About time," Aunt Tilly said and pulled her in for another hug.

Once released, Meg turned so that Tilly could lean on her as they walked to the solar. "I had no idea you were coming."

"I didn't either, my dear. Just a feeling I had that I wanted to see you. It seems your time at Ravensclyde has done you good."

"Very much so." Meg thought of Ronan and how he had touched her so gently.

"And the man?"

Meg swallowed, unsure of how much to tell Tilly. "He arrived recently and needed work. He's helping with odd jobs."

Aunt Tilly made an odd sound at the back of her throat. "And the furniture in the attic. Did you find anything that appealed to you?"

"Several pieces." She helped Tilly into a chair and sat beside her. "Some are being refinished or recovered. A few have already been dispersed throughout the castle after a good cleaning."

"That's good to hear, but was there anything in there that drew you?"

Maybe it was the way that Tilly's sharp blue eyes watched her so carefully, or maybe it was the tone her aunt used, but Meg had a feeling Aunt Tilly knew all about the mirror in the attic.

Her aunt suddenly smiled and sat back, both of her

hands resting atop her cane. "Ah. I see that you found it. I suspect that your new worker is Ronan."

"You know him?" Meg felt as if the chair had been yanked from beneath her as the world tilted precariously.

"I do. He's the one who put that glow in your cheeks, isn't he?"

Meg nodded woodenly, still trying to grasp what was going on. "If you know Ronan, then you let him out of the mirror?"

"That was me, aye. Newly married into the Alpin family, I just happened to find the mirror that had been hidden in the attic."

"You put him back in that prison. Why?" Meg couldn't believe her aunt could be so cruel.

Aunt Tilly glanced at the floor. "I didn't want to, but Ina said I must."

"Ina. I was on my way to see her when you arrived."

"She wouldn't tell you anything, Meg. You see, she told me to put Ronan back in his prison until it was time for him to be released again."

Meg stood, appalled and angry. "So Ina is a gypsy? Do all gypsies hate Ronan so much that they want him to suffer for eternity? Ilinca said he could earn his freedom. I've given it to him."

"It's not that simple," Tilly said softly. She let out a long sigh, her stare hard and unmoving. "Sit, Meg. Please."

She wanted to rush up to Ronan, or out to Ina, and demand to know the truth. Instead, Meg resumed her seat and waited.

Tilly rubbed her swollen knuckles. "Aye, Ina is a gypsy. As I'm sure you've figured out, there is such a thing as magic in our wonderful land. The gypsies have a way with curses that make them so unbreakable that not even another gypsy can destroy it.

"Ina knew of the mirror. Her family had remained on Alpin land to keep watch over the times Ronan was let out."

Meg's shoulders slumped. "The first time he was released from the mirror he ran away. It was a gypsy that sent him back wasn't it?"

Tilly's face scrunched. "In a way. It was also his prison that pulled him back. I wanted to help Ronan."

"Then why didn't you?"

"Ina said there would be another Alpin woman who would release him. There was a chance that he could earn his freedom at that time."

Meg licked her lips. "How does he earn his freedom?"

"Ina wouldn't tell me. Nor will she tell you," Tilly quickly said when Meg started to rise.

Meg huffed out a breath as she stayed seated. "I want to help him. He made a mistake, but he didn't kill Ana. She killed herself because she couldn't take rejection. Why should he be punished for that?"

Tilly reached over and set her gnarled hand atop Meg's. "Not everyone is as strong as you, my dear. Even in your darkest hour after that bastard ran off with your dowry and left you waiting at the altar, I knew you would come through it all."

"My chances at finding another man to marry are nonexistent, aunt. I have no dowry."

"For some, you won't have to."

Meg looked up at the ceiling as she once more thought of Ronan. "Wishful thinking on both our parts." Meg hated the pain she felt in her heart as she realized the truth of her words. "Ronan abhors marriage, and he has every right to after what his mother did to his father. He doesn't trust women."

"Do you...care...for him?"

Meg met her aunt's gaze. "I didn't think I'd ever be able

to have feelings like this again. Ronan barreled into my life, but he has opened my heart and my mind to the possibility that happiness could be mine. If I dared to reach for it."

"Are you willing to fight for him?"

"Fight for a man that will do anything to keep from being married?" Meg asked in disbelief. The answer swelled within her. "If there is even a wee chance I could have a future with Ronan, I would have to do it honestly. No manipulation, no lies, and no deceit. I would have to win him with my feelings."

Tilly nodded in approval. "If anyone can do it, you can. You keep saying you care for him, and that you have feelings, but is it love?"

Was it love? Meg recalled how he had taken her in his arms and kissed her with such abandon, touched her with unrestraint.

Made love to her as if there were no tomorrow.

Her stomach quivered as she recalled the hungry desire that had flared in his eyes right before he kissed her. He hadn't spent all his time with her, and the women of the castle had certainly taken notice of him. Yet he hadn't eased himself with any of them. Only her.

Was it because she held the key to whether he returned to the mirror or not? The euphoria blossoming within her withered at the thought.

"Meg?" Aunt Tilly called.

Meg rose to her feet, her stomach a ball of knots. "I've had a very long day."

"Of course," her aunt said with sharp eyes. "Why don't you send Ronan down to me?"

Meg nodded as she hurried out of the solar and ascended the stairs. Each step weighted her down until she felt as if she carried the world upon her shoulders.

Her hand shook when she raised it to knock on Ronan's

door. The door was yanked open, and Ronan stood before her, his eyes as troubled as before.

"You doona look well. Are you all right?" he asked.

Meg couldn't calm her heart it beat so fast. "Aunt Tilly just arrived. She would like to see you in the solar."

"All right. First, tell me what's wrong."

She hated the concern in his gaze. It made her feel special, and she knew better than most how easily she could be duped. She was afraid to ask Ronan why he was really with her, because she was terrified of the truth.

Meg tried to turn away, but Ronan pulled her against him, his strong arms wrapping around her. He held her to his chest, giving her comfort. "I doona know what I've done, but it wasna on purpose, whatever it is."

He was apologizing without knowing if he had even done anything. It would be so easy to love this man, to give him her whole heart and plan a life with him.

It all lay out before her, giving her a glimpse of what she could have.

Meg pulled out of his arms and met his gaze. "Thank you for today. I didn't think I could let a man that close again, but you proved me wrong. I'll have a good memory to wipe out the bad ones."

Ronan's heart missed a beat. Meg's speech sounded suspiciously like farewell. Her face was as pale as death, and her gray eyes filled with such sorrow that he searched his mind for a way to make it go away.

"What are you saying?" he asked.

"I'm saying you don't owe me anything for letting you out of the mirror. Don't feel obligated to woo me because you think I might get angry and send you back."

Ronan took a step back he was so shocked. It had never entered his mind that Meg would do that, which was more than odd since that's normally exactly how he would have approached her.

"That's no' what I was doing."

She backed away, a tight smile in place that didn't reach her eyes. "It's all right. I told you. I understand. My aunt is waiting for you."

Ronan stepped out of his chamber as Meg quickly walked away. He was so befuddled that he stared at her retreating back until she disappeared around a corner.

He had the unnerving feeling that Meg wanted nothing more to do with him. Anger replaced his bewilderment. There was only one person who could have turned Meg against him – Aunt Tilly.

R onan couldn't hold back his fury as he rounded the corner and walked into the solar. Only to come to a halt as he recognized the blue eyes staring at him. They were older, but there was no mistaking the kindness he remembered so well.

"Matilda."

Tilly smiled. "Hello, Ronan. It's been many years since I last saw you. While you look the same, age has changed me."

He walked around Tilly taking in the cane, wrinkled skin, and white hair. "I didna think to ever see you again."

"I'm sure you would rather not have seen me again."

It was true. "You did put me back in."

"Ina said I must. She told me that you would be released again."

He sat, her words muddling his already puzzled mind. "You have no idea what it's like in that prison. There is only darkness."

"I know." Her voice was low, regret in every syllable. "I'm sorry, Ronan, and though you may not believe it, I did it to save you."

His mother's and sister's duplicitous actions filled his mind. They too were always remorseful when they were found out. It never lasted long though. "Is that right? Tell me how."

"Ina said there was a chance for you to gain your freedom for good."

This had him sitting up straighter. He held Tilly's gaze and leaned forward. "How?"

"That I don't know. Ina wouldn't tell me. I believe it's because she doesn't know herself."

"Then how can she know this might be my chance?" he yelled. Ronan stood and paced the solar, Tilly's words battering him like a fierce winter storm.

Everything within him urged him to go to Meg. It wasn't something he had ever done before. He didn't even know what to say to her. He only knew that he had to make right whatever had somehow gone wrong.

"Why did you turn Meg against me?" he asked with his back to Tilly. He couldn't stand to see the triumph in her gaze.

"I have no idea what you're talking about. I asked her if she cared for you. That's all it took to send her upstairs."

Ronan leaned his hands against the stone hearth and dropped his chin to his chest. "She said she was ill when she came here."

"Did she tell you why?"

"Aye."

There was a beat of silence before Tilly said, "That man broke her. Meg has always been such a trusting, accepting soul. There isn't a mean bone in her body, and yet the worst kind of man offered for her."

"Could you no' see him for what he was?"

"He fooled everyone. Including his own family, who have since disowned him. None of that can change what happened. Meg was given a hard lesson of life, and because of it, she'll spend the rest of her life here."

Ronan lifted his head and faced Tilly. "You're going to allow her to remain here?"

"I've already spoken to my son. His main concern is his clan, as it should be, but this is a holding of the Alpins. We don't want it to fall into the wrong hands."

"You need to let Meg know."

"That's part of the reason I'm here. The other part was to make sure she found your mirror."

Ronan ran a hand through his hair. "She thinks I'm beholden to her for releasing me. She thinks that's why I...spend my time with her."

"I know exactly what you two have done. I shouldn't condone it, but Meg needed what you've given her, Ronan. And I think you needed what she has given you."

He wasn't sure what to say, so he remained silent. While his imprisonment had changed him, it hadn't changed his view of women. Meg had done that all on her own. She had also wormed her way into his soul, embedding herself there so that no other woman would ever compare.

"You told Meg of your view on women. I know I factored into that as well, because I told you that I would keep you free, and then sent you back. Do you view Meg in the same light as other women?" Tilly asked.

"Never. Meg is...different. She could have done a great many things to get me to do whatever it was she wanted in return for staying out of the mirror. But she didna."

"Are you beholden to her?"

"She let me out. Fed me, conversed with me, and told me she would never send me back. Of course I'm beholden to her. Just no' in the way she thinks."

Tilly's astute blue eyes narrowed on him. "And you taking her innocence? Was that your way of thanking her?"

If he answered honestly, Ronan could very well find himself back in the mirror because he was talking to Meg's aunt. Yet there was no other choice.

"Part of my punishment from Ilinca was a constant, aching need that only another's touch could relieve. When I fell out of that mirror I wanted three things. The sun, a goblet of ale, and a woman. And no' necessarily in that order."

"So you used my niece?"

"I wanted her, aye. It was a yearning clawing at me, persistent and ever present. Her easy smile, her guileless gray eyes, and her sweet voice. That first night I went looking to ease myself on a willing woman. I found one, but I couldna go through with it. I kept thinking of Meg. What happened between us wasn't planned. I might have wanted her, but I wasn't going to use Meg in that way."

Tilly's white head cocked to the side. "Interesting. Would you say you care about her?"

Panic set in. Was Tilly cornering him into marriage? As much as he didn't want to hurt Meg, he wouldn't be forced. "I care about my freedom."

"I'm not talking marriage," Tilly said angrily. "I'm merely asking if you care about my niece. Even if I wanted you two together, that's not my decision to make."

Ronan swallowed. Did he care about Meg? Caring meant the woman had some measure of control over him. He refused to turn out like his father.

Even as he opened his mouth to say no, he remembered his last conversation with Meg. She had cried no tears, nor had she tried to wring any promises from him. She had simply walked away.

The feeling was...crushing. He wanted to go to her and shake her. Just before he kissed her.

"I know that look," Tilly said with a slight smile that

would normally have set him on edge. "You do care for her, but you don't want to admit it. She's ready to give you up, Ronan. Are you ready to let her go?"

"Nay."

The word burst from him. He wasn't done with Meg – wasn't done kissing her, touching her…knowing her.

By the saints, how had he come to this? How had he fallen for an auburn haired beauty without even knowing it? More importantly, what did he do about it?

"Have you ever loved, Ronan?"

He looked at Tilly and frowned. "My three friends. I loved them like brothers."

"Then you know what it means to care that deeply for someone. Is it enough, though?"

"Enough for what?"

"To win Meg. She won't settle for anything other than all of you."

Ronan knew that meant marriage. He had been so adverse to it for so long that he wasn't sure he could go through with it.

"I had a long, happy marriage," Tilly said. "Oh, we fought. Everyone has their spats, but there's nothing better than a long night of making up."

He smiled in spite of himself. "You could be lying."

"I could be. Look around, Ronan. You've been at Ravensclyde for a month. You've seen unhappy people as well as happy ones. That is life. It's up to each individual to make the most out of what they have. You," she said as she climbed to her feet with the help of her cane, "have a second chance. So does Meg. The two of you better not muck things up."

She slowly walked to the doorway before she turned to him. "Because if you do, you'll be back in the mirror, and she'll have a very lonely life."

CHAPTER 9

Meg sat atop her bed without any candles lit and listened to the sounds of the castle. She had never minded the dark. It shielded her from prying eyes and hid the worst of her tears. She might welcome the darkness, but Ronan didn't.

She couldn't stop thinking of him, no matter how much she tried. Now, in the dark, she wondered how he had survived two hundred years trapped in the mirror without going daft.

He hadn't aged, hungered for food, or needed water. Whatever magic used must have made sure he wouldn't go insane either.

She let her mind wander over conversations she had with Ronan throughout the month. He was always quick with a smile and his charm. More often than not he made her laugh.

Little by little, he had become a constant in her life until she found herself wanting him with her. That want had somehow, inexplicably become need. He had shown her true desire. She recalled the story of his mother, and how he was cursed into the mirror.

Always it came back to that damn mirror. Without it she would never had met Ronan, and as long as the threat of him having to return to it hung over his head, she would never know if he was with her because he really wanted to be.

When the castle grew quiet, Meg rose and silently made her way out of her chamber to the stairs that led to the attic. She walked to the back room that held the mirror.

It stood as tall as a pillar and as eerie as an abyss. And yet Meg walked right up to it. She looked into the glass, but nothing of the room behind her was reflected.

She lifted her hand to the glass, ready to touch it, when she was suddenly spun away. Meg looked up into green eyes she had come to know so well.

"Doona test it," he whispered.

"The curse wasn't for me."

"It's no' something I want to prove. What are you doing up here?"

She shrugged, much too comfortable in his arms. When she tried to move out of his hold, he tightened his arms, preventing her. "When I can't sleep, I walk around the castle. What are you doing up here?"

"I came to see something."

"Did you find what you were looking for?"

"I'm no' sure yet."

Meg flattened her palms on his chest. "I better return to my chamber."

"Wait," he said hurriedly, almost nervously. "Just a few moments more."

She hesitated before she gave him a nod. This was a side of Ronan she hadn't seen before, and it intrigued her.

"Meg," he said, and then cleared his throat. "Have you spoken to your aunt again?"

"Nay."

"I'm sure she'll tell you in the morn, but your cousin is going to allow you to remain at Ravensclyde indefinitely."

Meg blinked at him. She didn't have to leave? She could call Ravensclyde her home? It seemed too good to be true. "Are you sure?"

"It's part of the reason your aunt came to visit."

Meg dropped her head against his chest, and felt as if a huge load had been taken off her shoulders. "I won't have to go to a convent or worry about finding relatives to allow me to stay with them."

"You get to make your own destiny. Including taking a husband."

She stiffened and slowly raised her head. If she could find a man who would take her without a dowry, then yes, there was a chance. But none of them would be Ronan. He had ruined her for any other man.

No one could give her that mischievous, wicked smile like he did. No one could make her toes curl with a single kiss like he did. No one could make her heart race uncontrollably just by being near her as he did.

"I don't think so." Was that dejection she saw on his face? Surely not.

"I see."

She frowned, wondering at the odd tone in his voice. "What about you? Will you leave the castle now?"

"I couldna even if I wanted to."

Meg ignored the little thrill that shot through her. "What do you mean? It's the mirror, isn't it?"

Ronan wouldn't tell her that it had been pulling at him for a week now. He had been ignoring it, but then he found himself in the attic that night. Imagine his surprise when Meg walked right up to it.

Fear knifed through him, and he had reacted instantly in

pulling her away. Even now, looking at the hated mirror, he wouldn't chance Meg being drawn in.

How much longer did he have before the mirror had him again? A day? An hour? Less?

He didn't want to go back into that dark prison without at least letting Meg know that she had changed his life. If only he had realized the chance he had and not ignored the feelings that had been growing.

But it was too late for him and Meg now. She no longer trusted him.

"I'm staying because I want to. I'm staying because of you, because I...love you, sweet Meg."

Ronan didn't know what he thought would happen, but her silence was deafening. It was what he deserved. He had been going through the past weeks as if his life was his to control once more.

All those wasted hours he could have been wooing Meg to love him. They had been glorious days, and he was thankful they would get him through more centuries in the darkness until – if – anyone ever released him from his prison again.

Knowing he loved Meg and she didn't return his feelings was painful. It must have been what Ana experienced, and why she took her own life.

"You love me?" Meg asked in a soft voice.

Ronan couldn't stop touching her. His hands reverently cupped her face. "I didna realize it until tonight when you were putting a wall between us. I had to let you know before..."

"Before what?" she pressed.

He smiled, his heart breaking inside his chest. "My time here is up, sweet Meg."

Her gaze darted to the mirror. "I said you could remain. I'm not sending you back."

"I know. It's the curse. When I'm released, I guess I go through a test of sorts." At least now he knew what he needed to earn his freedom – love.

He could have had that with Meg, he knew it in the depths of his soul. If only he had realized what he would need to fight for. But it was too little, too late.

"You can't leave," she said, her voice becoming shrill. "I'm not ready for you to leave."

"Neither am I."

Ronan tried to tell her he loved her again when the edges of his vision went black. He could hear Meg screaming his name, but it sounded far away, and growing fainter by the moment.

He blinked, and the next instant he was back in the mirror. The desolation was severe, the despair intense.

The anguish fierce.

His sweet Meg was gone from him forever. He threw back his head and bellowed, putting every ounce of regret into it.

Meg slammed her hands against the mirror, the inky glass unswayed by her attack. She hollered for Ronan again and again, but he didn't answer.

She refused to let him go, even as the fear for the love growing inside her overwhelmed her. Meg sank to her knees, her hands sliding down the mirror as the tears came.

"Ronan. I love you, too."

Suddenly Meg was thrown backwards as a blinding white light erupted from the mirror. Something was tossed out before the light disappeared again.

Meg looked over to find Ronan on his side unmoving. She hastily crawled to him and rolled him onto his back. "Ronan," she called as she touched his face and smoothed back his hair. "Ronan, open your eyes and look at me."

A relieved laugh erupted from her when his lids opened to pin her with his green gaze. "Did you say-"

"Aye. I love you," she interrupted him as she dashed away tears. "I'm terrified of what will happen now, but I couldn't deny the truth, especially when you were back in the mirror."

He pulled her down atop him and kissed her deeply, passionately. Ronan then rolled them over until he leaned over her.

"I doona want to waste another moment. Stand by me for eternity, Meg. Be my wife."

"I'd love nothing better."

EPILOGUE

Two weeks later

Ronan couldn't believe he was actually getting married. The fortnight had seemed an eternity as he waited impatiently to make Meg his own.

Tilly had remained at Ravensclyde getting everything in order for the wedding. The entire castle had come out for the event.

Ronan looked around the bailey at all the smiling faces, including Tilly's son Angus and his wife. Angus had pulled him aside and offered Ravensclyde as his and Meg's home as long as they held it for him.

He had found a home at Ravensclyde, a life that seemed brighter than he could have ever hoped. The only thing missing were his friends. Ronan would do anything if he could have Daman, Morcant, and Stefan standing with him.

It was a bittersweet moment missing his friends so terribly while being so happy. The melancholy, however, diminished when he caught sight of Meg standing on the steps of the castle.

She looked enchanting in a gown of deep green. Her auburn locks flowed freely down her back with a simple circle of white and yellow flowers around her head.

Her smile was wide as she made her way to him. Ronan took her hand as soon as she was near. He feared she might run away or change her mind about marrying him if he didn't.

"I'm yours," she whispered with a wink.

Ronan felt the grip on his heart ease. They faced the priest as the ceremony began. Ronan couldn't believe magic had taken him from his home into a prison, but it had also delivered him to Meg.

More magic had happened when love blossomed, and now he was going to have her for the rest of his life.

Applause erupted as the ceremony ended, and Meg faced him once more.

"You're officially mine," he told her. "You willna get away from me now."

"You have me forever."

"That willna be long enough," he whispered before he sealed their vows with a kiss.

THE
HUNGER

ROGUES OF SCOTLAND - BOOK TWO

DONNA GRANT

NYT BEST SELLING AUTHOR OF *THE DARK KINGS SERIES*

PROLOGUE

Highlands of Scotland:
Summer, 1427

There was something about being with friends.
Morcant Banner never thought he would consider
three men not related to him brothers, but there
was a connection between Stefan, Daman, Ronan, and
himself that none could deny. Even more so than the
brothers he did have by blood.

Even now as they waited in the valley for Ronan to join
them, Morcant basked in the summer sun, contentment
settling around him. All his worries vanished when he was
with his friends.

Because they accepted him for who he was.

Because no one else would.

The sound of a horse's whinny had all three of them
looking to their right and the rider atop the mountain.
Ronan. Morcant smiled, anticipation for the evening
building.

Ronan leaned forward slightly. His horse pawed at the

ground and then raced down the mountain at breakneck speed. Stefan shook his head at Ronan's recklessness, while Morcant and Daman laughed.

Morcant held his stallion with a firm hand as the horse yearned to race as well. Morcant got him under control just as Ronan arrived.

"About time," Stefan grumbled crossly.

Ronan raised his brow. "You might want to rein in that temper, my friend. We're going to be around beautiful women this night. Women require smiles and sweet words. No' furrowed brows."

There was laughter from everyone but Stefan, who gave Ronan a humorless look.

"Aye, we've heard enough about this Ana," Daman said as he turned his mount alongside Ronan's. "Take me to this gypsy beauty so I can see her for myself."

Ronan's lips compressed. "You think to take her from me?"

Daman's confident smile grew as his eyes twinkled in merriment. "Is she that beautiful?"

"Just you try," Ronan dared, only half jesting.

"Be cautious, Ronan. You wrong a gypsy, and they'll curse you. No' sure we should be meddling with such people," Morcant said as he shoved his hair out of his eyes. He knew the stories of the gypsies, and it gave him just enough caution and prudence that might not otherwise be there.

Then again, the young gypsy women were known for their beauty and seductive ways. Morcant couldn't say no to that. Hell, what sane man could?

Ronan laughed and reined in his jittery mount. "Ah, but with such a willing body, how am I to refuse Ana? Come, my friends, and let us enjoy the bounty that awaits." He gave a short whistle and his horse surged forward in a run.

Morcant and the others remained behind for a moment as they watched Ronan take the lead as he always did. It had begun a decade earlier when they chanced upon each other during Highland Games between their four clans. After that, they made sure to meet up regularly until they were as inseparable as brothers. The four formed a friendship that grew tighter with each year that passed.

"I'm no' missing this," Morcant said and gave his stallion his head.

The horse immediately took off. Behind him, Morcant could hear the thundering of Stefan's and Daman's horse's hooves.

Ronan looked over his shoulder, a wide smile on his face. He spurred his mount faster. Not to be outdone, Morcant leaned low over his stallion's neck until he pulled up alongside Ronan.

One by one, the three caught up with Ronan. A few moments later, Ronan tugged the reins, easing his stallion into a canter until they rode their horses four abreast. A glance showed that even Stefan's face had eased into lines that some could consider almost a smile.

The four rode from one glen to another until Ronan finally slowed his horse to a walk. They stopped atop the next hill and looked down at the circle of gypsy wagons hidden in the wooded vale below.

Need pounded through Morcant. It was always the same. Women. He loved women. They were meant to be sheltered and protected, and made love to for hours until they were boneless and sated.

He made it his life's mission to woo and pleasure as many women as he could. His mother said it seemed as if his soul searched for something – or someone.

In fact, it was the opposite. Morcant wasn't looking for

anyone that would tie him down. His duties to his clan were all he would ever need or want.

"I've a bad feeling," Daman said as he shifted uncomfortably atop his mount. "We shouldna be here."

Morcant's horse flung up his head, and he brought his mount under control with soft words. "I've a need to sink my rod betwixt willing thighs. If you doona wish to partake, Daman, then doona, but you willna be stopping me."

"Nor me," Ronan said.

Stefan was silent for several moments before he gave Ronan a nod of agreement.

Ronan was the first to ride down the hill to the camp, and Morcant was right on his heels. He watched in interest as a young beauty with long, black hair came running out to greet Ronan in her brightly colored skirts. Ronan pulled his horse to a halt and jumped off with a smile as Ana launched herself into his arms. Ronan caught her and brought his lips down to hers. It was a reunion of lovers, and Morcant began to scan the female faces for his own. After all, why spend the night alone when there were willing women around?

Ronan and Ana spoke quietly before Ronan turned her toward them. "Ana, these are my friends, Daman, Morcant, and Stefan," he said, pointing to each of them in turn.

Her smile was wide as she held out her arm to the camp. "Welcome to our camp."

Morcant didn't wait on the others to dismount. He'd already found what he was looking for. He dropped the reins to allow his horse to graze freely and walked between two wagons into the center of the camp.

He glanced behind him to find Stefan following. Morcant paused when he noticed the indecision on Daman's face. It was long moments until Daman slid from his horse and gathered the reins of all four mounts to tether them together.

"I'll keep watch," Daman said as he sat outside the camp near a tree.

Ronan wrapped an arm around Ana and walked away, his voice calling, "Your loss."

Morcant gave a nod to Daman and then continued on his way to the woman he'd seen sitting on the steps to her wagon, her bright turquoise and yellow skirts dipping between her legs while she braided a leather halter for a horse.

"Och, but you're a bonny lass," Morcant said as he leaned against the side of the wagon.

Her dark eyes cut to look at him suspiciously. "I'm alone for a reason."

"And that is?"

"Not your concern," she said and went back to her braiding.

Morcant moved so that he stood in front of her. It took several moments before she lifted her black gaze to his. Her dark hair was down, the thick waves falling over her shoulders, begging to be touched.

"A woman should be protected. Why do you no' have someone protecting you?"

She shrugged and glanced around her. "I am protected. Look around. These people, my people, are my protection."

"But you're lonely."

It wasn't a question, and when she paused in her plaiting for a second time, Morcant stepped closer. "Why are you alone?" he pressed.

"My grandmother foretold that I would meet my husband on my travels, and that I must remain pure for him. That husband would give me a baby that would unite the gypsy clans in Romania. If I were to remain pure."

Morcant couldn't believe her words. Even if the foretelling were true, which he highly doubted, the gypsy was beautiful with her olive skin and large eyes. "It's difficult to refuse the pleasures of the flesh," he said as he guessed what had happened by the regret in her gaze.

"More than I ever imagined."

"Such a waste to leave someone so lovely on her own. Your family should be with you."

"I was part of a great prophecy that I ruined. My family shunned me," she said in a whisper, her eyes locking with his.

"I'm Morcant."

Her lips softened into another smile. "Denisa."

He closed the small gap between them. "I offer nothing more than pleasure."

"I shouldn't," she said softly.

Morcant touched her face with his fingers before he rubbed his thumb along her lower lip. "There's nothing wrong with giving in to your desires. You are sensual and beautiful. You were made to experience pleasure."

Without a word, she set aside the leather strips and stood before ducking into her wagon. Morcant smiled when her hand slid between the curtains and held one side open for him.

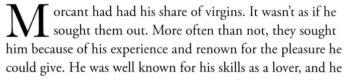

Morcant had had his share of virgins. It wasn't as if he sought them out. More often than not, they sought him because of his experience and renown for the pleasure he could give. He was well known for his skills as a lover, and he made sure never to leave a woman unsatisfied.

But the gypsy had lied to him. She hadn't given in to another man. He had been her first, which couldn't be good any way he tried to look at it. Why had she lied? He couldn't piece it together, but it didn't matter. He wouldn't be around long enough to learn the truth.

Denisa lay sleeping on her side, her long, black hair tangled and damp with sweat from their exertions. He had pleasured her until she was limp but just as always, nothing stirred within him.

He found his own release, but there was a weight, a deadness that filled him with each woman he slept with. Sometimes he felt as if it might swallow him whole.

Morcant leaned up on his elbow and lightly kissed Denisa on her forehead. He rose and dressed quietly. Now that his needs were seen to, he would sit with Daman until the others finished.

The night was shattered with an anguished scream, a soul-deep, fathomless cry that was wrung from the depths of someone's soul.

"What the hell," Morcant said as he hurried to exit the wagon still fastening his kilt.

His gaze snagged on Daman, who stood standing outside the wagons staring at something with a resigned expression on his face. Morcant turned to see what had caught Daman's attention, and found Ronan, shirtless with his hand on the hilt of his sword as he stood looking at an old woman who gazed down at something in the grass.

That's when Morcant spotted the bright pink and blue skirts of Ana, Ronan's lover. Even in the fading light of evening, there was no mistaking the dark stain upon the grass as anything but blood. Unease rippled through Morcant when he saw the dagger sticking out of Ana's stomach with her hand still around it. The night of pleasure and laughter vanished.

They needed to leave. Morcant shifted his gaze to Stefan, who stood amid a group of gypsies. Stefan gave him a nod.

Morcant began to softly, slowly pull his sword from his scabbard. The gypsies would blame Ana's suicide on Ronan.

The only way they would get out of this alive was by killing them all.

"Ronan," Stefan said urgently.

Morcant waited for Ronan to attack, but before Ronan could, the old woman let loose a shriek and pointed her gnarled finger at him. Ronan's eyes widened in confusion and anger.

Morcant heard a rustle behind him as Denisa poked her head out of the wagon. He glanced at her to see sadness fill her eyes. "What is going on?" he demanded in a quiet voice.

"Ana was Ilinca's granddaughter. She's using her magic to keep Ronan in place as she levels her curse upon him."

"Curse?" Morcant felt as if he'd been kicked by a horse. Daman had been right. They should have listened to his warning and never entered the camp.

It would be a miracle if they made it out alive.

Words tumbled from Ilinca's mouth, her wrinkled face a mask of grief and fury. Morcant didn't need to comprehend the words to realize Denisa was right, that Ilinca was cursing Ronan.

Morcant wasn't going to stand still and wait. With his sword in hand, he rushed to Ilinca, ready to take her head. He was a mere four steps away when she turned her furious gaze on him, and froze him in his tracks.

Morcant couldn't move no matter how much he tried. He couldn't shout a warning to Stefan, couldn't demand that Daman get away.

All he could do was watch helplessly as Ilinca went back to cursing Ronan.

The ever-present rage exploded in Stefan and he let out a battle cry worthy of his clan as he leapt over the fire toward Ilinca. But once more, the old gypsy used her magic to halt him.

Her gaze shifted to Daman. Morcant prayed Daman

would get help, but they had never left each other behind before. It wouldn't start now. Daman glanced at the ground and inhaled deeply. Then, with purposeful strides, he crossed some unseen barrier into the camp.

Morcant watched as Ronan squeezed his eyes shut, his body fairly vibrating with pain. And then he was gone, vanished as if he had never existed.

Ilinca faced Morcant next. She looked to Denisa's wagon, and her anger grew, becoming palpable. More incomprehensible words fell from her lips.

Morcant didn't have time to think of anything as his sword flew from his hand and pain exploded in his head. He squeezed his eyes shut, but there was no blocking it out. It went on for eternity.

When it finally died, Morcant discovered he could move. But when he opened his eyes, there was nothing but darkness.

And silence.

"This is for ruining Denisa and the foretelling that would unite all gypsies. For that, I curse you, Morcant Banner. Forever will you be locked in this place alone until you earn your freedom."

Morcant didn't feel anything. No heat, no cold, no wind, no rain, no hunger, no thirst. There was no light, no sound, no stirring of anything. He was utterly alone.

Not once had he ever been afraid, but he was now. He sank down and dropped his head in his hands. He hadn't been able to help Ronan, and he didn't know what had happened to Stefan and Daman. How was he to help any of them now when he didn't know where he was or how to get out?

Morcant squeezed his eyes closed and began to hum. Anything to break up the silence.

CHAPTER 1

1609 Scotland

Leana lifted her face to the wind and closed her eyes. There was a touch of fall upon the air, a nip of icy chill that hinted at the winter to come. She loved autumn, but winter was her favorite season. There was something peaceful and beautiful about the country blanketed in white.

The wind died away, and Leana opened her eyes to see the mountain's gentle slope to the valley below. The small village was all she knew. The people were good and kind. They were simple folk who lived simple lives.

They also meant well, but sometimes they didn't know when to leave well enough alone.

A gust of wind whipped her skirts about her legs violently. Leana adjusted the basket in her hands and turned around to finish her hike up the mountain to the other side where she could find the herbs she searched for.

Leana had walked the hills and mountains alone for as long as she could remember. The fact that the village was in the middle of Clan Sinclair meant that they were rarely raided by other clans. Not to say that the younger men of the village didn't join in with others and raid their closest neighbor – the MacKays.

As soon as she entered the forest, Leana let out a sigh. The forest always relaxed her. It was why she chose to remain in her cottage alone instead of moving to the village. She didn't understand the girls her age who were focused solely on finding a husband. There was more to life than a man.

Leana was alone, but she wasn't lonely. People tended to get the two confused, or assumed that she must be lonely because she was alone. Truth be told, people irritated her. They presumed, interfered, or simply tried to tell her what to do. As if any of it would work. Yet, no matter how many years passed, they continued on as they were, claiming it was for her own good.

As if they knew her well enough to know what was good for her.

Leana stopped and set her basket down as she knelt next to a bog myrtle shrub. She broke off several stems. The plant was used for a variety of applications, such as including it in her bedding to ward off insects, and occasionally adding it to her candles to help put her to sleep, especially when she combined some lavender into the wax, as well.

When she finished, Leana rose and continued her stroll through the ferns and trees. She found a small meadowsweet bush. Not only was it a great herb to cure headaches or calm nerves, but the leaves could also be used to treat sores. Leana took only a little of the meadowsweet so there would be more later.

She replenished more of her stock of herbs on her walk. Leana strolled leisurely through the trees, touching them as she passed. There were some so huge, her arms couldn't wrap half way around them. There were others so tall she was sure the tops brushed the clouds.

Songbirds chirped happily, filling the air with a continuous melody that seemed to grow louder and louder. Leana saw a wildcat out of the corner of her eye, but she knew better than to try and coax the animal to her. It would stay hidden until she left.

After another half hour of walking and collecting herbs, Leana sat against a tree and leaned her head back. Her eyes drifted shut and her mind began to drift as it often did when she was in the forest.

Except it wasn't the brush of a breeze on her cheek she felt. It was…emptiness. This was no dream. She calmed her racing heart when she realized she was having a vision. At first, there was nothing but darkness all around her sucking all the light. She couldn't see her hand in front of her face. Slowly, gradually she began to make out the shape of a man. He was down on one knee, hunched over so that his left hand was braced on the ground. He fisted his right hand and then spread his fingers, only to repeat the movements again and again. His sandy blonde hair hung loose and wavy around him, hiding his face from view.

He wore a saffron shirt and kilt, along with black boots. There was nothing that could hide the hard sinew that bunched in his arms and shoulders, or the fury that radiated from him as intensely as the rays of the sun.

Suddenly, he stilled. Then his head slowly turned to her, and he pinned her with his yellow-brown gaze that flared as bright as a topaz.

Morcant stood. He sat. He crawled, he kneeled, he even lay prone, but nothing helped. He shouted, he whispered. He cursed.

And he prayed.

His hand missed the feel of his sword. He missed the weight of the weapon, the leather-wrapped pommel, and the way the blade sounded when he swung it. The sword was his pride and joy, it was the only thing that meant anything to him other than the men he considered brothers – Stefan, Ronan, and Daman.

Where were they? Had the gypsy killed them? Perhaps she threw them in a prison like him. Saints, he hoped that wasn't the case. He didn't know how long he had been in the darkness, but he knew it was a considerable amount of time. Or perhaps it had only been a blink in time.

The fact he didn't need to eat or sleep worried him at first. That was soon forgotten as he realized the one thing that he couldn't relieve or ignore was his cock. He was in a constant state of arousal, and if he touched himself, it only made the need double.

Was this his punishment for sleeping with the lovely Denisa? She'd said she wasn't a virgin, but Morcant knew he would've likely taken her even if she had been honest. He had wanted a woman, and she was beautiful and willing.

He fell to his knee and closed his eyes as he concentrated on remembering what it felt like to hold his sword. He fisted his hand, just to spread his fingers wide and fist his hand again and again and again.

His balls tightened, and his cock jumped as a swell of desire shot through him. In his mind, he recalled how it felt to sink into the warm, wet flesh of a woman's sex, to have her legs wrap around him.

Sweat broke out over him as he fought not to grab his

cock and attempt to ease the devastating, engulfing hunger of his body. He fell to one knee and braced himself with his left hand, his fingers splayed upon the ground.

Not once in all his years before had he denied himself sex. The act allowed him pleasure, as well as the chance to lose himself for a few moments before he realized just how devoid his life truly was.

Morcant didn't know how long he remained in that position until he was able to think past the need clawing through him. When he could take a deep breath, he had the sensation that he was being watched.

He opened his eyes and slowly turned his head, but he saw nothing. Nothing but black as far as he could see. What he wouldn't do to see some color, even if it were the gray skies that could last for weeks in his beloved Scotland.

As dark as it was, Morcant could see himself when he looked down, but if there were anything or anyone else in the cursed place, he couldn't see or hear them.

He clenched his teeth. Morcant tried to remember Denisa's face and body, tried to recall how it had felt when he had lain with her, but he couldn't remember anything about her. There had even been a few occasions where he forgot her name.

When that happened, he would go through everyone he knew and recount their names as well as what they looked like because his fear was that he would lose himself in the blackness.

Perhaps he already had. His friends might be trying to wake him up, and he didn't even know it.

Or he could be dead and this was Hell.

He wouldn't claim to be a saint, but neither had he done enough to have his soul condemned to Hell. It could be purgatory, or it could be nothing. How many times had Morcant gone over this in his head? How many times had he talked out loud, hoping that something might make more sense if he heard it?

He was losing his mind. Bit by bit, little by little, the longer he remained in this wretched place, the more of him was taken.

He fought against it, but it did no good. The gypsy had seen to that.

CHAPTER 2

L eana's eyes snapped open, her heart pounding against her ribs. She wasn't sure what she had witnessed.

Everything had been too real. The darkness, the stillness. Then there was the man himself. She heard his ragged breathing, sensed the battle he waged within himself. She felt the warmth of his skin and was pierced by his topaz eyes.

As her breathing calmed, Leana recalled the man's face. She only had a glimpse, but his image was embedded in her mind. Sharp eyes, slender nose, hard jaw, sunken cheeks that accentuated his cheekbones, and too-wide lips. Whether she wanted to remember him or not, she didn't have a choice.

Leana shook her head to clear it. It had to have been a dream. There was no such man about the area, nor such a place of blackness. She always dreamed in the woods, though they weren't really dreams. She sometimes saw the future. It was just glimpses, barely blips of images that came to her, but days, weeks, or even months later, what she dreamt would come to pass.

Excitement blossomed in her chest at the thought that

she might get to see the man. That emotion died a swift death as she recalled his anger. No, it would be better if she forgot the dream and the man.

Leana got to her feet and dusted herself off before reaching for her basket. She began to walk back to the cottage, and that's when she realized how noisy the forest was. Halting, she looked up to the branches and saw birds everywhere.

All around her birds perched, looking down at her as they sang loudly. In all the times Leana had been in the forest, she had never seen so many birds or heard them singing so deafeningly. She lifted her skirts in her free hand and lengthened her strides. The day was an unusual one, and she wanted it behind her.

Leana hadn't gotten far when she slipped on the dead leaves. Her basket flew from her hands as she struggled to keep her footing and not tumble down the steep slope of the mountain.

She cried out as her feet came out from beneath her and she fell on her rump, sliding as she did. Leana grasped a passing tree and managed to stop herself. She pulled herself into a sitting position. The birds were fluttering now, their songs getting louder.

Leana covered her ears and looked down the mountain to her basket that had crashed against a giant oak, her herbs scattered. She stood on shaky legs and slowly made her way to the basket. It wasn't until she began to gather the herbs that the birds started to swoop around her. Leana hurriedly tossed the herbs into her basket, looking up as she did.

Her hand closed around something cold and metal. As soon as it did, the birds stopped singing. A moment later, their wings halted as they returned to the branches. The stillness was unnerving, but it was nothing compared to the utter silence.

Leana turned her head and looked down to see what it was she had grabbed. She frowned and pulled it out from beneath the ferns to reveal a sword. She marveled at the size of it. Even with both her hands on the pommel, there was still room. It was made for a man with large hands, a man with strength enough to wield such a weapon.

Slowly, she withdrew the weapon from the scabbard to look upon the blade itself. It was flawless. She tested one edge by running the pad of her thumb across the blade and saw a small line of blood bubble from her skin.

Why would anyone leave such a weapon behind? Leana fit the sword back into the scabbard. Whatever the reason, the weapon was now hers. She would learn to use it just as she had her brother's bow and arrows. It wasn't going to be easy, but she was more than capable of taking care of herself. And she would prove it once again.

Leana carried the sword in one hand and the basket in the other. She rose and turned around, only to freeze. Not five feet from her lay an unconscious man with long, sandy blonde hair in the same tartan she had seen in her vision. The sword fell from her numb fingers. She could only stare in shock. It was as if her vision had brought him to life.

She set the basket down carefully and hesitantly walked to him. Leana knelt beside him. Several seconds passed before she reached out and warily moved a portion of his hair that covered half his face.

As soon as she did, there was a flutter of wings as the birds suddenly took to the skies and flew away. She watched them for a moment before she turned her attention back to the man.

Leana was enraptured by the striking male. His skin was deeply tanned, and there was a short beard of a darker blonde than his hair covering his face that did nothing to hide the hard lines of his jaw and chin.

She let her fingers brush over the beard, amazed at how soft the bristles were. That's when her gaze snagged on a scar that ran along his face from his right temple into his hairline. It was jagged and looked as though it went deep. How she wanted to know what caused such a scar.

Her gaze leisurely drank in his amazing face from his brows that matched his beard, to his crooked nose, to his mouth. Her eyes then drifted lower to the open expanse of his saffron shirt that revealed lean muscle honed to perfection.

Leana swallowed hard and, unable to help herself, pulled open his shirt a little more. She told herself it was to look for a wound, but she knew it was to see more of such a fine specimen. He was unlike any man she had ever encountered – or was likely to see again.

His skin was warm, as if the sun had been upon him. Something that was difficult in the deep shade of the tall trees. She bit her lip as she flattened her hand upon his chest. Beneath her palm, she could feel the steady beat of his heart. His breathing was even, but that didn't explain why he was unconscious.

Leana began to worry that there really was a wound she couldn't see. She forgot her exploration of his fine body and began to smooth her hands gently over his torso. She touched his side, only to have his fingers clamp around her wrist. Her eyes jerked to his face to find him staring at her. She opened her mouth to speak but didn't get a sound out as she was suddenly on her back with him leaning over her.

"Who are you?" His voice was deep, raspy, as if it hadn't been used in awhile.

She was taken aback by the intensity of his golden brown eyes. "Leana."

"Is this a trick?" he asked with a frown.

Leana shook her head, all too aware of his very male

body atop her. She liked the feel of him entirely too much. His muscles. His weight. His…hardness that pressed into her stomach. "Nay."

His topaz eyes lifted from hers to glance quickly around. "How am I here?"

"I don't know. One moment you weren't, and the next you were. I was attempting to see if you had an injury." She twisted her wrists that he held in each hand to remind him he had a hold of her.

His frown faded when he looked at her wrists, and then he slowly returned his gaze to her. Gone was the confusion, replaced by blatant desire. Leana's blood heated instantly, and her nipples tightened at the look in his eyes. If he could make her feel like that with just a look, what would happen if he touched her?

Morcant fought against the desire, rallied against the vast hunger to sate himself on such a woman until neither could move. He remained still and prayed the lass did the same. If she moved, he wasn't sure he would be able to keep himself in check. As if sensing how perilously close he was to losing control, she grew so still she was barely breathing.

He couldn't believe he was out of the darkness. His mind was a jumble of questions, as his senses were bombarded with sounds and sights. He wanted to soak it all in, but he couldn't make himself move off the woman.

She was a bonny lass with rich, brown hair and eyes as blue as the sky. Those eyes watched him carefully, her fear kept hidden. She stared at him, unblinking, as if she were trying to decide if he were real.

Her heart-shaped face was beyond lovely. There was something in the curve of her full lips and the direct stare of her sky blue eyes that was both accepting and curious. He longed to stroke his fingers down her smooth cheek to her neck, and lower to her breasts pressed against him.

Her soft curves that cradled his body were only clouding his mind. His cock ached to be inside her, to relieve the torment that had been his for countless days.

"You were in the darkness," she said in a soft whisper.

His brow furrowed as he recalled sensing someone watching him not long before he was suddenly jerked out of his prison so hard that he blacked out. "How do you know that?"

"I...I saw it."

"Impossible."

She lifted a brow. "As impossible as you suddenly appearing? Were you in darkness?"

He debated whether to answer her. Who in their right mind would believe a word he said about such a place? Then again, if she *had* seen him, she might be the only one who would believe him. "Aye."

"That place was awful," she said with a shudder.

His desire faded as he thought of his prison and his friends. Morcant rolled off her to sit with his arms resting on his knees. "How did you see me?"

"I don't know," Leana said as she sat up and picked leaves from her long braid. "I sometimes see things that eventually come to pass."

"You see things?" he asked curiously as he turned his head to look at her.

She shrugged and looked down at her faded blue gown. "I don't tell people that normally."

"Who am I to tell?"

There was a hint of a smile as she cut her eyes to him. "True. Where were you, when I saw you?"

"What did you see?" He wanted to know how long she had watched him.

"Not much. I saw you kneeling. I could sense your anger and frustration."

He looked back to the trees. "My ever-present companions."

"Why didn't you leave such a place?"

"I tried. Many times. It was my prison, I suppose you could call it."

Leana's head turned to him. "Prison? Who put you there?"

"A gypsy." Morcant looked at her to see her eyes widen.

"I've heard rumors of the power of gypsy curses. You must have angered her greatly."

Morcant grunted as he recalled that awful night, though Ilinca's fury was mostly directed at Ronan. He knew Stefan and Daman well enough to know both of them would search for him and Ronan until their deaths.

He knew by Leana's brogue that he was still in the Highlands, but he didn't know how far he was from his clan. The sooner he started toward home, the sooner he could meet up with Stefan and Daman and help them find Ronan, because if he could get out of his prison, then so could Ronan, wherever he was.

"Where am I?"

"The Sinclair clan."

Morcant briefly closed his eyes. He was days away from home. Then another question occurred to him: just how long had he been in his prison. "What year is it?"

"1609. I gather by the muscle jumping in your temple that my answer wasn't what you wanted?"

He laughed, though there was no mirth in the sound. "I knew I was confined for a long time, but I didna think it would be nearly two hundred years."

"Two hundred?" Leana asked with wide eyes. "That can't be correct."

Morcant rose to his feet and walked to a spot of sunlight that filtered through the trees. "The last time I saw the sky, it was the Year of our Lord 1427." He turned his head to her. "I was with three of my closest friends. All I could think about while in the darkness was finding them. Now I know that's impossible, at least for two of them."

"Why?" she asked and climbed to her feet.

"The gypsy that cursed me, Ilinca, was furious over her granddaughter's suicide. She blamed my friend, Ronan. I was trying to help him when she threw me into the darkness. If she didna kill Ronan, he could be in a similar prison."

"And the other two friends?"

Morcant fisted his hands as he itched for his sword. "They'll either have been smart and gotten away, in which case they're long dead, or..." he trailed off as he considered what could have happened.

"Or," Leana pressed.

"Or they were imprisoned like me."

Leana smoothed out her skirts and eyed him. "If I didn't have glimpses of things to come, or if I hadn't seen you before you appeared, I'd think you were daft. If I were you, I wouldn't repeat any of this to others. Good luck finding your friends."

He nodded his thanks and watched as she bent to pick up a basket. It wasn't until she grasped something else that he realized it was a sword – *his* sword!

Morcant wasn't going anywhere without his sword.

CHAPTER 3

Leana hadn't gotten three steps before she heard the man following her. He set her on edge, reminded her, as no one else could, that she was alone, likely never to know the touch of a man.

"Hold up, Leana," he said as he hurried to catch up.

She didn't slow her steps. Every time she looked at him, she wanted to wrap her arms around him and beg him to lie atop her once more so she could feel his weight again. It should be wrong for a man's body to feel so good atop her.

"I think you freed me," he said.

She glanced at him. "Perhaps. Make use of it and find your friends."

"I should repay you."

"There's no need," she said as she strode up the hill at a brisk pace.

He stopped and said, "To be honest, I was wondering if I could beg a meal. I have no coin or belongings with which to trade. I doona even have a weapon."

Leana's steps slowed and then halted. She tightened her grip on the sword. Giving it to him wasn't an option, but she could feed him. She turned to face him. "I don't even know your name."

"Morcant Banner, lass," he said with a bright smile.

She knew with such a sexy, rakish smile like his that there were few women who had refused him anything. "Well, Morcant, you have a grand adventure ahead of you. I can't in good conscience send you on your way without a meal."

"That's verra kind of you," he said and closed the distance between them. He reached for the sword, "Let me help you carry that."

Leana easily dodged his hands. "I'm capable of carrying it myself."

He held up his hands and flashed that charming grin. "Forgive me. I just wanted to help."

She continued walking, and he kept pace with her. Leana let the silence go on for a while. He smiled and acted as if everything was fine, but he couldn't hide the pain and confusion in his beautiful topaz eyes.

Leana covertly watched him out of the corner of her eye. He kept fisting his hands, just as she saw him do while in the darkness. The weight of the sword in her hand made her wonder if it was simply a coincidence that she'd found the weapon right before he had appeared – or if the sword were his. There was no doubt he was a man accustomed to having a weapon.

She wasn't as taken aback by his story as others would be because she had encounters with the gypsies before. She had seen, firsthand, what some of them were capable of when they were wronged.

Magic wasn't a word she bandied about, and yet, it was a word she knew all too well, and not just from her experience with the gypsies. Nor did it have anything to do with her visions.

No, the villagers spoke the word often in regards to her.

They said her use of herbs to heal was unexplainable, magical. Perhaps it was magic that helped her know which herbs to use for what. She didn't know or care.

Morcant was an oddity, much like herself. Is that why she felt the need to help him? Or was it because she found him all too appealing?

"Did you eat while in the darkness?" she asked to fill the silence.

"Nay. I wasna hungry or thirsty, though I find I'm famished now."

She glanced over to find him looking at her, his eyes watching her curiously. "Do I have leaves in my hair?"

"Nay," he replied softly, a half smile upon his lips. "I just didna expect to finally get out of my prison and be confronted with such a lovely vision."

Leana held back her snort. She didn't take his words to heart, because she knew while she might look good to a starving man now, he wouldn't remember her afterward.

"You doona believe me?" he said, his voice filled with surprise.

Leana reached the top of the steep incline and shrugged. "You said you didn't feel hunger until you were released. I suppose you didn't feel a man's need until now either."

"You'd be wrong, lass."

His words were laced with fury, causing her gaze to jerk to him. Leana saw the truth shining in his eyes. He hadn't suffered just the darkness. He'd endured unending longing, as well.

She swallowed and quickly looked away when his gaze dropped to her breasts. Leana recalled all too well how delightful he'd felt atop her. "In the valley is a small village. On the edge of town is a widow who lost her much older husband during the winter. She'll be more than willing to take you to her bed."

"You think you know me well enough to know what I want?"

She tried to ignore the scorn in his voice. "I know men."

"I've known a lot of women, but I doona claim to know you because of it."

Leana pushed the stray hairs out of her face from the wind. "It isn't difficult to know a man. You're ruled by your cock, your stomach, and bloodshed."

"Is that so," he replied with a cool look. "Tell me then, what type of man am I?"

Every instinct screamed for her to walk away and forget his challenge, but when had Leana ever walked away from anything? It was a trait that got her in trouble more times than she could remember. Instead, she faced Morcant and locked gazes with him.

"You're the type of man who easily charms. You're the type of man who is used to getting whatever he wants. You're the type of man who leaves a string of broken hearts wherever he goes. You're the type of man who gives his word to another man, but never to a woman."

For long moments, he simply stared at her. Then he said, "I doona deny loving women. They are meant to be protected and sheltered. They were made to be loved by men, to be brought unimaginable pleasure. If it's wrong that I've given women ecstasy, then condemn me."

"You've already been condemned by the gypsy," Leana pointed out.

"Aye. You've the right of it. I no' only went with my friends, but I did find a willing bed partner before that."

"If she was willing, then why did the gypsy curse you?"

He raked a hand through his long blonde hair and blew out a deep breath as his gaze shifted to the valley and the village. "The woman I bedded told me she'd already had another man before me. She lied."

"She was an innocent?" Leana asked in shock.

Morcant stiffly nodded his head. "I've had women say they were virgins when they were no', but I've never had one claim to be experienced and no' be."

Leana swung her gaze to the village. "Did you confront her with it?"

"What good would it have done?"

"None, I suppose." She turned to the right and began walking.

Morcant's heavy footfalls fell in behind her. "You doona live in the village?"

"Nay."

"What will you tell your husband about me?"

Leana glanced over her shoulder. "Nothing. I don't have a husband."

"Your father, then?"

"He's dead, as are my brothers, my sister, my mother, and my two uncles."

She was a bit surprised when Morcant didn't ask why she lived alone, but she was glad she didn't have to explain it. The rest of the walk to the cottage was done in silence, making her aware of his every move, his every breath until she was anxious to put some distance between them.

Leana jerked to a stop when Morcant's hand suddenly snaked out and grasped her upper arm, drawing her to a stop. Her head snapped to him, realizing too late that she didn't know how to use the sword to defend herself. The one weapon she could use, was inside the cottage.

"How long have you been gone, lass?" he whispered as his gaze surveyed their surroundings.

"I left after the noon meal."

He gave a quick look to the sky. "It's been hours. It's no' wise to walk blithely in there without first ensuring there are no' enemies about."

"The only enemies we have this far onto Sinclair land are the few raiders from the MacKays."

Morcant pointed to the ground a few feet in front of them. "That boot print is much larger than yours. Far afield or no', you can no' be too careful."

A shiver raced through Leana. There was no denying the proof of Morcant's words. "There's been talk over the past few months, but I didn't believe any of it. Old men talk of the past and how things were."

"What are they saying?"

She pulled her eyes away from the ground and the boot print to Morcant. "The MacKays lost many of their warriors in last fall's battle with the Frasers. The Frasers then raided the MacKays and took all their sheep. The MacKay laird was killed trying to get the sheep back, and the clan has been in an uproar ever since. Many have left the clan, and the ones who remained took to raiding during the winter to keep from starving."

"In other words, the men who remain are more bandits and criminals than clansmen," Morcant said with a frown.

Leana swiveled her head from one side to the other looking through the dense trees set behind the cottage to the stream that ran on the left side. "A new laird stepped forward, and he's working to unite his clan once more, but it's been a slow process."

"It doesna bode well for your clan if the raiders are making it this far in without being seen." Morcant made her face him. "Remain here while I have a look inside."

Leana didn't have to be told twice. She was rooted to the spot, watching as Morcant walked cautiously toward the door. She was struck anew with his masculinity and strength.

He bent and picked up a log of wood stacked by the door, the muscles in his forearm flexing as his fingers wrapped around the firewood. The way he stalked the cottage, the way he saw and heard every sound, reminded her of a predator closing in on his prey.

Her breath locked in her lungs when he slowly opened the door and slipped inside. Leana kept waiting to hear a crash as he came upon an intruder, but a moment later he walked back outside.

Morcant put a hand to his lips to keep her quiet when she started to speak. Leana's eyes followed him as he walked around the cottage with the same alert and vigilant motions as before. When she lost sight of him, Leana's gaze jerked to the other side of the cottage and waited for him to reappear. When he did, he walked casually, replacing the log as he did.

"Whoever was here is gone now," he said. "It isna a safe place for you to be alone."

She walked past him through the door into the cottage. "It's my home. I'm not leaving it."

"You say that as though I'm no' the first to mention it to you."

"Because you're not." Leana set down her herbs on the table before standing the sword next to her bow and quiver of arrows alongside the hearth. "I'll have some food ready shortly."

She heard the chair scrape the boards as he pulled it out and sat. Leana tried to ignore Morcant, but his very presence sucked all the space from the tiny structure.

"What happened to your parents?" he asked.

Leana paused in chopping the carrots. "No one can escape death when it comes for you, and it comes in various ways. My mum died years ago during childbirth. My youngest brother, who was stillborn, is buried with her."

"You mentioned other brothers."

"I had four older brothers and one younger. All sought glory and readily answered the call to go raiding or into battle. Each time one left, they didn't return," she said as she reached for another carrot.

A large hand covered hers, stilling her hand before she could move. Morcant was close behind her, his heat seeping through her clothes. When had he moved? She hadn't heard him, hadn't sensed he'd left the chair.

"That couldna have been easy."

Goosebumps rose along her skin as his baritone voice spoke softly near her ear. "My father and one of my uncles left to get revenge on the deaths of my youngest brother slain in battle. As soon as word reached us that they were unaccounted for, my other uncle left to join the fighting. It was a week later that all three were returned to me for burial."

Morcant's hand lightly squeezed her. "They shouldna have left you."

"I had my sister." Leana could've sworn he moved closer. She closed her eyes and fought not to lean back against him.

"Where did she go?"

Leana looked down at Morcant's hand atop hers. Her heart missed a beat when she felt his warm breath against her cheek. How was she to think coherently with him so close? Didn't he understand that he set her off-kilter, that she couldn't think of anything but his nearness? "She married a man from the village and died nine months later while birthing her first babe."

"And the bairn?"

She closed her eyes, recalling how she fought to keep the infant alive. "A fever took him. Not even my skill with herbs could save him. Just like everyone else, he left me."

CHAPTER 4

Morcant didn't think Leana knew how telling her words were. He could feel her pain and loneliness, the anger and resentment. His first instinct was to take her mind off of her troubles by kissing her, but something stopped him.

His body ached for relief, to sink between her thighs and seek the pleasure that awaited him. Leana's body was more than appealing. Her independence was as beautiful to him as her face and her figure.

He didn't know what stopped him from seducing her. The fact that she didn't push him away as he touched her hand and molded himself to her should have spurred him onward.

Could the darkness have changed him? Did the years there remembering Denisa and her lie alter him? Or was it the countless faces of the women he'd bedded that went through his head constantly over the two hundred years of his confinement, reminding him of the emptiness he felt in their arms that stopped him?

He wanted relief. He wanted pleasure.

But he didn't want that empty feeling in his chest that always occurred after the satisfaction wore off – and occasionally before.

Morcant found he was content to stay as he was touching Leana. He craved conversation almost as much as he longed to be touched. It hadn't hit him until that moment. His chest constricted at all he had lost – his family, his friends...his life.

How had he taken the everyday exchanges with his friends, the unintended brushes against another, or a lover's caress for granted? Morcant closed his eyes against the agony.

All of it was crashing upon him now, and he didn't think he could stand beneath the weight of it all.

When Leana's head dropped back against his chest, he brought his other hand up and set it at her waist. He wanted to turn her around and kiss her, but even the comfort they were giving each other now was enough to heave off the depression that threatened.

Morcant slowly opened his eyes. "Why have you no' found a husband?"

"So he can leave me, as well?" she asked without any heat in her words.

"You need someone to protect you."

"I protect myself. I learned how to use the bow and arrows, and I'll learn how to use the sword."

His sword. Morcant wanted it back, but he wouldn't leave her undefended to do it. As skilled as he was, he could get another weapon quickly enough. "That sword wasna made for a woman. It was meant to be in a man's large hands."

"I'll learn."

"No doubt," he whispered as he looked down at her face.

Her lashes fluttered and her eyes opened. He gazed into her sky blue eyes, lost in the utter blueness, drowning in the absolute acceptance he saw.

"You're hungry."

For much more than food, but Morcant didn't correct her. Leana had been nothing but kind. He wouldn't ruin things by seducing her only to leave her. Too many had already abandoned her. He wouldn't add his name to the list.

"I respect your independence, Leana, and even if you learn how to use the sword, against a group of men, you'll be overtaken easily."

She straightened and moved her hand from beneath his. "I know. I'm often reminded of how easily I can be over-powered."

"You're speaking of someone in particular." Morcant didn't know how he knew such a thing, only that he did. He returned to his seat, missing her touch, missing her warmth. "Who are you talking about?"

"His name is William," she said and chopped the carrot with a hard stroke. "He's been after me to marry him for years."

"So he loves you."

Leana threw him a look. "Nay. William doesn't like to be denied anything."

"If a man willna take no for an answer, it's more than just being denied."

She dumped the carrots into a pot and shrugged. "William thinks I cannot survive without a man."

"And you plan to prove him wrong?" Somehow that made Morcant smile. If there was a woman that could do it, he imagined it would be Leana.

"I've done it this long. I can continue."

Morcant never paid that much attention to women while they cooked, but he found his gaze locked on Leana. There was nothing sexual about her movements, and yet, just watching her eased the storm within him.

Had anyone told him before that he would find contentment watching a lass cook, he'd have laughed them out of his clan.

There was no doubt Leana was capable. She had to be in order to live so far from the village on her own. The spring and summer months would be the easiest for her, but the fall and winter couldn't be easy. The idea of her starving left him frowning.

"Who hunts for you?"

She pointed to the bow and quiver of arrows next to his sword. "I learned to use the bow. I also fish in the river and have my own chickens and geese. I'm not without food."

"Apparently no'," he mumbled

She used her shoulder to move hair out of her face. "There's nothing wrong with being alone."

"Other than being lonely?" he asked. "You can no' claim no' to be lonely, lass."

Her chopping paused for a heartbeat. "On occasion."

"Do you no' want a husband and bairns?"

"I did at one time."

Intrigued, Morcant sat forward so that his arms rested on his knees. "What happened?"

"I was left alone. Then I took a good look at what was available in the village, and realized I'd rather be alone."

Morcant scratched his beard. "I doona believe a bonny lass such as yourself didna have offers from men of other clans during Highland Games and such."

"I had one or two," she said flippantly.

That's when he comprehended what she wasn't saying. "You didna want to leave your land."

"Aye." Her response was barely a whisper.

"If you were part of my clan, I wouldna allow you to remain alone. If you didna wish to marry, I'd ensure there was someone checking in on you and helping when you needed."

She chuckled, smiling over her shoulder at him. "You say that as if you've ruled a clan before."

Morcant leaned back in his chair and looked away. Until that moment, he hadn't allowed himself to think of what was now out of reach. Once again, wave after wave of regret, guilt, and fury assaulted him. All because he had let his cock rule him.

He knew that wasn't the only reason. Even if he hadn't taken Denisa's maidenhead, he would have defended Ronan, which would likely have landed him in the same predicament.

"Morcant?"

His gaze jerked to Leana to find her half turned to him, her forehead furrowed in question. "My father was laird," he explained. "I was the second son of four. My father was killed in an ambush along with my mother, and my elder brother came close to dying. I took over while he recovered."

"And after?" she pressed.

"After, I was there for my brother. I did what was needed."

"But you enjoyed leading."

For the first time, Morcant admitted to what he hadn't even been able to confess to his friends. "Aye. Verra much."

"I know you want to find your friends, but is it wise to return to your clan?"

"Probably no', but that's the best place to begin."

She nodded and turned back to the food. "I've not stopped to ask how you're feeling. You seem to be taking all of this so...well."

"What I feel willna change how things are."

"You can't just ignore your emotions."

He smiled then. "Och, lass, but you sound like my mother."

Leana ducked her head, but he didn't miss the small

smile that tilted up the corners of her mouth. She had no idea how charming she was, how uttering mesmerizing he found her.

He fisted his hands, not for his sword, but because he longed to touch her again, to slide his fingers into the long, cool length of her dark hair and hold her against him as he sampled her inviting lips.

Morcant suddenly stood. If he remained, he would do something stupid like try to touch her again. "I'm going to..." He trailed off since he didn't know what to do. "I'll be outside," he finished and stalked from the cottage.

Once outside, he drew in a deep breath and fought against the desire that raged. Would he ever be rid of it? If he eased himself now, would he find relief? He briefly thought of going to the village and finding the widow Leana had spoken of, but the thought of leaving Leana alone didn't sit right with him.

Morcant couldn't explain the silent urging telling him he had to remain close to her, as if he were being forewarned of something. He couldn't ignore the warning any more than he could pretend he wasn't adrift in a time he didn't know or belong in.

He walked to the stream and knelt against the grass before he splashed the cold water on his face. With water dripping from his beard, he looked up and let his gaze roam over the rugged landscape.

Unable to resist, he plunged his hands back into the water. How he had missed the feel of it on his hands. One of his favorite things was to swim, and he had been denied that for far too long.

There would be a loch somewhere close, and Morcant would find it soon. Then he would spend hours in the water making up for lost time.

He dropped his chin to his chest as he pulled his hands

from the stream. He was being tugged in several directions. There was his need to find out what had happened to Daman, Ronan, and Stefan, the desire to protect Leana, and then his wants like swimming, laying upon the ground and staring up at the sky, holding his sword in his hand, and riding upon a fast steed.

If he remained, he could accomplish two of the three, but then how could he face himself every day if he didn't learn about his friends?

Morcant sat, the uncomfortable weight of decisions settling over him. He hadn't minded the decisions while he acted as laird, but that was for the clan, not for himself.

As late afternoon turned into evening, Morcant watched the sun sink behind the mountains and the sky turn to orange and deep red with a smile upon his face. The sunset would be seared into his memory, not just because it was beautiful, but because it was the first time he had seen color in over two hundred years.

And he had no one to share it with. His smile faded as he thought of Leana. He wanted to call her out to join him, and as he was about to do just that, he stopped. Being too close to her was a temptation he didn't need. Leana had been kind. The least he could do was keep from touching her.

Morcant let out a breath and leaned back on his hands. As the sky darkened, it reminded him too much of his prison, causing him to become agitated and anxious. He stood and walked to the forest to gather wood. After he stacked it by the cottage, he checked the gate holding the chickens. Next, he walked the perimeter of the cottage looking for anything out of the ordinary.

Only when there was nothing else for him to do did he return to the stream and pace back and forth hoping the trickle of water would calm him as Leana did.

But it didn't.

Morcant dropped his head back as he clenched his teeth. Then he opened his eyes and saw the stars. The pinpricks of light reminded him he was no longer in the darkness.

His breathing evened and his heart stopped racing. A bright light to his left drew his gaze. Morcant turned his head and spotted the full moon that crept over the mountains. The simple beauty of it held him transfixed, captivated.

CHAPTER 5

Leana stood in the doorway of the cottage staring at Morcant. The way he looked at the moon hit her right in the heart. She didn't think he realized the joy and sheer delight his expression stated.

Since she had found him and he woke, he'd kept himself tightly controlled, but eventually, he would come unwound. Remorse weighed heavily upon him. Even with that weight, he stood proud and strong, almost as if daring the world to try and crush him.

She had never been courageous enough to do that. It was all she could do to face each day, and yet a small victory came with each evening.

Leana was drawn to Morcant. She couldn't deny it, nor did she want to. He placed no demands on her. He accepted her for who she was. She wondered if that was just the type of man he was, or if it was because he was in a world two centuries later than when he had last seen it?

She shook her head. Nay, Morcant might be struggling to come to terms with things, but that's not why he treated her the way he did. Perhaps that was the reason she hadn't pulled away from his touch earlier.

The simple truth was that he confused her. He made her forget her need to be independent and free of a man's rule. All Morcant made her think of was heated touches, sighs of ecstasy, and nights of pleasure.

She licked her lips, wondering what it would be like to kiss him. In all her years, she'd had only one kiss, and that had been from William when he first tried to woo her. It had been rough, sloppy, and wet.

Morcant's kiss would be the exact opposite. It was the easy way he moved, as if he were one with the world, as if he knew he owned it and didn't care what others thought that made her so certain.

His touch earlier had been light and gentle, but insistent enough so that she knew he was there. Her stomach trembled just thinking about how he had held her securely, and how she had given in and rested her head back against him.

Did he have any idea how much that little bit of weakness had cost her? She didn't think he did, nor did he fathom how much she gained from setting her burdens on his wide, thick shoulders for a short time.

Leana stepped from the cottage and made her way toward Morcant as if some unknown force pulled them together. It frightened her, this undeniable power that ruled her body. Mostly because it felt...right.

She stopped a few feet from him. He was bathed in moonlight as he tilted his face upward with his eyes closed. The complete happiness on his face made her heart skip a beat.

"Even with my eyes closed I can see the light," he said softly. His head turned to her as his lids lifted to spear her with his topaz gaze.

That's when she realized it was the night that reminded

him of his prison. She'd had a glimpse of it and knew first hand the utter darkness that once surrounded him.

Leana closed the distance between them and tugged a strand of his hair caught in his beard. "There is light all around you."

"Aye," he whispered and ran a hand down her face. His gaze intensified as he caught and held hers. "None more so than what stands before me now. You've no idea how beautiful the moonlight looks on you."

She wasn't sure how to respond. Leana began to back away, when his hand halted her with the soft grasp of her arm.

"Doona leave. Please," he pleaded. He glanced away, his smile replaced with a frown of regret. "I've been alone so long I no longer remember how to act. Forgive me if I upset you."

"It's me," she hurried to say. "I don't know how to act when receiving a compliment."

Leana could once more feel the heat of him they were so close, and again, she didn't want to move away. She wanted to be closer. All too clearly, she recalled the feel of his muscles as she had touched him earlier. Her gaze lowered to his chest. His shirt still hung open, giving her an eyeful of hard sinew.

Her mouth went dry as she thought about his shirt and kilt being gone, his body bared to her to explore as long as she wanted. The uncontrollable, irresistible need was making her forget everything else.

With her heart pounding, she raised her gaze to his face. Palpable desire hung between them. Her mouth went dry when his eyes dropped to her lips. Her lips parted of their own accord as if seeking his kiss.

"Supper is ready," she blurted out.

Just like that, a wall came down, shutting him away. "Of course."

Leana closed her eyes as he walked past. She wanted that

kiss. So why had she spoken? Why couldn't she have let it happen?

Because you know he'll leave you like the others.

Yes, that was part of it, but the other part was that she was too afraid to take the chance of finding anything so wonderful, only to realize it wasn't hers to have.

Leana turned on her heel and followed Morcant into the cottage.

~

It was the longest night of Morcant's life. Leana's meal had been amazing, even if the conversation was stilted. She hadn't asked him to stay, and he hadn't tried to talk her into it.

She expected him to go to the village but he hadn't. Though he probably should have. Instead, Morcant remained in the woods behind Leana's cottage watching over her.

Unable to sleep, his mind was in a whirlwind. His thoughts drifted from his friends, to Ilinca who had cursed him, to the family he no longer had. However, mostly he thought of Leana.

The woman was driving him mad with desire, and she didn't even know it. He found it ironic that in the past, he would have simply moved on to another woman.

It wasn't just that he didn't want to find another woman but that no other would do. He had done no more than touch Leana, and yet the longing to have her was greater than anything he had ever experienced.

An eternity later, the sun finally broke the mountains. Morcant decided it was time to learn more about the village and the threat from the MacKay clan. Until he knew how imminent the threat was, he couldn't start to look for his friends.

Leana walked to the cottage with the hare dangling from her fingers and the bow in her other hand. It didn't take long to skin the rabbit and set it to roasting over the fire. She dusted off her hands and looked around her home. Morcant had made it seem small, but without him in it, it just seemed...empty.

Her gaze snagged on the sword. She claimed to be able to take care of herself, and in most cases she could, but Morcant was right. She couldn't stand against more than one man if attacked.

Leana grasped the pommel with her right hand, and with her left, removed the scabbard from the sword. The weapon was so heavy that she had to hold it with both hands as she walked outside.

She was never more thankful of living alone as she was when she tried to swing the sword. The weight of it caused her to lose her balance as it swung downward. She had no choice but to let go of it as she fell.

With a sigh, she climbed back to her feet and started again. Each time she fell, she got back up and kept trying. It didn't take long for her arms to begin shaking from the weight of the sword. If she continued, she was liable to take her foot off.

Leana was putting the sword back in the house when she heard a horse approach. She quickly notched an arrow and aimed it in the direction of the rider. Even when she spotted the dark red hair of William, she didn't lower the arrow. He reined his horse quickly, causing the animal to turn to the side and snort in protest.

"What are you doing, Leana?" William asked gruffly. "You know it's me."

She raised a brow. "So?"

"Lower the weapon, damn you."

"What do you want?"

He glared at her weapon a moment. "I came to see if you were all right. There's talk that someone saw you with a man yesterday."

"That's none of your concern."

"It is," he said affronted. "You're mine, Leana, you just doona realize it yet."

She rolled her eyes. "When did you hear about this strange man, William? Yesterday? Before or after you were at the pub? If you were so concerned for me, then you should've come immediately."

His face went red with anger. "That's no' fair, woman, and you know it."

"Thank you for the concern, but as I've told you, I don't need it."

"You do," he stated, his face still red as he started to dismount.

Leana pulled back the string on the bow. "I wouldn't do that unless you want this arrow in your gut. Find yourself a wife. The widow has all but thrown herself at you. Besides, you sleep in her bed nearly every night."

"How do you know that?" he demanded taken aback.

She didn't bother answering, and a heartbeat later, he swung his horse around and galloped off. Leana lowered the bow. It was a good thing William had been far enough away not to see how her arms shook holding the string.

"So that was William."

Leana jerked around to find Morcant standing at the side of the cottage with his arms crossed and a small smile playing about his wide lips. "How long have you been there?"

"Long enough to tell you that if you're going to use that sword, you're going to need someone to teach you."

She looked inside the cottage to the sword lying on the

table. "It's a heavy sword."

"It was made for a man."

"You've seen swords made for women?"

He shook his head. "Nay, but that doesna mean it can no' be done."

"That's your sword."

He stared her a long while, and then gave a single nod.

"I found it just before you appeared," she explained. "Why didn't you just take it from me."

"As you said, you found it."

Leana set the bow and arrow aside. "You could've over-powered me at any time. You could've taken it when I wasn't looking."

"I'm no' that kind of man."

"Nay, you're not."

Once more, she was held by his topaz gaze. His long, sandy blonde hair was pulled back in a queue, making his face look harsher.

He dropped his arms and pushed away from the cottage. He hesitated a second before walking slowly to her. "William is a big man, but the imprint we found yesterday was bigger."

"Which means it was someone else."

"Aye. Are you worried?"

She wasn't as long as he was there, but he had to find his friends. Leana couldn't ask him to stay. It wouldn't be right. "Did you come back for your sword?"

"Nay."

"Did you come back to tell me about the boot print?"

He shook his head.

"Then why did you come back?"

"I never left."

Leana tried to hide her surprise. Her voice was breathless as she asked, "Why?"

"You, Leana. I'm here because of you."

CHAPTER 6

"**I** don't understand."

Morcant wasn't sure he did either, but he wasn't going to fight the draw he had to Leana. Every time he did, it felt as if he were pushing against fate.

He halted several paces from her. "I tried leaving this morning. I got as far as the village before I turned around."

She blinked slowly, her lips parting slightly.

Morcant shrugged. "I didna even have to enter the village to discover the people are afraid. The castle near here, Ravensclyde, do you know it?"

"Aye. Everyone does," she answered.

"Apparently, the Sinclair clan has grown while I've been imprisoned. Your laird has several castles, as well as stewards. The lord of Ravensclyde is coming this way with men."

Leana rubbed her forehead as she looked around. "I see."

"War is likely coming." And for once, Morcant wasn't keen to join in.

"You think I should leave, don't you?" she asked, meeting his gaze.

"The fact your laird is sending men is good. Depending

on where they set up, you might be safer here." He then moved to the wood piled at her door and chose two long sticks. Morcant tossed one to Leana. "If you're going to use a sword, then you need to know how to wield it."

"I thought you said it was too big."

"It is, but knowing how to handle a sword may one day save your life."

She swung the stick. "You would teach me?"

He liked that he surprised her. Leana thought she knew men, but she didn't know him. "First, you must keep your balance at all times. Center yourself."

Morcant demonstrated, and Leana quickly mimicked him. She was a quick study, picking up everything he taught her with ease. It wasn't long before they were sparring with the sticks. The smile on her face made something break apart in his chest, something that seemed to...free...his heart.

Every chance he got, Morcant touched her. Whether it was a brush of their bodies as he turned her one way or another, or their hands touching when he guided her arm for her. Each time he came in contact with her was like being zapped with lightning.

He easily deflected the downward arc of her stick and sidestepped to come up behind her. Morcant grasped the long braid of her brunette locks and tugged her backward. "You should've gone left."

"Your sword was going right," she said in frustration.

Morcant turned her head by tugging on her braid so that she looked up at him. He had a hard time concentrating with her lips so close. "Watch your opponent's body, no' their eyes. My body told you I was going left while my eyes fooled you."

Silence fell between them, drowned out by the desire that raged like a wildfire. Leana's chest heaved from exertion and color infused her face. Her sky blue eyes were bright, watchful.

His gaze dropped to her mouth. Never had a woman tempted him as she did. He fought against the deluge to no avail. He hungered for a taste of her, craved to plunder her mouth until she clung to him.

The restraint he was exhibiting was something new, and he found he hated it as much as he had hated the darkness. In all his years with women, not once had he ever denied himself. He still wasn't sure why he was doing so now.

It was just a kiss. A simple kiss.

Morcant dropped his stick and wound his arm around her waist. His gaze returned to hers to discover another kind of flush had overtaken her, the flush of desire. His balls tightened in response.

His cock swelled when she also dropped her stick and turned so that she could wind her arms around his neck. If he had been uncertain of what Leana thought of him before, he had his answer now.

Gradually, his head lowered until their lips touched. Morcant moaned at the feel of her soft mouth. He cautioned himself to go slow, but passion had him fully in its grip.

Her fingers dug into his shoulders. Morcant angled her head so that he could reach her better. He slid his tongue against her lips, seeking entry. She parted her mouth, her tongue meeting his hesitantly.

He was burning from the inside out. Leana's inexperience only heightened his desire. His hand on her braid tightened as he deepened the kiss. Pleasure erupted, engulfing them. Every time Morcant tried to slow things down, she would moan. The kiss took on a life of its own. He was mindless with need.

Somehow, he found the willpower to end the kiss. He was gasping for breath, his eyes closed as his body shook with the need to have another taste of her. Morcant rested his forehead against hers, desperate to get some measure of control.

When he cracked open his eyes, he saw Leana was as out of breath as he was. She watched him with her beautiful eyes.

"Why did you stop?" she asked in a soft whisper.

He bit back a groan. The woman had no idea how seductive she was. "Before the gypsy, I took women as I wanted. I left them pleasured, aye, but without any thought of them. I only wanted to ease myself. Two hundred years in solitude has changed me."

"Your actions, but not your desires."

Morcant shook his head. "Nay, it didna dim my desire."

He frowned as she stepped out of his arms and walked backward to the cottage. As she reached the door, she paused before she turned and walked inside.

For long moments, Morcant stayed where he was. If he went inside, he wasn't sure he could stop himself from kissing her again but neither could he walk away.

He drew in a deep breath and followed. As he stepped into the cottage, he looked around for her. Morcant finally spotted her standing by the bed with her back to him. She was unbraiding her long, dark hair.

When she finished, she shook out the length so that it fell down her back in a curtain of brunette waves that he couldn't wait to slide his fingers through. Then she turned around and locked her gaze with his. It didn't register with his brain why she had the blanket wrapped around her shoulders until she let it fall.

Whatever control he found outside vanished in an instant as he took in the sight of her nude body. Her breasts were full, but not large. Her dusky pink nipples hardened beneath his gaze, making him long to take one into his mouth.

His gaze lowered to her slim waist and gently flared hips, to the triangle of dark curls at the juncture of her thighs and down her slender legs.

"By the saints, you're beautiful."

There was no walking away now. Morcant knew it and accepted it.

He strode to her and plunged his hands into her dark locks as he dragged her against him. Her hands landed on his chest as her eyes flashed with excitement.

"Are you sure?" he asked.

Her smile was slow as it tilted upward. "More sure than I've been of anything."

Morcant hissed in a breath when her hand shoved aside his saffron shirt and met his skin. His eyes closed while she leisurely stroked his chest. His gaze snapped open when she moved. He stopped breathing when she knelt in front of him, her eyes locked with his so that her face was even with his straining cock.

Her cheek brushed against the fabric of his kilt where his arousal stood out. But it wasn't his rod that her fingers found. It was his boots. One by one she removed his boots, and then she grasped his cock through his kilt. Morcant moaned. The pleasure was exquisite, but pure torture.

Morcant unpinned his kilt and let it fall. Then he jerked off his shirt to find Leana standing before him once more.

He caressed down her arm with the backs of his fingers, completely enthralled with her. He didn't know why she had chosen him, and it didn't matter. All that concerned him was giving her pleasure.

Leana wasn't sure what had come over her. After the wild kiss that sent her reeling, she couldn't imagine not seeing where the desire would take her in Morcant's arms.

She took in the superb body before her and sighed in appreciation. Scars littered his body, proving he wasn't afraid to fight. She placed her hands on his trim waist and stroked upward to his corded stomach and thick, wide shoulders. His crisp chest hair was at odds with his warm skin. She became breathless when his arms wrapped around her, pressing her breasts against him.

Leana raised her eyes in time to see his head lower once more. As soon as their lips met, she opened her mouth for him. The fire that had taken them outside surged again. She held nothing back. Whatever he demanded, she readily gave.

The kiss grew fierce the more the passion and desire grew. His hands were everywhere, touching her, learning her. Leana was floating on a cloud of pleasure that continued to expand with each heartbeat.

Suddenly, he had her on her back on the bed. She looked up at him, watching as he bent and closed his lips around a nipple. Leana sank her fingers into the covers and moaned.

He suckled and licked first one nipple and then the other until she was moaning endlessly. Desire coiled tightly within her.

Her back arched as he skimmed his hand between her breasts down her stomach. Leana was panting, her hips moving on their own. She didn't know what would come next, but she knew as long as she was in Morcant's arms, he would take care of her.

His large hand rested on her thigh as he kissed her stomach. When he pressed her legs apart, she only hesitated a fraction of a moment.

Leana lifted her head when he settled between her legs. His gaze met hers as his mouth hovered over her sex. Then his tongue came out and he licked her.

Her head dropped back while her hips rose to meet his tongue and the pleasure that wound through her. She didn't know such bliss could be had. Leana sucked in a breath when his tongue found a spot that sent her barreling toward some unknown pinnacle.

The climax slammed into her, knocking the breath from her as wave after wave of pleasure filled her. There wasn't time for her to recover from that before he slid a finger inside her.

Leana whispered his name, as the passion grew too intense. Soon, her hips were rocking in time with his hand as his finger stretched her.

Morcant had never seen such a beautiful sight before. Leana's dark hair was spread around her, her head moving back and forth, and her soft cries of pleasure filled the cottage. Seeing her peak the first time had been amazing, but he wasn't close to being finished with her. He ached to be inside her, but he wouldn't rush anything.

He joined a second digit with the first to stretch her so she could accommodate him. As he increased his tempo, his thumb swirled around her swollen clit. That's all it took for her to orgasm again.

A satisfied smile pulled at his lips to see her body flushed with pleasure. While she was still in the throes of her climax, Morcant entered her.

She was so tight, her walls so slick that he almost spilled before he was fully inside her. He gritted his teeth and slid deeper until he felt her maidenhead. With one hard thrust, he tore through and seated himself fully.

Leana's body went taut for a moment before she relaxed. Her eyes opened to stare up at him. He smoothed her hair from her face and kissed her. As soon as she shifted her hips, he knew she was ready for more.

Morcant lifted his head and caught her gaze as began to thrust, slowly at first, but steadily building as they held each other, lost in the ecstasy.

Their bodies slid against each other as they hurtled toward pleasure. Morcant held his orgasm off as long as he could, but the moment he felt her walls clench around him, he gave in. For the first time, he found the peace that had been lacking after sharing his body with a woman.

Lost in each other's eyes, something profound and vital snapped into place within Morcant, something he knew would change him forever.

CHAPTER 7

Leana fell asleep in Morcant's arms, feeling secure and sheltered as she never had before. She rested her head on his chest with his arm around her.

Sated and exhausted, Leana hovered in the place between sleep and wakefulness. She drifted through the space as if searching for something. Suddenly, she saw a man with long, dark brown hair and pale green eyes smiling down at a woman with auburn hair and gray eyes.

The vision shifted to the man riding upon a white steed with his face set in hard lines. He withdrew a sword from the scabbard at his waist as he nudged the horse into a run. Her view expanded to take in her cottage and the stream, as well as a group of men armed and ready for battle.

Leana's eyes snapped open. It took her a moment to realize she was no longer lying on Morcant's chest. He was now leaning over her, his face lined with worry.

"You cried out. Was it a dream?" he asked.

She put her hand to her forehead and shook her head. "It was a vision."

His frown deepened. "What was it?"

"You must understand that what I see could happen tomorrow or two years from now."

"Just tell me," he urged as he took her hand and brought it to his mouth to kiss.

Leana tugged on a strip of sandy blonde hair that had come loose from his queue. "I saw a man and a woman. They were obviously in love."

"Did you recognize the couple?"

"Nay. Next, I saw the man riding upon a white horse as he drew his sword. I saw him ride into battle against the MacKays."

Morcant rolled to his back and brought her with him. "If you doona recognize the man or the woman, then what do we do?"

"Nothing. Whatever I saw is coming, which means the MacKays will attack."

"Did you notice where the battle would take place?"

Leana closed her eyes and held him tight.

"Leana?" he pressed.

"Here. The battle is here."

"Shite," Morcant stated in a low voice. "The worry I saw in the village combined with what you told me about the MacKay clan means your vision will happen soon."

She swallowed hard and opened her eyes. "I suppose the couple could be from Ravensclyde."

"Most likely."

By his tone, Leana knew his mind was already focused on the upcoming battle. For once, she was considering going somewhere else. Perhaps she would leave with Morcant to search for Ronan and his other friends.

Leana rolled from him and rose from the bed. She walked to the table where his sword lay and lifted it in both hands. With the sword balanced between her hands, she turned back to Morcant.

"This is yours."

He slowly sat up. Then he threw off the blanket and swung his legs over the side of the bed as she approached.

She smiled at his questioning look. "You're a warrior, Morcant, a Highlander. You should never be without your sword."

"There's something else I should never be without," he said as he set aside the sword and pulled her between his legs. "You must have magic like the gypsies because you've bewitched me, Leana."

"I've no magic."

"Aye, lass, you do," he whispered.

Leana cupped his face. "You don't have to stay because of me. I know you want to search for your friends."

"I stay because I want to."

"And your friends?" she asked.

He looked away, which caused her heart to twist.

Leana licked her lips and braced herself for the inevitable. "If the gypsy put you in such a prison, it's likely she did the same to the others. Gypsies don't like to kill. They like to curse people."

"I feel as if they're still alive. Somewhere."

"Then you need to find them."

His gaze slid back to her. "You think I'm going to leave like everyone else."

It wasn't a question. "Your leaving won't be a surprise. From the beginning, I knew you wouldn't stay. I thought you left this morning."

"You think you're that easy to leave?" He posed the question in a soft voice, his gaze narrowed slightly.

Leana shrugged and let her hands drop to his shoulders. "I'm not going to trap you into staying. I don't regret making love to you. I don't regret a single moment that you've been in my life. You have an important role to play, Morcant, or the gypsy wouldn't have kept you alive."

"Important?" he asked with a snort. "No' verra, if I was taken from my family who needed me most."

"Perhaps it wasn't your family who needed you, but your friends."

"Why was I released from my prison now? Why this time? Why no' earlier or later?"

Leana shrugged as she gave a small shake of her head. "I don't know the answers."

His frown smoothed out, his face taking on a thoughtful expression. "I think I do."

"Why?"

Morcant waved away her words. "Ilinca said I would be released from the prison when I earned my freedom. I didna do anything to earn it."

"Perhaps being released was a test."

"Aye, my thoughts exactly. And if I've been released, then there is a chance that Stefan, Ronan, and Daman have, as well."

Leana felt as if Morcant were slipping further and further from her grasp. Which was silly, because she knew he was never meant to be hers to begin with.

She hadn't lied. Morcant was meant for something important, and the longer he stayed with her, the longer it would take him to find his friends and learn what it was that he was meant to do.

"You need to look for your friends. You're far from home, but they may not be," she reminded him.

He nodded absently. "Come with me."

Leana was so taken aback by his words that she could only gape at him.

"Come with me," he urged again. "What is holding you here? With a battle about to occur outside your door, why no' come with me. Help me look for my friends. Be with me."

Leana looked around the cottage. She didn't have anything holding her, but if she left, she would take a chance that Morcant would never leave her.

Was that something she could do?

Was it something she wanted to do?

"Talk to me, Leana," he urged. "What are you thinking?"

"I don't know what to think. We just met."

He raised a brow. "I'm no' denying that, but can you honestly say you doona feel that there is something between us?"

"I don't deny it. I've not been able to ignore it since I found you lying unconscious in the woods. It's almost as if we were..." she trailed off, unable to say the words.

"Meant to be together," Morcant finished for her. "You say I'm here for a reason. I say you found me for a reason."

She wanted to accept what he said, but she knew first-hand how life could deal a terrible blow. She'd suffered through enough of them already.

"You doona want to be here for the battle," he continued. "I'll protect you as best as I can, but the middle of a war isna a place for you."

Leana ran her fingers through his hair. "Will you bring me back?"

"If that's what you want."

"It is. I ask nothing more of you."

He smiled mischievously and lightly slapped her bare bottom. "And if I want more from you?"

"We'll have to come to some sort of agreement," she said sternly, then ruined everything by laughing.

He pulled her onto the bed, and then covered her body with his. Morcant grew serious then. "You may no' realize it, but I'm no' the same man I was when I was cursed. My mother often said I was searching. I used to laugh at her, but I think she was right. None of the other women broke through my walls or caused me to feel as you do. I think I've been searching for you."

Leana blinked away the moisture that gathered in her eyes. "That's impossible. You lived two centuries before me."

"But I'm here now." He gave her a quick kiss. "Rest. We've a few hours before supper."

Morcant was thankful that she didn't argue, and even more thankful when Leana fell asleep quickly. When her breathing evened out, he rose and dressed, strapping his sword at his waist.

Then he quietly left the cottage and began to scout the area. If there was going to be a battle, that meant the MacKay clan had already chosen this area. Morcant wanted to know why. He also expected to find someone from the MacKay clan keeping watch somewhere.

The man wasn't anywhere close to Leana's, but that didn't mean he hadn't seen Morcant. If Morcant could find him, then that would give the Sinclairs a chance to stop the MacKays before an attack.

Morcant glanced back at the cottage. He hated leaving Leana alone, but it was imperative that he stop the battle before it happened. He had a terrible feeling that Leana would get caught in the middle. It left him with a knot in his chest that grew by the second.

He made his way into the woods and picked up a trail. Morcant followed it as night descended. The trail took him from one mountain to another, leading him far from Leana. Just as he was about to turn around and start again in the morning, he saw a fire in the distance. Morcant withdrew his sword and started toward it.

As he drew near, he spotted four horses and only three men sitting around the fire. Morcant knew he could take them, but he had to wait for the fourth one. He couldn't chance the man coming up behind him.

Not when he finally had something to live for.

A half hour went by with the men talking of how the upcoming battle with the Sinclairs would play out before the fourth man returned carrying a brace of hares. He tossed them down next to the three sitting before the fire. Morcant crept around to the side of the camp and plunged his sword into the one standing before they knew what was happening.

Before the other three could react, Morcant kicked one in the face and spun to dodge a blow from another sword. He yanked his sword from the first man and sunk it into the second.

He looked around for the third man and saw him disappear into the night. Morcant grimaced as he glanced down at the one he'd kicked in the face who lay with his head bleeding from hitting a rock.

Morcant doused the fire and checked to make sure the man was dead before he took off after the last foe that happened to be headed straight toward Leana's.

CHAPTER 8

Leana knew it was a vision she was seeing. Perhaps it was the pounding of her heart. Maybe it was the way Morcant looked at her as if she were his entire world. Or it could be the happiness, the completeness she felt standing next to him with their hands linked.

Whatever it was, Leana felt whole for the first time since her mother had died. In the vision, she no longer felt that ever-present fear that she would always be alone.

The vision slowed, allowing her time to take it all in and really see everything. It was a first for her, and it frightened her to the marrow of her bones. But nothing like the surprise that ripped through her when she noticed the graying at Morcant's temples.

She was seeing the future – many years into the future.

Leana remained in the vision until it ended. She slowly opened her eyes, not bothering to wipe the tears that fell from the corners of her eyes and into her ears as she lay on her back.

Why had she been shown that? Why had she seen the

very thing that could heal her shattered heart and give her a life she wanted more than anything?

Nothing worked like that.

Just as magic wasn't supposed to exist.

Who was she to determine what was right and what wasn't? Who was she to dare question the workings of fate or destiny?

Leana turned her head to the side, but she already knew Morcant wasn't there. She waited for the certainty that usually always came when she knew someone wasn't going to return, but she didn't feel that coldness.

She rolled off the bed and quickly washed. There was no explanation for the urgency that pushed her, but she didn't question it. Leana dressed and was in the process of brushing her hair when the ground began to shake.

There was only one thing that could cause such a tremor. Horses.

She threw open the door and stepped outside to see an army descending.

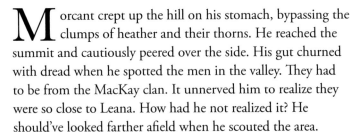

M orcant crept up the hill on his stomach, bypassing the clumps of heather and their thorns. He reached the summit and cautiously peered over the side. His gut churned with dread when he spotted the men in the valley. They had to be from the MacKay clan. It unnerved him to realize they were so close to Leana. How had he not realized it? He should've looked farther afield when he scouted the area.

Morcant spied the man he was chasing rush toward a large, barrel-chested man with a hard face. The two exchanged words, and a moment later, the leader motioned three men to him.

It wasn't long before the three were mounted and headed out. Morcant didn't need to be there to know that the leader had sent them to Leana's. He slid out of sight and got to his feet. Morcant didn't know the area that well, but that didn't slow him as he raced toward Leana.

Morcant climbed over boulders, leapt across gaps, and used the force of running downhill to help him keep the three men in sight. The horses were faster, but they couldn't move over the terrain as he could.

His lungs burned as he pumped his legs faster. Over the next rise was Leana's cottage. She was alone, no one there to protect her. That thought made him push himself even harder.

It seemed fate was set against him. The faster he ran, the further away the men got. Still, he didn't give up. He took a chance and climbed a boulder, jumping across three of them in an effort to close the distance.

Morcant cleared the first one with no problem. He glanced down, noting a fall would certainly break his leg. The second was just as easy until he went to jump from it to the third and his foot slipped.

He was prepared when he fell upon the third boulder on his hands and knees. His fingers helped to grip as he got his feet beneath him, and then he leapt to the ground and began running again.

As he ran up the slope, he withdrew his sword, letting out a battle cry as he did. The three men jerked their horses to a stop and faced him.

Morcant smiled when one of his opponents raced his horse toward him. The man couldn't know that was a training technique he learned from his father. Morcant continued right at the horse until the last minute where he feigned to the left, the steed missing him altogether.

The other two quickly jumped from their horses, swords at the ready, and attacked.

There was nothing so familiar as his sword in hand and a battle going on around him – even if it were three men against him. Those were usually the odds he faced, and he managed to come out the victor.

Then again, he'd had his friends to watch his back.

He was on his own this time, and it was never more apparent than when he felt a sting across his back just as he moved to the right.

Morcant pivoted and found that the third man had joined in the fight. The three attacked at once. He blocked one of the swords and punched another of the attackers in the face, and even though he tried to shift his body to dodge the oncoming sword, it still sliced across the top of his thigh.

He bellowed in fury, swinging his sword down and into the top of one of the men's shoulders. Morcant pulled his sword out of the dead man and turned to the other two as dozens more came running down the hill from Leana's.

The sound must have alerted the MacKays because in the next instant, a full-scale battle was on. Swords clang, men yelled, and blood coated everyone and everything.

Morcant bumped into someone from behind. He glanced down at the plaid and knew the man wasn't from the Sinclair or MacKay clans. They were soon fighting back to back, just as Morcant had done with his friends countless times.

～

Leana stood at the top of the hill, her gaze riveted on Morcant. Her stomach dropped to her feet when she saw the blood running down his right leg from a wound. There was also blood coating the back of his shirt, which meant there was an injury there, as well.

She couldn't take her eyes off the way he moved – effortlessly, gracefully...smoothly. He didn't waste a single movement. Everything he did went to cutting down his enemies as if they were nothing more than pesky insects.

"I've seen him train, but this is the first time I've truly seen him in battle."

Leana turned her head as Lady Meg came to stand beside her. Her auburn hair was in a neat braid, and her gray eyes were trained on her husband – Ronan Galt – the new lord of Ravensclyde.

Meg's eyes shifted to her. "The man you recently came across? You said his name was Morcant?"

"Aye, milady."

"Please," Meg said with a smile. "There's no need for that. What is Morcant's surname?"

Leana glanced at him again. He spun and sank his sword into an opponent that was coming at Ronan from the side. At the same moment, Ronan slashed open the chest of another who had his sword aimed at Morcant.

Ronan. It couldn't be. Could it?

Leana turned back to Meg. "It's Banner. Morcant Banner."

"I knew it," Meg said and hastily blinked her eyes. She peered at Leana hard. "What do you know of Morcant?"

If Meg's Ronan were the same Ronan that Morcant searched for, then Meg would know of the gypsies and the curse. Leana took a deep breath and said, "He appeared out of nowhere from a prison of darkness that he endured for two centuries."

Meg's hand gripped her arm. "Does Morcant remember anything?"

"Everything," Leana said. "He was getting ready to leave to search for Ronan and the others."

"They're fighting back to back and don't even know."
Meg shook her head as she smiled. "I can't believe this."

Leana couldn't either. The men from Ravensclyde
outnumbered the MacKay clan two to one. It didn't take the
Sinclairs long to subdue their enemy.

The last two fighting were Morcant and Ronan. By the
way they shifted from one side to the other fending off
attacks from all sides, they had obviously done this many
times. As the last of the MacKays fled back to their land,
Morcant lowered his sword, his chest expanding as he took in
a deep breath. Leana took a step toward him when he turned
to her.

His topaz gaze met hers. She began to mentally think of
all the herbs she would need for his wounds, when a smile
slowly began pull up his lips. So many of Leana's family had
been lost in battle that she was unaccustomed to someone
like Morcant.

She smiled, the last fragments of the walls surrounding
her shattering. Her heart was exposed, bare...and yet, she had
never felt so shielded as she did at that moment.

Leana glanced to Morcant's left to find Ronan staring in
shock. She had forgotten him for a moment, but it was time
that Morcant's conscience be eased. She slid her gaze back to
Morcant and tilted her head in Ronan's direction. Morcant's
brow furrowed slightly, but he then turned his head and
looked directly at Ronan.

"Well done," Meg said. "I think that's the first time I've
seen my husband unable to find words."

Leana wanted to watch what happened between Morcant
and Ronan, but her attention was called away by the men
who needed their wounds tended to.

She reluctantly turned away, hoping that it wouldn't be
long before Morcant returned.

It took a moment for Morcant to realize the man standing before him wasn't an illusion that his brain had created after the battle. The man's dark brown hair was still long but trimmed and neatly held back by a leather strip at the base of his neck. The pale green eyes were openly staring with a hint of doubt and bucketsful of hope.

"Morcant?"

He couldn't believe that the man standing before him was Ronan, because if it really weren't, Morcant didn't think he could handle it.

"Morcant?" Ronan said again, his head cocked a little to the side. "Is it really you? Is it really possible?"

It was the voice and the mannerisms that confirmed it for Morcant. "Ronan?"

Morcant was all smiles as Ronan pounded on his back as they embraced. He pulled back and looked into the eyes of his friend. "It really is you."

"Aye," Ronan said with a chuckle. "I didna think to ever see you again."

"I know what you mean. Where were you?"

The smile dimmed from Ronan's face. "In a place with no sound or light."

"I was in a similar place."

Ronan stepped back and looked up the hill. "I was freed by Meg."

Morcant followed his gaze to see a woman smiling down at Ronan. He immediately thought of Leana, but he couldn't find her. His first instinct was to go looking for her, then he realized she wouldn't leave her home.

"We've been married almost six months now," Ronan continued. "I never thought I could find a woman to love, much less think about marrying, and yet it happened."

"I'm happy for you." And he was, but he was also ready to be alone with Leana again, to hold her in his arms and feel her body against him.

"How were you freed?"

Morcant shrugged and turned his attention back to Ronan. "I doona know. One moment I was in the darkness, and the next I was looking up into Leana's face. I was about to set out looking for you, Daman, and Stefan."

"I've no' found anything about any of you until today." Ronan rubbed his jaw. "How long have you been out?"

"A couple of days."

"A lot can happen in a few days," Ronan said, his gaze penetrating.

Morcant merely grinned. "Aye, old friend. A verra lot can happen, like being freed from my prison, discovering a beauty who has visions of the future, learning I can no' breathe without her, and finding you again."

"It's taken me a long while to forgive Ilinca for what she did. I didna realize she did the same to you."

"I'm no' yet ready to forgive her, but I have to wonder if she knew what awaited us in the future."

Ronan shrugged and sheathed his sword. "I no longer care. If you can be here, then there's a chance that Stefan and Daman can, as well. First things first, you need to see to your wounds."

Morcant hadn't felt them until that moment. He and Ronan walked up the hill together. He still couldn't believe that it was actually Ronan beside him. But it no longer mattered how they had come to be in their dark prisons, or how they got out of them and found each other again.

Morcant reached the top of the hill and looked through the men milling about to find Leana. She moved from one man to another tending wounds. Her touch was light and her smile easy as she saw to the injuries, leaving many a man staring after her with lust in their eyes.

"She's the one who's caught your eye?" Ronan whispered.

Morcant couldn't take his eyes from her. "She's the one who captured my heart. Without even trying."

He limped away from Ronan and made his way to Leana as she finished with her last patient. She turned and caught sight of him, halting instantly. Her long brunette tresses hung freely about her, only adding to her allure.

Without a word, she took his hand and pulled him into the cottage. He sat at the table as she knelt before him.

"You were magnificent out there," Leana said as she began to wipe the blood from him.

Morcant closed his eyes at the feel of her hands on him. "All I could think about was killing them before they reached you."

"You did it."

He sighed and opened his eyes. "With the help of Ronan. Was he who you saw in your vision on the white horse?"

"The very same," she said with a grin as she looked up from the wound on his leg. "I had no idea he was your friend. Do you know what that means, Morcant?"

"That Daman and Stefan could be out there?"

She nodded and pressed some leaves that instantly stopped the pain against the wound. "What happens now?"

"What do you mean?" There was something in her tone that worried him.

"You've found Ronan. Will you return with him to Ravensclyde?"

"No' without you."

Her blue eyes snapped to his. "You acted as laird of your clan. You know what it is to lead. You can't seriously mean not to go."

Morcant touched her face. "Ronan hasna asked it of me,

but even if he does, I'm no' going anywhere without you. Why do you no' understand that? I need you, Leana, like I need the water, the sun, and the breath in my body. I don't ever want to be without you."

She stared at him, her face not showing any emotion, and Morcant knew true fear. He didn't know what he would do if she didn't want him.

"I know how much this land means to you. If you want to stay, then allow me to remain with you."

Still she didn't utter a sound.

Morcant was going to have to say the words, words he'd never thought to speak. Words he feared would scare her away. "Leana, I always thought I'd be alone. I never expected to find you. I didna even know I was looking for you." He looked down at his hands covered in blood and winced because he could only guess what he looked like after battle. "This isna the right time."

"It is," she insisted, putting her hand on his legs to keep him sitting. "Finish. Please."

Morcant frowned, unsure if she wanted to hear what he had to say, or if she just wanted him to get it over with. He parted his lips to speak when Leana held up a finger.

"Wait." She quickly and effortlessly finished cleaning his leg before winding a strip of material around it with fresh leaves. "I don't think this one needs stitching. Let me see your back."

He shifted so she could reach him. A smile formed when she grabbed a knife and sliced off his ruined shirt. With a grunt, she set a bowl of water and a towel in front of him.

"Wipe your face and arms," she ordered as she got to work on his back.

Morcant didn't say a word as she worked and he cleaned himself. He was mystified, baffled by her, and yet he couldn't get enough.

In no time at all, she stood in front of him expectantly. Morcant blinked, anxiety taking him again now that it was time to say the words. He took her hands and got to his feet.

"You were saying you didn't know you were looking for me," she urged, her eyes bright and expectant.

The iron grip of nerves loosened their hold. "Aye, I didna know I looked for you, but I was. Now that I have found you, I doona want to let you go. Ever." Morcant swallowed hard. "I've never said these words to another woman. I love you, Leana."

Her lids closed over her eyes as she stood still. A heart-beat later, she leaned forward and rested her head on his chest as Morcant wrapped his arms around her. "I love you," she whispered.

Morcant held her tight. "It's all right, my love. I've got you, and I willna ever let you go."

"You'll need to say that every day."

"Thrice a day at the verra least," he said with a grin. He rested his chin on her head and took in a deep breath. "Is this what peace feels like?"

"I don't know. I've never felt it before. It's a little scary."

"Aye, but we've each other."

Leana lifted her head to look into his face. "I like the sound of that."

"Then how does forever sound?"

"Amazing."

Morcant felt as if his heart would burst from his chest he was so ecstatic. He wanted to shout and dance, and at the same time he wanted to make love to Leana. A few days ago he was in Hell.

Then an angel found him and showed him heaven.

One month later…

Ravensclyde as he had been doing for the past ten minutes waiting on Ronan. "You know he wouldn't leave you waiting if there weren't a reason."

"Aye," Morcant said testily. "Where the devil is he?"

"Right here," Ronan said as he entered the solar with Meg on his arm. "I apologize for the wait, my friend. I was dealing with some matters about the castle."

Leana wondered at the way Meg was grinning widely and looking between her and Morcant. Leana's gaze returned to Morcant to find his gaze narrowed on Ronan.

"Why did you call me here?" Morcant asked.

Ronan nodded a greeting at Leana. "I wanted to talk to you the day I found you, but Meg insisted the two of you needed some time alone."

"Thank you," Morcant said with a bow of his head to Meg. "Leana and I appreciate that."

Leana stood when Morcant walked to her and threaded

his fingers with hers. In the month they had been together, their love had deepened. She found not only a lover, but also a friend, someone she could share her deepest desires with.

Ronan cleared his throat. "Morcant, Leana, Meg and I want to offer you both positions here as family."

Leana expected Ronan to want Morcant with him, but she hadn't expected to be included in the offer. She looked at Morcant to find him staring at her. She squeezed his hand to let him know she would support whatever decision he made.

"Morcant," Ronan said into the silence. "You know we were brothers without the bond of blood. I know you always wanted to be laird, but there's no other man I'd rather have at my back in battle."

Morcant turned to her. "What do you think?"

The fact he asked her opinion was one of the many reasons she loved him. "I want you to be happy."

"And you?"

"I'm happy wherever I am. As long as I have you."

Morcant's gaze turned dark with desire as he pulled her against him. "Ah, my bonny, Leana. To be separated by centuries, and yet we found each other – against all odds."

Leana had tears of joy filling her eyes when Morcant turned his head to Ronan and said, "We accept. Right after Leana marries me."

She laughed through her tears. "Name the place."

"Here. Now," Morcant replied with a grin. "Marry me this day, Leana."

"Aye."

Ronan's bellow for the priest was drowned out as Morcant kissed Leana completely, thoroughly, as though eternity was theirs for the taking.

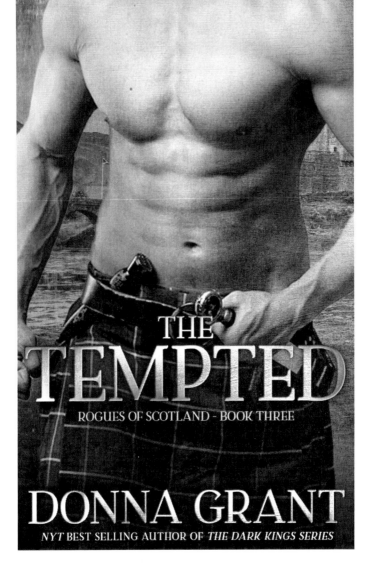

THE TEMPTED

ROGUES OF SCOTLAND - BOOK THREE

DONNA GRANT

NYT BEST SELLING AUTHOR OF *THE DARK KINGS SERIES*

Highlands of Scotland:
Summer, 1427

There were only a handful of things in Stefan
Kennedy's life that he was thankful for. His three
friends – Ronan, Daman, and Morcant – made up
the majority of them.

If it weren't for his friends, Stefan knew he would already
be dead. The anger inside him was a living beast. He couldn't
control it, and he stopped trying long ago. No one had given
him a reason to try and keep it in check until he met
Morcant, Ronan, and Daman that fateful day.

It was by happenchance that he even went to the Highland Games. He almost hadn't, and he still didn't know what
had made him go. But he had. Everything changed upon
meeting his friends. Only with them did he have reason to
restrain his rage.

His horse snorted, shaking his great head. Stefan patted
his steed's neck as he waited with Morcant and Daman for
Ronan to arrive. The valley between the two mountains was

wide. The summer sun was warm, and a breeze ruffled his horse's white mane.

Above them, the shrill cry of a golden eagle broke the silence. Stefan glanced up at the bird to see it soaring upon the wind currents before flapping its great wings.

Stefan's attention was snapped to the right at the sound of a horse's whinny. He spotted the rider atop the mountain. Finally. Stefan's patience had been wearing thin. Morcant's smile when he saw Ronan had Stefan glancing at Daman, who was also grinning.

Ronan's horse pawed the ground, and a moment later, he leaned forward on his mount. His horse raced down the mountain. Morcant and Daman laughed while Stefan shook his head at Ronan's wildness. Then again, that same thread ran through all four of them. It was just one of many reasons they'd become friends.

Morcant had to hold his young stallion with a firm hand as the three waited for Ronan to reach them. Daman's mount danced sideways, just as Morcant finally got control of his horse and Ronan arrived.

"About time," Stefan grumbled to Ronan.

Ronan raised his brow. "You might want to rein in that temper, my friend. We're going to be around beautiful women this night. Women require smiles and sweet words. No' furrowed brows."

Stefan was used to such words, so Daman and Morcant's laughter didn't bother him. Stefan shot Ronan a humorless look.

"Aye, we've heard enough about this Ana," Daman said as he turned his mount alongside Ronan's. "Take me to this gypsy beauty so I can see her for myself."

Ronan's lips compressed. "You think to take her from me?"

Daman's confident smile grew as his eyes twinkled in merriment. "Is she that beautiful?"

"Just you try," Ronan dared, only half jesting.

"Be cautious, Ronan. You wrong a gypsy, and they'll curse you. No' sure we should be meddling with such people," Morcant said as he shoved his hair out of his eyes.

Morcant wasn't generally the voice of reason among the four. That was normally reserved for Daman, but Morcant's comment gave Stefan pause. Most clans didn't allow gypsies on their land for long. Even though their bold colors and beauty were intriguing, there was no doubt they could be dangerous.

Ronan laughed at Morcant and reined in his jittery mount. "Ah, but with such a willing body, how am I to refuse Ana? Come, my friends. Let us enjoy the bounty that awaits." He gave a short whistle and his horse surged forward in a run again.

Stefan's well-trained mount stood still, his ears pricked forward as Stefan watched Ronan. The three remained behind for a moment as Ronan took the lead as he always did. Each had found their place within their small group. What began by chance a decade earlier had grown into their own clan. After they'd met at the Highland Games, they'd made sure to meet up regularly until they were as inseparable as brothers. The four formed a friendship that grew tighter with each year that passed.

"I'm no' missing this," Morcant said and gave his stallion his head. The horse immediately took off.

Stefan shared a look with Daman, and as one, they nudged their mounts forward. It wasn't long before they caught up with Morcant. Ronan looked over his shoulder, a wide smile on his face. He spurred his mount faster. Morcant then leaned low over his stallion's neck until he pulled up alongside Ronan.

Stefan loosened the reins, and his horse closed the last bit of distance to come even with Ronan a moment before Daman rode up beside Morcant.

A few moments later, Ronan tugged the reins, easing his stallion into a canter so they rode their horses four abreast. Being with his friends and riding along the craggy, windswept mountains were the only things that could make Stefan forget who he was.

His soul felt almost...free.

How he cherished his time with his friends. Without them...well, he didn't want to go down that road. Not now. Not when he was in such a fine mood.

The four rode from one glen to another until Ronan finally slowed his horse to a walk. They stopped atop the next hill and looked down at the circle of gypsy wagons hidden in the wooded vale below.

Stefan focused his gaze on the circle of wagons and the gypsies walking around. There was a large fire in the middle of the camp, and as far as Stefan could tell, no one else was with the gypsies.

"I've a bad feeling," Daman said as he shifted uncomfortably atop his mount. "We shouldna be here."

Morcant's horse flung up his head, and he brought his mount under control with soft words. "I've a need to sink my rod betwixt willing thighs. If you doona wish to partake, Daman, then doona, but you willna be stopping me."

"Nor me," Ronan said.

Stefan was silent for several moments. Never before had he abandoned his friends, and he wasn't about to start now. Unlike Morcant, who wanted to fuck every woman he came across, Stefan tended to only sate his body when he could no longer stand the need.

He would go into the camp with the others, even if only to watch their backs. Stefan gave Ronan a nod of agreement.

Ronan was the first to ride down the hill to the camp, and Morcant was right on his heels. Stefan nudged his horse into a gallop as a young beauty with long black hair came running out to greet Ronan in her brightly colored skirts. Ronan pulled his horse to a halt and jumped off with a smile as the woman launched herself into his arms. Ronan caught her and brought his lips down to hers.

Stefan pulled his horse to a halt beside Morcant's, and a moment later, Daman rode up on Morcant's other side. By the look of Daman's tightly held lips, he wasn't happy.

Ronan and the woman spoke quietly before Ronan turned her toward them. "Ana, these are my friends, Daman, Morcant, and Stefan," he said, pointing to each of them in turn.

Her smile was wide as she held out her arm to the camp. "Welcome to our camp."

Morcant quickly dismounted and dropped the reins to allow his horse to graze freely. He then started to walk between two wagons towards the center of the camp before he hesitated.

Stefan wasn't going to sit atop his mount as he waited for Ronan and Morcant to sate themselves. He dismounted and patted his horse.

"I'll be back," he mumbled and followed Morcant into the camp. He met Morcant's gaze when Morcant glanced his way. It was Morcant's pause that had Stefan looking back at Daman. Indecision warred on Daman's face.

Stefan didn't move as he waited for Daman to make up his mind. Finally, Daman slid from his horse and gathered the reins of all four mounts to tether them together.

"I'll keep watch," Daman said as he sat outside the camp near a tree.

Ronan wrapped an arm around Ana and walked away calling, "Your loss."

Morcant gave a nod and continued on to a woman sitting on the steps to her wagon, her bright turquoise and yellow skirts dipping between her legs while she braided a leather halter for a horse.

It was long moments before Stefan reached the fire in the middle of the camp and nodded to the three men sitting there.

"Welcome," the youngest of them said. He had black hair and eyes, and wore a bright red shirt and black pants.

The elder of the other two had stark white hair cut short. He was carving a piece of wood into a buck and motioned to the rock next to him. "Have a seat."

Stefan glanced at the third man, middle-aged, with just a hint of white in his dark hair at the temples. His dark eyes were welcoming as he stood and spooned some soup into a bowl then handed it to Stefan.

"Thank you," Stefan said and sat. He sampled a bit of the soup and nodded at the rich flavor. "It's good."

"Of course it is," the youngest said with a laugh. "Our food is excellent."

The elder lifted his eyes to Stefan, his bushy white brows raised on his forehead. "You're friends with Ronan?"

"I am."

"Close friends?"

Stefan paused in his eating. "I consider him a brother, as I do Morcant and Daman."

"When does Ronan plan on marrying Ana then?"

Stefan swallowed. Marry? Apparently, they didn't know Ronan at all. Ronan was as opposed to marriage as the Devil was to Heaven. It wasn't like Stefan could tell them any of that, but surely Ana knew.

Ronan wasn't the type to take a woman to his bed unless she knew from the beginning there would never be more from him. Ronan wasn't cruel, but he also didn't lead a female on.

"He's no' mentioned it to me," Stefan finally said.

The youngest chuckled. "If Ana has her way, it'll be tonight."

"He's all she can talk about," the middle-aged man said. "By the way, we've not introduced ourselves. I'm Yanko. This is my son Luca, and my father Guaril."

Stefan nodded his head to each of them. "I'm Stefan Kennedy."

Despite talk of Ronan's impending marriage that he knew nothing about, Stefan finished his meal listening to the three men chatter of their travels. He didn't understand their need to move from place to place. It was almost as if they couldn't remain still. It was partly due to the fact that no one would allow them to remain, but it was also in their blood to wander.

When Guaril finished his carving, he handed it to Stefan to inspect. Stefan was impressed with the skill displayed. Guaril had perfectly captured the likeness of a red deer from the hooves to the eyes to the antlers.

"This is fine craftsmanship, Guaril."

Luca smiled. "My grandfather is a master. We sell many of his carvings."

"I keep trying to teach Luca as I did Yanko," Guaril said with a grin directed at his grandson. "But he lacks the dedication."

Yanko slapped his son on the back. "I was the same. He'll grasp it soon enough."

"Here," Guaril said and tossed the small dagger to Luca.

Surprised, Luca caught it and then held it up over his head causing even Stefan to smile as the three laughed.

The night was suddenly shattered by an anguished scream, a soul-deep, fathomless cry that was dredged from the depths of someone's soul.

Stefan was immediately on guard. He searched the camp and saw Ronan first. He stood outside of Ana's wagon, shirtless with his hand on the hilt of his sword, looking at an old woman who was staring at something in the grass.

The next instant, Morcant hurriedly exited a wagon still fastening his kilt. Stefan slowly stood and glanced behind him to find Daman standing outside the circle of wagons with a resigned expression.

"Who is that?" Luca asked in a strangled whisper.

Stefan turned his gaze back to Ronan and the old woman. That's when he saw the bright pink and blue skirts of the body in the grass. It was Ana, a dagger still sticking out of her stomach. Their night of fun and revelry was over.

By the looks exchanged amongst the gypsies, there was no way Stefan and his friends were going to be able to leave without a fight. The smiles from the gypsies turned to glares of hatred and disgust.

Stefan noticed Morcant's gaze. He gave Morcant a nod to say he was ready for battle because that's exactly what was about to happen.

The gypsies in the camp stood still, almost afraid to move. Ronan's face was twisted with denial and sorrow while Morcant slowly began to pull his sword from his scabbard.

"Ronan," Stefan said urgently, trying to snap his friend to attention. It was going to take all of them to get out alive. Stefan palmed the hilt of his sword and waited.

There was a moment of utter silence, as if the world were holding its breath. Then the old woman let loose a shriek and pointed her gnarled finger at Ronan. Ronan's eyes widened in confusion and anger.

"Ilinca will make him pay," Luca whispered.

Yanko cut his gaze to his son and said, "Enough."

But Stefan didn't need to hear more. He looked at the old woman again. Her grief shone plainly, clearly. So did her anger.

Words, hurried and unfamiliar, fell from Ilinca's lips. The language was Romany, and Stefan didn't need to understand them to know that nothing good could come from whatever she was saying.

The longer Stefan stared, the more he realized Ronan was being held against his will. His pale green eyes were wide with confusion. The same time Stefan drew his sword, Morcant rushed Ilinca.

The next thing Stefan saw was Ilinca shifting her gaze to Morcant. Instantly, he was frozen in place, no more able to move than Ronan. With Morcant taken care of, Ilinca returned her gaze to Ronan and continued speaking in the strange language.

Stefan couldn't believe that Morcant and Ronan had been halted with merely a look from the old woman. He let loose his rage, let it fill him until he shook with it. He released a battle cry and leapt over the fire toward Ilinca. Stefan hadn't gotten two steps before the old gypsy pinned him with a look that instantly jerked him to a halt.

Stefan was momentarily flabbergasted at the feeling rushing over him, the force controlling his body. He tried to move his arm, his head, anything. But she had complete control. He couldn't even get his lips or voice to work.

The only thing he could move was his eyes, and he wished to God he wasn't able to see what was going on. He hated the helplessness, the utter powerlessness he felt. When he got free – and, he would get free – he was going to take Ilinca's head.

Ronan had no more killed Ana than he had. Ilinca had no right to blame any of them for Ana's weakness. The longer the old gypsy held Stefan in place, the more his fury grew, consuming him with a blind rage that blocked out everything but the gypsy.

Ilinca's gaze held his for a moment, seemingly undeterred by his wrath. She looked behind him.

Daman.

Stefan tried to shout for Daman to get away before she got him, as well. Stefan knew Daman wouldn't leave, and when a satisfied smile crossed the old gypsy's face, Stefan knew Daman had walked into the camp.

Stefan didn't have time to think about that as Ronan suddenly squeezed his eyes shut while his body shook with pain. In the next instant, he vanished.

Naaaayyyyyy!

The bellow welled up in Stefan's mind but it never passed his lips. No sooner had the old woman looked at Morcant than he disappeared, as well.

Then Ilinca returned her gaze to Stefan.

I'm going to kill you!

She smiled coldly, as if she could read his mind. The pain started slowly but built quickly. It seeped into every nerve, every crevice of his body.

It burned, it bit. It slashed, it gutted.

It ravaged.

Stefan held Ilinca's gaze, daring her to give him all that she had. Had he not been held up by her magic, Stefan would've been on his knees, doubled over from the piercing, searing pain that went on and on.

His vision began to fade until there was nothing but

blackness. Stefan fought against Ilinca's hold, against his vision loss and his inability to help his friends.

The pain grew to such a degree, he could feel his heartbeat begin to slow. Stefan's wrath doubled, his rage expanded until it exploded within him.

The next thing he knew, he was lying on a floor of stones. Stefan rose up on his arm and looked around for Ilinca so he could kill the gypsy witch.

Except there was nothing but darkness and silence.

The silence was eerie and the dark was cold, malicious.

He managed to get to his knees before he grew dizzy. He fell forward onto his hands and took huge gulps of breath.

"You're here, Stefan Kennedy, because you are empty inside," said a female voice all around him, crackling with age. "For that I curse you. You will be locked in this place until you get the chance to control your rage. If you fail, you'll spend eternity here."

Stefan sat back on his haunches with his hands on his thighs. It looked like he would never get out of whatever hell the old gypsy had put him in.

That thought only made his fury grow.

He got to his feet and felt...nothing. There wasn't even a stirring of air. No cold, no heat, no sound, and definitely no light. He wasn't thirsty or hungry or tired.

What he was, however, was totally and completely alone.

Stefan knew that feeling well. It hadn't been around in a decade, but it was familiar nonetheless. It had remained his constant companion after his mother had died, right up until Ronan, Morcant, and Daman befriended him.

Where were his friends? Ronan and Morcant had disappeared in front of him. Did that mean Ilinca cursed them, as well? Could they be in this same prison?

Stefan grunted. "No' likely."

Ilinca wouldn't be so kind as to put all four of them in the same place, not where they might find each other. As for Daman, Stefan knew his friend was most likely cursed, as well.

Something snapped inside Stefan. It was the part of him that his friends kept in check, the part that fell away after his mother had died.

This time he knew it was gone for good, and he welcomed the anger as he began to plan how he would kill Ilinca.

CHAPTER 1

Highlands, 1609

Morvan exited her home and looked to the morning sky as she stretched. There was a nip in the air, a hint that autumn would soon arrive. She surveyed the wooded landscape around her and sighed with pleasure. There was nowhere else she would rather live. The trees helped to cut the wind during the harsh winters, but that's not why she preferred the forest.

Some called her magical.

Others called her cursed.

All Morvan knew, was that the forest was her home. She understood the plants and animals. If that made her cursed, then she would gladly accept the mantle.

She combed her fingers through her hair to push the heavy length out of her face, then quickly plaited it and tied it off with a strip of leather.

"What is in store for me today?" she asked, her steps light and eager as she walked the short distance to the loch.

The mountain was steep in places and the rocks many as

she made her way down to the water. She stopped just before she left the trees when she saw a herd of red deer drinking on the opposite bank of the narrow strip of water.

Morvan waited, taking in the sight of the impressive herd. They knew her scent, but she didn't want to intrude. It wasn't until the last of them had had their fill and trotted away that she continued to the loch.

She sat against a grouping of rocks and pulled an oatcake out of her pocket. It was rare for her not to be at the loch first thing in the morning. As she ate her breakfast, Morvan contemplated the day.

Normally, there was a set area she would walk looking for animals that were in need of healing. Though the village thought her touched, there were those who didn't hesitate to ask for her skills if one of their animals were sick.

The day before had been spent at the miller's tending to the injured hoof of one of his sheep. Perhaps it was that she had been kept from the woods by helping the miller that she felt the need to just wander the forest and see what she could find.

With the oatcake finished, Morvan dusted off her hands and got to her feet. She turned to the right and began walking. As soon as she stepped back into the woods, a shiver ran down her spine. She halted instantly. The forest had been her home all her life, and not once had she ever felt such...foreboding. As if fate were warning her that something was coming.

Or was already there.

Morvan touched the nearest tree, a tall evergreen. The bark scraped her palm and pine needles crunched beneath her feet. The smell of pine permeated the air.

"What is it?" she asked the tree.

She didn't expect an answer, but since she lived alone, she

found it better to talk to the plants and animals rather than not talk at all.

Morvan took a deep breath as the music of the forest assaulted her. The wind whistling through the leaves, the creak of the limbs, the sweet songs of birds. Every animal, every plant contributed to the beautiful music.

When Morvan was just a child, she'd discovered that she was the only one who could hear the melody. She let her hand trail down the trunk of the tree as she lifted her foot and took a step. Then another, and another.

There wasn't another chill, but she still couldn't shake the feeling that something was going to happen. It didn't make her turn around though. Morvan didn't turn away from anything or anyone. She slowly walked through the forest, stopping every now and again to admire a bird or flower.

It didn't take long for her to relax as the tranquility of the woods seeped into her. She lost herself in the forest. She was spellbound by the serenity, enthralled by the peacefulness.

Morvan suddenly stopped and looked around. She knew every inch of the woods – especially the boundary between the MacKay's lands and those of clan Sinclair that she was never to cross.

How then had she crossed the border?

With her heart pounding, Morvan hastily glanced around to make sure no one was hiding in the foliage. She took a tentative step back, appalled to realize she was much farther onto Sinclair land than she'd first thought.

Morvan swallowed nervously. Tensions between the Sinclairs and her clan, the MacKays, were high, especially after a recent skirmish. The last time she was in the village near the keep, she'd heard that there was trouble within the castle. The new laird, Alistair, was bent on peace while his younger brother Donald, still upset over not becoming laird, wanted war.

She didn't want to be responsible for starting the war simply because she'd crossed the boundary by accident. It was so stupid of her. She knew better. No matter how many times she gave herself up to the woods, she had never ventured off her clan's land. Ever.

From the moment she'd woken that morning, she'd felt as if there were something particularly different about the day, something not quite normal. Morvan hadn't questioned it further though, and that's apparently where she went wrong. She should've remained in her cottage.

Morvan spun around and walked back toward her clan's land as fast and quietly as she could. She didn't know this side of the forest like she did her own, and it complicated things. Twice, she had to retrace her steps and take a different route. Sweat beaded her forehead as she lifted her skirts to free her legs in an attempt to move faster.

It was a distressed bleating that brought her to a halt a second time. Morvan closed her eyes and sighed. There was an injured animal calling to her for help. But the longer she remained on Sinclair land, the more she put herself and her clan in peril.

Her shoulders slumped even as she turned toward the sound. No amount of danger could keep her from helping an animal in need.

Morvan followed the cries, recognizing them as being from a red deer. A few moments later, she moved aside foliage and caught sight of the majestic buck that had his impressive antlers tangled in the branches of a tree.

The buck caught her scent before he saw her, and it set him to jerking his antlers in a renewed attempt to get free. Morvan began to hum softly and walked toward the frightened animal. The louder the buck cried, the more his hooves flailed and his legs kicked, she louder she hummed, all the while moving slowly and calmly.

THE TEMPTED | 179

She slowed and cocked her head to the side when she caught the buck's gaze. "Easy now, handsome. I'm here to help."

The buck let out a snort, his black eyes wild with fatigue and fear. Morvan remained where she was, hoping the animal would calm a bit to allow her to get closer.

The humming helped, but she had to touch him before she could really help him. The longer she waited, the more the buck's frenzy would double. By the marks on the tree from his antlers, and the grooves in the ground from his pawing of the earth, the poor animal had been stuck for some time.

With only five feet separating them, Morvan took a deep breath and moved closer. As soon as she did, the buck kicked out a hoof. Morvan grunted as it slammed into her stomach, knocking her backwards.

She clutched her abdomen but kept eye contact with the buck. Pushing past the pain, Morvan once more walked to the deer. He kicked her twice more in the legs before she was finally able to put a hand on his flank.

Instantly, the animal calmed. Tears gathered when she felt how the buck shook beneath her palm. She hummed and softly stroked him while walking around to his other side.

"It's all right now. I'm here to get you loose," she whispered in a sing-song voice that matched the tune she was humming.

The buck closed his eyes. Morvan ran her hand up to his spine, then forward to where his antlers sprouted from his head. She kept one hand on him at all times and slowly turned his head this way and that to get him free.

For the next ten minutes she worked, sweat dripping down her face. The buck's breathing had calmed, but he needed food and water quickly.

Suddenly, the thick antlers came free. Morvan released

the animal as he stumbled backwards a few steps. His black soulful eyes blinked at her for a heartbeat. Then he walked to her and lowered his head enough so that she could rub his forehead.

"You're welcome," she whispered with a smile. "Go now. The forest is calling to you."

The buck turned and leapt over a fallen tree before he bounded out of sight. No matter how many animals she saved, their gratitude afterwards always made her teary.

Morvan leaned against a tree and gently touched her stomach, knee and shin where the deer had kicked her. She was lucky not to have any broken bones, but there was definitely going to be bruising. Despite the injuries she'd sustained, it was worth it to save an animal.

She turned east to return to MacKay land and had only gone a few steps when something urged her to go left. Morvan tried to fight the compulsion, but the force was too strong. Trepidation made her hands clammy. Four times she tried to turn around, and each time the force compelling her grew stronger.

Morvan gave up fighting and allowed the compulsion to take her where it would. To her horror, she walked deeper onto Sinclair land toward a rock structure that seemed to burst out of the ground and stretch to the heavens. Every step she took left a sinking feeling of doom that spread through her.

Quickly, she found herself at the structure, staring up. Morvan tried to turn around, but the force wouldn't loosen its hold. With a sigh, she began to climb up a steep incline riddled with moss-coated rocks. By the time she reached the top, she was winded and weary. Precipitation began to fall in a soft drizzle that quickly increased. Morvan blinked through the rain.

All around her were massive boulders that dwarfed her.

Morvan saw an opening to a cave and dashed. She didn't know where to go next. The feeling that had been guiding her was gone. She hoped that meant she'd reached her destination, but as far as she could tell, there was no animal for her to help.

"Which means what, exactly?" she mumbled in frustration.

Not only was she on Sinclair land, but she was also miles away from her woods. She wished she were back in her cottage sipping a mug of tea.

Morvan poked her head out of the cave and lifted her face to the sky but saw nothing but gray. The storm could be over in a moment, or it could linger for hours. She didn't like the idea of climbing back down the slope, especially after the rain had made the damp stones slick. But she couldn't remain there anymore either.

Morvan glanced over her shoulder to the dark cave behind her. She didn't know how far back it went, or what might be living inside, and she didn't want to find out.

A look out of the cave once more revealed boulders that almost looked as if they were placed in a maze-like pattern. But that couldn't possibly be right. No one but giants could lift those boulders, and there were no giants.

The atmosphere suddenly became ominous, foreboding. It wasn't the weather, but...almost as if a dark presence were causing the shift. There was no denying the malevolence, the cruelty permeating the very air.

Morvan didn't like the place. She wanted to get as far from it as she could.

With no weapon in sight, she walked out from the shelter of the cave and went back the way she had come to return to her cottage. Only it was blocked by a boulder. A boulder that hadn't been there before.

Magic. Her mind voiced the word she wasn't prepared to let past her lips.

Morvan looked up at the rock that seemed to reach the heavens. She tried to find a way around it, but both sides were melded into the rock on either side of it leaving her walled in. She spun around and faced the narrow path between the other rocks. If she wanted to leave, she was going to have to walk the trail.

Her heart thumped a slow, dreadful beat in her chest. The first step was the hardest. With every one after, she expected something to jump out at her from behind one of the boulders. She heard something behind her, but when she tried to turn around and see what it was, a voice in her head screamed for her not to. Morvan wisely kept her gaze ahead of her.

The path led her on a continual soft incline this way and that. Normally she knew her way instinctively, but she was so turned around that she didn't know if she would ever find home again.

The rain was at least letting up enough so she could see a little ways ahead of her. That was how she saw the wall of rock. It towered before her, carved with thousands of markings of various sizes.

As a child of the woods, Morvan kept her Celtic roots close. She recognized the carvings as those of the Celts. By their worn look, these were ancient. It was as if the wall was important to the Celts. Why else would they carve all of these symbols into it? There was also a slight humming coming from the stone, as if it were alive.

Magic, her mind whispered again.

Magic had brought her to the cliff, and magic filled the air. Why had it chosen her? That dark feeling from earlier was now gone. It had dissipated after she'd left the cave.

Morvan began to wonder if there were some kind of entity guiding her. It made her shiver with fear – and wonder.

No matter how many times she looked at the ancient Celtic symbols, she kept coming back to a carving of a wolf. The carving was larger than her hand, the knotwork exquisite.

She knew the wolf could be literal or symbolic. And it could mean any number of things. The Old Ways taught her that a man marked with the symbol of the wolf was fearless, brave, and rarely compromised. They were the men who became heroes in the heat of battle. They would not back down, and they would take no quarter. They thrived on challenges. Their character was impeccable, and they lived by a creed of honor.

What did that mean for her, however? There were a few instances in history when a woman was marked with a wolf, but those times were rare. Besides, Morvan knew her place. She was anything but a wolf.

She stared at the etching for long moments. Another overwhelming feeling filled her. This time, she felt the need to touch the wolf etching, to run her fingers over it. She didn't know why it was so important.

Or why she hesitated.

Morvan swallowed and gave in to the need. As soon as her fingertip came in contact with the symbol, there was a loud boom, and a gust of air from the stone that sent her flying backwards.

CHAPTER 2

One moment Stefan was encased in darkness, and the next he was standing in the rain. He didn't stop to wonder why he was out of his prison. He ducked behind the first stone he saw, crouched down, and looked around for an enemy.

His hunt had begun. It was the same hunt he swore he would take if he ever got out of the hellish place Ilinca had put him in. The gypsy would pay for what she had done to him and his friends. All Stefan had thought about was the gypsy's death, of how he would take her last breath. Until the old woman was dead, he couldn't rest, couldn't think about his friends.

He pushed his long, wet hair out of his face and stood. He needed to know where he was. Stefan climbed atop the boulder and surveyed the area.

There was nothing about the forest that looked familiar, but he recognized the trees and the mist-covered mountains. He was still in Scotland, and that meant it was only a matter of time before he found the gypsy.

Stefan leapt to the ground, landing with bent knees. He

wouldn't put it past Ilinca to send someone after him, but the old woman had no idea who she'd put into that darkness. If she thought he had nothing but anger in his heart before, now it consumed him.

He went from boulder to boulder. There was someone up ahead. He could hear their breathing as well as a grunt of pain. Stefan lifted his lips in a sneer. So, Ilinca hadn't taken long to send her first assassin.

Stefan rushed from behind the boulder. He didn't have a weapon, but with the fury inside him, his hands would be enough. Just as he rounded the next rock, he saw a tangle of dark skirts as a woman used a boulder to get to her feet. Woman or man, it didn't matter. Anyone sent by Ilinca would die.

Then the woman turned to face him and he saw her arresting face. That one moment of hesitation surprised him as much as it did her. But Stefan was already on a collision course, and there was no time to alter his direction.

Time slowed, allowing him to see her nutmeg brown eyes widen and her lips part in surprise. Stefan managed to slow himself, but it wasn't enough. The woman stepped back to get out of his way, only there was nothing behind her. Her arms flailed, and those big eyes of hers filled with panic. Then she was gone.

Stefan slid to a stop, one foot going over the side of the cliff as dirt and pebbles followed the woman down. He leaned over the side and spied the body amid the thick ferns and jagged rocks below.

He wanted to forget the woman, but he couldn't. It wasn't just her eyes, it was her face. Creamy skin unblemished except for a small, dark mole at the corner of her right eye. Inky black brows that matched her long braid gently arching over her eyes. High cheekbones and full lips made for kissing.

The woman wasn't Romany. Her skin wasn't nearly dark enough, but that didn't mean she hadn't been sent by Ilinca.

Stefan stared down at the unmoving form of the woman for long moments. She was most likely dead anyway. The odds of her missing any of the rocks were slim. Besides, he had a gypsy to kill.

~

Pain, ferocious and intense, roughly dragged Morvan awake. She inhaled, and then wished she hadn't as agony reverberated through her. She was afraid to move and make the pain worse. Yet she couldn't remain where she was.

Drops of water fell on her face. Morvan opened her eyes and looked at the sky, blinking from the rain that had slackened to a light drizzle.

She wiggled her toes, thankful that it seemed nothing was wrong with her legs. Next she moved her fingers, again feeling nothing amiss with her upper body other than her ribs. Gingerly, she rolled onto her side, gasping at the pain. It took several attempts before she was able to move to her hands and knees. That's when her arm began to throb.

Morvan looked at her left arm, but there was no tear in her dress or any blood. She could move her arm, so she didn't suspect it was broken. Her ribs, however, already bruised from the buck's kick, were the worst of everything.

Keeping her breathing light, Morvan eventually made it to her feet. Then wished she hadn't when she grew dizzy. She was able to grab hold of a tree growing between two rocks to steady herself. She stood silently for several moments waiting for the world to stop spinning. Morvan closed her eyes and evened her breathing. That's when she recalled the man.

He'd looked as wild and untamed as the animals in the forest. His eyes, a stunning hazel mix of blue, green, and gold, were stony and feral. Half of his face was hidden by his long, light brown hair.

But it was his lips formed in a cold, hard line that frightened her most of all.

There was no compassion in the man, no kindness or gentleness. He'd shown that when he hadn't tried to help her when she'd lost her balance. The fact he also hadn't come down to see if she were alive or dead spoke volumes.

It reminded Morvan why she chose the forest and animals over the village and the people within. She understood animals and their behavior, but people she could never fully grasp. One of her downfalls was believing people spoke honestly, when in fact they never did.

Animals didn't lie or deceive. Animals didn't betray or manipulate. They didn't exploit or abuse, steal or cheat.

Morvan opened her eyes and held her sore left arm against her battered ribs. It was going to be a long walk home.

∽

Stefan circled the area to get an idea of any potential threats, but all he found was the woman. To his amazement, she was on her feet, though she looked the worse for wear. Her skin was pale, and by the way she held her left arm, she was injured. Yet the woman didn't shout for help or wait for someone to find her. She began walking.

Stefan once more chose to ignore the female. She was alive, and apparently knew where she was going. He, on the other hand, had hunting to do.

Ilinca.

He had no idea how many days had passed while he paced and fumed inside the darkness where she had confined him, but it didn't matter. Whether it had been a few days or several years, he would find the gypsy.

There was no holding back his fury – nor did he want to. He fed the rage, nurtured the wrath until every bit of gentleness and humanity his friends cultivated in him vanished.

He was the monster his mother feared he would become.

He was his father.

Stefan used to fear he would become his father, but now he embraced his lineage, welcomed it with open arms. It would be what freed his friends. It would be what helped him kill Ilinca and break whatever magic she'd used to put him in that dark hell.

By then he would be too far gone to ever be among people again. But it was a price he would gladly pay once he knew Morcant, Daman, and Ronan were liberated from Ilinca.

Stefan didn't walk the forest. He stalked, he hunted. He moved as quickly as a hare, as silently as a hawk, and as deadly as a wolf.

The farther he went from the stone cliff, the sharper his senses became. He didn't care how long it took him to find Ilinca, he wouldn't stop. If he had to walk the length and breadth of Scotland a hundred times over, he would do it. Nothing and no one would stop him from his mission.

The gypsy took him from the only family he had, the brothers who kept him from giving in to the monster inside him. For that, she would pay with her life.

Stefan paused when he heard water. It seemed like eons since he'd heard such a sound. It was…musical. Unable to forget it, he shifted from his path and went towards the sound of the flowing water. When he reached the stream, he simply stared.

The rain stopped and the clouds parted long enough for a ray of sunlight to shine upon the water. The glint of the light off the surface made it appear golden, and caused Stefan to raise his hands to shield his eyes from the brightness.

Suddenly, he found his mouth dry. He was so thirsty. He took stock of everything before he walked to the stream and knelt beside it. Stefan cupped his hand and brought handful after handful of water to his mouth.

When he was satisfied, he took in the majestic view of the mountains rising all around him. Even with the gray sky, there was nothing more beautiful than the Highlands.

It made him think of his friends. They were the only reason he was sane enough to recall their names. It saddened him that he would never be able to talk to them again. He didn't want them to see what he had become. All three would try and change him, and they would never stop.

But there was no changing him back to what he was. The monster was loose. The anger had become a living, breathing thing inside him that nothing could defeat.

This was how his life was always meant to turn out. His mother had tried to change his future, but there was only so much she could do once his father refused to acknowledge Stefan's existence.

Just thinking of his father sent a wave of fury rumbling through him. Stefan could still remember his father's stony look, his callous laughter when Stefan was six and ran away from his mother to go to his father.

That's the day he learned he was a bastard. It was the day the monster inside him was born.

It was also the day he learned the only person in the whole world who cared about him was his mother. She tried to help him control his anger, anger that was passed from his father onto him. If not for his mother, Stefan would've been lost to his monster, just as his father had succumbed to his.

For the next ten years, it was just Stefan and his mother. Then his mother died suddenly. Stefan had been terrified of the anger inside him, but there wasn't fear now. Now, he embraced it.

He rose to his feet and started back to the trees when a sound to his right drew his attention. His head jerked around and he saw the woman from earlier stumble out of the forest to the stream.

Stefan hid behind a tree and watched her. She had leaves sticking out of her braid, or what hair remained in the plait anyway. Her gown had patches of mud and dirt on it. After she drank, she wrung out the water from her skirts and hung her head.

As she sat there, Stefan was shocked to see a buck walk up to her. When the buck lowered his head, Stefan thought the deer might attack her. To his surprise, the buck pawed the earth as if to get her attention.

When the woman lifted her head, she looked at the deer and smiled. He couldn't tell what she said from the distance, but she was talking to the buck. Stefan grew more confused when the woman draped an arm around the deer's neck and it helped her back to her feet.

Stefan shook his head and turned away. There were still several hours of daylight left. He walked another ten minutes before he found a road that cut through the forest.

He remained hidden as a man on horseback rode past. Stefan took note of the plaid and the sword the man carried. It didn't take long for Stefan to decide to follow the man even though it took him back in the direction he had come from.

Stefan hadn't been following the rider long when the man drew his mount to a stop and simply sat there. Stefan couldn't see the man's face because of his cloak and hood, but the man was being cautious. A moment later, he clicked the horse back into a walk.

Stefan was glad of his decision to follow the rider when

they came to a castle. He recognized the preparations taking place. With all the activity, it was apparent the clan was gearing for war. He took note of the number of warriors this clan held.

Stefan crept closer to the castle and overheard someone mention the name Sinclair. If he was on Sinclair land, then that meant he was only a hundred miles or so from where he was last with his friends.

He turned and made his way back to the forest. Now that he knew where he was, he knew which direction he needed to go. Which was where he had been headed to begin with.

Stefan easily made up the time he'd lost by following the man. He found the stream again and kept going, running low and fast. As the sun began to set, he crested a hill and saw smoke curling from the trees. Hunger rumbled in his stomach and he decided to check it out.

Surprise ripped through him when he found a small cottage and the same woman from the cliff. Instead of being inside tending to her wounds, she was feeding the chickens while barely keeping on her feet. It was while she tried to bring in more wood that she collapsed.

Stefan waited a few moments to see if she would wake. When she didn't, he walked from the trees and squatted beside her. He moved aside the black hair that had fallen over her face to look at her.

Why had she been so far from her home? What had she been doing on that cliff?

He didn't want those questions running through his mind, and he certainly didn't want the answers. He stood, intending to turn away when he recalled her face up on the cliff right before she fell. He had no idea how he'd gotten on the cliff, and there was a chance something similar had happened to her.

A sliver of emotion churned in his gut. He felt responsible for her injuries. That's the only reason he bent and gathered her in his arms and stood. He kicked the door to the cottage open and walked inside to the bed before he set her down. As he pulled his arms from beneath her, his hand touched her skin and he felt the coolness.

If the lass could live after such a fall and make the trek all the way to the cottage, fate had a plan for her. That's the only reason Stefan hurriedly removed her wet boots, stockings, gown, and shift.

As he was pulling the blanket over her, he spotted the huge bruise covering her left side. Stefan tucked the blanket tight, threw a log onto her dying fire and walked out, intending to forget her.

CHAPTER 3

Morvan was on her side when she woke. She opened her eyes and looked into the flames in the hearth. The last thing she remembered was trying to get more wood to stoke the fire. When had she gotten it? More importantly, when did she get undressed and into bed?

She clutched her side and slowly sat up, realizing she was naked. Something was definitely wrong because she never went to bed naked.

Morvan wrapped the blanket around her and stood to walk to the window. She looked out the shutter to see the faint glow of the sun just breaking over the mountain. Her stomach rumbled loudly. She turned away from the window and walked to the table where she cut a piece of bread and added a slice of cold ham to it. Morvan ate four pieces of ham and two portions of bread before she retrieved a clean gown and petticoat. Her boots and stockings also in her arms, she walked from the cottage.

She had never walked down to the loch in nothing but a blanket, but there was no one about to see or disturb her, so

Morvan didn't worry. She was more concerned with the missing hours she couldn't remember.

Had she fallen so hard that she would lose time? Surely if that were to happen, it would've happened right after she woke from the fall off the cliff. She hadn't hit her head on any rocks, but that didn't mean her brain hadn't been addled a bit by such a rough tumble.

When Morvan reached the loch, she draped her clean clothes over a low-hanging branch along with the blanket. Then she walked into the water. It was cool against her skin, making her catch her breath at the contact. When the water reached her hips, she dove under, remaining beneath until her lungs began to burn.

When she surfaced, she played in the water for a bit, trying to relax after the day before. It wasn't just her injuries or the fall, it was the fact she had been on Sinclair land for a long time. As far as she knew, none of the MacKays had seen her, but she also didn't want to go into the village and find out if she was wrong.

Morvan gathered sand from the bottom of the loch and began to wash. She was so out of sorts that she'd forgotten her soap at the cottage. When she finished, she walked to the shore and wrung out her hair.

It wasn't until she was walking back to her clothes that she had the suspicion someone was watching her, which was ridiculous. No one would want to spy on her.

She used the blanket to dry off and then hurriedly dressed. Only then did she look around, but she could find no indication that anyone was there.

"I'm just rattled," she murmured.

That had to be the excuse. After the man had come out of nowhere on top of the cliff and she'd fallen, she hadn't been the same. Well, that wasn't exactly true. It had begun yesterday morning. She still couldn't pinpoint exactly what it was, but everything about the day before had been a little off.

Morvan gathered the blanket and made her way back to the cottage. She needed to mix some herbs to help with the pain of her ribs, not to mention a poultice to deal with the ugly bruising.

Once inside, she made the tea and added some herbs for the pain. While she drank the mixture, she combed out her hair, which proved difficult with her ribs. When the tangles were all out, she left her hair free and ventured back into the woods to look for the herbs she would need for the poultice.

If she had been thinking clearly yesterday after she'd helped the buck, she would have gathered them then. She'd used her last bit on the blacksmith's horse two days earlier when it had come up with a lame leg.

Morvan brought some oatcakes with her since she was still hungry from missing two meals the day before. She wasn't twenty steps from her cottage when she found a hare caught in a trap.

She looked around because she hadn't set the trap. Someone else had. Someone else who had been close to her cottage. Morvan bent and touched the frightened hare. The animal instantly stopped fighting and stayed calm as she removed the vine from its hind leg.

"Off you go," she said and watched it hop away.

It wasn't that she minded someone hunting. Everyone had to eat. What disturbed her was that it had been done so close to her cottage, and she hadn't even known about it.

Out of the corner of her eye, Morvan saw movement. She jerked around, but there was nothing but a fern leaf swaying. Before she could react to whatever was out there, she heard a group of men stomping through the forest. The fact that the sound was coming from the direction of her laird's castle meant that her clan was probably marching off to war.

Morvan quickly hid behind a large oak and plastered her back to the bark. The men were getting closer. They were talking in low tones, but the mood was dark and dangerous. She didn't want them finding her because her clan or not, she wasn't exactly welcome.

Men on their way to battle were likely to do all sorts of things to a woman alone. If everything she knew about her clan were true, then it was only the roughest, meanest warriors who remained.

Suddenly, there was a shout from one of the men. Everything went silent for a heartbeat, and then chaos erupted. There was no clang of swords, yet there was no denying the sounds of battle. The shouts of pain, the bellows of outrage, and the grunts of the dying could clearly be heard.

Had the Sinclairs ambushed her clan?

Morvan glanced around the tree and saw her clan. And one man attacking them. She gaped in astonishment that one man could do such damage to a group of fifteen men. He was quick and agile, swift and lethal. He used no sword, just his hands and a dagger.

As the man pivoted away, she caught a glimpse of his face. It was the same man from the cliff. She was mesmerized, captivated.

Six of her clansman left alive ran back the way they had come as the man fought a seventh. She covered her mouth with her hand as her clansman fell. The man from the cliff stood among the dead breathing heavily. He started to turn away when one of the six who'd run off returned and threw a dagger that landed in the man's thigh.

The stranger's face turned deadly, as feral as a wild animal's when he locked his gaze on his attacker. In quick order, he had her clansman in his grip, and the man died quickly and violently.

Morvan knew she couldn't be seen by the man. Even as he staggered and slammed against a tree, she knew she had to leave. She waited until he pulled the dagger from his thigh before she took a step back. She held her breath when her foot landed on a stick and it split, the sound as loud as a crack of thunder in the silence of the forest.

The man's head jerked around to her and their gazes locked. He pushed away from the tree, and she saw the blood seeping from various wounds on his arms and chest. Though his eyes were wild and focused, his body wasn't responding as it had before. He took two steps toward her before he went down on one knee.

He growled, his face twisted with anger – at her or himself for not rising, she didn't know. Her heart ached as she watched him try to get up. It reminded her of the elk she'd seen be taken down by an arrow the winter before. The massive animal had fought the death that awaited it, it struggled and scraped to get its legs underneath it, only to stagger a few steps and fall back down.

Which was exactly what the stranger was doing.

Morvan couldn't stand to see any animal suffer – even a man. At the same time, the stranger was still in the grips of battle. He wouldn't stop until she was dead.

She lifted her skirts and started running. Even with her heart pounding and her breath rushing, she could hear him behind her. The only thing in her favor was the fact that she knew this forest better than anyone. She ran in the opposite direction from her cottage, her gaze directly in front of her to the stream. There was no use looking behind her. All her concentration was needed to maneuver around trees and rocks.

She could hear him closing in, knew he was about to

grab her. Morvan caught a glimpse of the stream through the trees. She was so close. All she had to do was get him to the water. She knew where the shallow spots were. If he fell into the deep part, it would give her time to get away.

Morvan shrieked when her head was jerked back as the man grabbed the ends of her hair. She swatted her arm behind her and connected with him. It was all that was needed to get him to release her.

With renewed drive, she pumped her legs faster. A smile formed when she came to the stream and headed for the shallow part. Luck was on her side as her boot hit the shore of the water.

Suddenly, she was slammed into from behind. The water came at her quickly, and then she was on her back looking into hazel eyes. She watched, confused, as his anger faded and clarity filled his eyes.

He kept her from going under the water by shifting, his hold easing considerably. With his chest heaving, he frowned down at her. Blood gushed from his wounds, and he blinked, fighting to stay conscious.

A tremor went through him as he released her and fell back. Morvan warily sat up and discovered the stranger had passed out. If any of the MacKays arrived and found him, they would kill him instantly. She should want his death, and yet, the same feeling that urged her to the cliff the day before screamed at her to heal the man.

She might live on MacKay land, but she didn't consider them her clan. She didn't have a clan. The forest was her home, the animals within it her family. So she didn't feel as if she were betraying a clan who didn't want her.

Morvan stood in the water and looked around to find a secluded section where she could hide the stranger. Using the water to help, she pulled him to the spot she'd selected. It took awhile between his weight, her ribs, and her heavy skirts to pull him as far out of the water as she could.

Then she rushed around finding the herbs she needed to staunch the bleeding. She packed the leaves and flower petals into the wounds and tore off strips of her shift to bind them in place.

When she finished the last one, she sat back and looked at the man. He was tall and muscular, a Highlander in every sense of the word. Never had she seen someone kill with their bare hands, but that's exactly what he had done – to ten men.

Morvan looked down at her hands to see the blood upon them. She rinsed her hands in the water as she took in the man's face. His face was all hard angles, but with his hollowed cheeks and full bottom lip, he was striking.

Unable to resist, she ran the back of her fingers along his cheek and then sank her fingers into his thick hair. His deep brown eyebrows were a shade darker than his hair and slashed over his eyes. Now that his forehead was no longer furrowed, he looked younger and much calmer.

"Who are you?" she whispered.

He slept on, unaware of her question. That was just one of many she had, however. She hoped he would wake in time to answer them, but she doubted he was the kind of man who would give answers if he didn't want to.

Her world of solitude and silence had been shattered, and there was nothing she could do about it. There was a possibility her clansmen wouldn't come to her cottage. It was a slim one. At least the stranger had a chance to escape. If he woke in time.

Somehow, she didn't think he was the kind of man to lie around no matter how severe the wound. No, he would be up and gone as soon as he woke. Which was probably a good thing.

Morvan sighed. Besides stitching them, she had done all

she could for his wounds. It was too bad he wasn't awake. She found herself wanting to hear his voice to see if it matched the virile, muscular visage of the man she had witnessed in the heat of battle.

Then again, she would be better served getting as far from him as she could.

CHAPTER 4

S tefan's eyes snapped open to see thick, puffy clouds lazily drifting across a blue sky. He felt like roasted arse and he didn't know why his feet were wet inside his boots.

He raised his head and saw the stream, and then he remembered the woman. He recalled his anger directed at her. He'd grabbed her, and it was like a veil had been lifted from him. Everything became calm and clear for a moment.

The same had happened the night before when he'd carried her into her cottage, but he hadn't realized it until they were in the water.

Stefan couldn't recall what had happened after touching the woman, or before he was chasing her through the forest. Why had he chased her? It was the same woman from the cliff, and the same woman he'd watched swim in the loch that morning. But that shouldn't have made him go after her.

He ran a hand down his face and sat up, grimacing at the pain that assaulted him from his chest, arms, and thigh. Someone had tended to his wounds, and if the material binding him were any indication, it was the woman.

If she'd run from him, it was because she was frightened. Why would she then tend to him?

There was only one way to find out.

Stefan started to get to his feet when he heard a snap of a limb. He slowly pulled his boots out of the water and turned so he could look over the foliage covering him when he saw six men, all wearing blue and green tartans.

"Find him," demanded the tallest of the men. He carried a sword in his meaty fist, a look of rage contorting his face.

Stefan remained hidden as he watched the men follow tracks to the stream. They waded across and began looking for another trail.

"The tracks stop, Donald," one of the men said to the leader.

Donald's gaze looked up and down the stream, pausing for a moment near where Stefan hid. "We tracked him this far, we can find his trail again. The bastard will pay for killing our clansmen."

Stefan might have holes in his memory, but his wounds combined with the fact that he woke at the stream made it a safe bet that he was who the men were looking for. The longer he remained, the sooner they would find him. Stefan waited until the group – minus the leader - were out of sight up stream before he decided to go in the opposite direction. He kept bent over and had only taken one step when voices reached him.

"Look who we found," came a man's voice full of laughter.

Stefan paused, though he wasn't sure why.

"Were you here?" Donald demanded.

A feminine voice said, "I'm always here. The forest is my home."

Stefan looked over his shoulders and saw the woman, her

black hair in a neat braid as she held Donald's gaze with her chin high.

She was brave and fearless despite one man towering over her, and another behind her holding both of her arms. It was the perfect time for Stefan to get away. Why then did he remain?

"I hear the whispers of you," Donald said in a hard voice, his lip lifted in a sneer. "You and your magic."

"I don't have magic," the woman protested.

Donald gave a snort. "I could have you burned. Tell me what I want to know, and I'll leave you alone."

"I have no magic," she said again through clenched teeth.

A third man walked around the group and stopped at the water's edge. He looked back and said, "Donald, Morvan is known as a healer of sorts. Perhaps she was...unaware...that she was helping a man who is an enemy to us."

Donald regarded Morvan for a moment. "Did you find a stranger and heal him?"

Stefan's gaze was glued to Morvan. It was an unusual name for a particularly unusual woman. He used the group's diverted attention to steadily move away from his hiding spot and into the forest, careful that he didn't encounter any more men.

Stefan didn't stop until he was on the other side of the group, and then he crouched down behind a pine. It brought him closer to Morvan, and to his dismay, he was drawn to her in a way he couldn't explain.

No matter how he tried, he couldn't shake the feeling that he was meant to be there to help her.

"Tell me true, Morvan," Donald said. "He killed your clansman. He needs to be caught and punished."

For long moments, Morvan held Donald's gaze. Then she finally said, "Aye, I came upon a man and tended him."

"Where?" Donald asked tightly.

Morvan pointed to where Stefan had been. While the leader and one of his men went to look, Morvan was held in place by the guard.

Stefan waited until Donald and his man were nearly to where Morvan had left him before he came out from behind the tree. He kicked Morvan's guard in the back of the knee, dropping him down while snapping the man's neck.

Morvan twisted away and turned to gape at him. "You should be gone," she whispered urgently.

There wasn't time for Stefan to respond as a shout from across the stream brought the leader's attention to them. Stefan grabbed Morvan's hand - feeling the same calming sensation he recognized from before – and jerked her behind him.

Her brown eyes were wide with fear, but she didn't argue. Stefan took a deep breath and faced his attackers.

For the second time that day, Morvan watched the stranger battle. As injured as he was, he moved as if he didn't feel anything, as if he hadn't lost all that blood.

The man she faced a moment ago wasn't the same one who had chased her earlier. The clarity was still there, but for how long? As MacKay men came at him, she saw the blood-lust take him again. At least that's what she thought at first.

The more he fought, the more she saw the anger return. It was like it consumed him, took him. The more the men came at him, the more the fury showed. One by one, the men of her clan died by the stranger's hand. It wasn't until he was battling Donald that she knew she had to stop him.

Morvan shouted, hoping to get the stranger's attention. When that didn't work, she walked closer. "You must stop," she said. "There has been enough killing."

She stepped over the fallen men as Donald and the stranger punched each other. The stranger had divested Donald of his sword early on in the fight, and it was all hand-to-hand now.

Suddenly, the stranger had Donald on his back, choking him. Morvan hurried to the men, knowing that the stranger might very well turn on her again.

"Stop," she said and touched him.

Just as before, she felt a tremor go through him. He didn't release Donald, but he loosened his grip and turned his head toward her.

"No more killing," she said again and looked into the man's hazel eyes. Morvan glanced down at Donald to find him watching them.

The man looked back at Donald and slammed his fist into Donald's jaw, knocking him out. The man then got to his feet and faced her.

"You can no' go back," he stated.

His voice was as deep and silky as she imagined it would be. It sent a thrill through her that clumped low in her belly, urging her to take note of his fierceness – as well as his protection of her.

The lucidity had returned to the man again. Had her touch done that? In animals yes, but she hadn't known it to work on humans. Then again, he was more beast than man when in battle.

"Did you no' hear me, lass? Donald knows you've helped me. Twice, I might add. He'll kill you."

Morvan glanced back in the direction of her cottage. "No one knows this forest like I do."

"He'll find you eventually. Come with me," he urged.

She looked down at the hand he held out to her. "I don't even know your name."

"It's Stefan. Stefan Kennedy."

"Where are we going?" she asked as she took his hand and he led her towards the water.

"As far from here as we can get. Is there another clan who will take you in?"

Since their only option was to cross the stream, Morvan lead him to the shallow part when she drew up at his words. "What? I thought you were from the Sinclairs."

"Nay. My clan is far from here."

The day was growing grimmer by the moment. Morvan crossed the stream, but as soon as they were on the other side, Stefan took the lead.

"How far is it to Sinclair land?"

"Not far," she said staring at his back. There was more blood on him, and she would guess that his other wounds were bleeding again. "We should reach the border in about thirty minutes."

He held a tree limb up for her to duck under. "Do you know anyone there?"

"Nay. It appears the Sinclairs and MacKays are about to go to war."

They walked in silence for a bit. Then Stefan stopped and turned to her. "What did you do to me?"

Morvan blinked. "Do? I tended to your wounds."

"Nay. You touched me and...you calmed me."

She looked at the ground and gave a shake of her head. There was no use denying it. "I tend to the animals of these woods."

"Meaning?" he pressed in a soft voice.

"I heal them or help them if they're trapped."

"Like my hare earlier?"

She jerked her gaze to him, once more finding herself ensnared by his hazel gaze and thick, dark lashes. "I didn't know it was yours. There is nothing special about me. I merely take the time with the animals, and I'm calm with them. That in turn calms them."

He took a step toward her, closing the distance so their bodies were nearly touching. His gaze was probing, searching. "Call it what you will, but there is something special about you, Morvan. No one has been able to pull me back like you have. And both times, only with a simple touch."

"Pull you back from what?" she asked softly.

"You saw me. You saw the monster I become when my fury gets ahold of me."

"How often does that happen?"

"Any time I get angry."

She could feel the heat coming off him. He was intense, forceful, and dangerous. He set her on edge, and he made her ache for something she couldn't name. It was a growing feeling inside her, one that began the day before.

"What makes you angry?" she asked.

One side of his mouth lifted in a smile, but there was only desolation in his eyes when he said, "Everything."

He turned and continued on their path. Morvan fell in step behind him, wondering what turned a man like Stefan so furious all the time.

"I'll make sure you're safe," he said over his shoulder. "Then I must leave."

Morvan knew she should leave well enough alone, and yet she found herself asking, "To return to your clan?"

"Nay. I'm hunting the gypsy who ruined my life."

Morvan decided it was best to keep from asking more questions. She kept up with his fast pace, even as her ribs ached. The tea she'd drank that morning, and again at noon before the MacKays arrived at the cottage, was helping control the pain. But only just.

Not once did she ask Stefan to slow. She hoped she

would be able to shake the gloomy feeling once they crossed onto Sinclair land, but it only grew with every step she took.

When dusk came, Morvan looked up to discover that Stefan had brought them back to the cliff where she'd first seen him. Thankfully, he didn't make the climb up.

"We'll stop here for the night," he said.

When he started to walk off, she stood in his path and gave him a shove back. "Sit so I can look at your wounds."

It looked like he might argue for a moment, but then he sat on a boulder and lifted a brow.

Morvan first looked at the damage he had done to his previous wounds before she examined the fresh ones. "The new ones don't look that bad, but I need more herbs for your leg and the wounds on your chest from this morning. Stay here until I get what I need."

To her surprise, she didn't have to go far to gather the herbs. As she made her way back to the cliff, she happened to see Stefan stand up. His shirt was gone and water dripped down his bare chest from the small pool of water where he had been washing.

She let her gaze wander over his finely sculpted muscles from his shoulders and arms, to his chest that narrowed to a V at his waist. She was too intent on his wounds before to notice the many scars that crisscrossed his entire torso. Despite the scars – or perhaps because of them – his body was amazing. He was a warrior in the truest sense of the word. She didn't know of another who could fight a group of men twice in one day and come out the victor both times.

She let her eyes slowly travel back up his chest, her hands wishing they could feel his warm skin, to know the shape of his muscles. When she looked into his face, Stefan was staring at her.

Morvan wasn't a maid. She'd once given her heart – and her maidenhead – to a man she'd thought loved her. Even if she were a maid, she would've recognized the desire in Stefan's eyes.

It had been so long since she'd felt such yearning stir that she feared it as much as she craved it.

Stefan tossed aside something that Morvan only belatedly realized was his ruined shirt. She walked to him, their gazes never breaking. When she reached him, she pushed him back to sit on a rock and knelt between his legs. She saw a droplet of water fall from the end of his hair to his collarbone. Without thinking, she covered the drop with her finger and spread it over his chest.

His skin was warm, his chest hair crinkling beneath her palm. Morvan's blood pounded through her as desire coiled tightly.

She went from wound to wound washing them and packing them with herbs before taking more of her shift to use as bandages. Every time she touched Stefan, it became harder and harder to keep her hands from him. He was like a magnet drawing her to him.

There were no words spoken. She felt his gaze on her face even as she kept her eyes on his magnificent body. If she looked up, she might give in to the desire that was slowly consuming her.

When she finished dressing his wounds, she set aside the herbs. After a moment, she lifted her eyes. She didn't flinch away when his hand cupped one side of her face. He pulled her to him the same time he lowered his head. Their lips brushed once, twice, seeking, searching.

A moan rumbled in Stefan's chest as his arms wound around Morvan and pulled her closer. He deepened the kiss, the passion flaring high, the desire erupting brightly.

CHAPTER 5

Stefan knew he should soften the kiss, but he couldn't. The longing, the desire was too great. Touching Morvan affected him in ways he couldn't describe, but kissing her set his blood afire.

Her hands roamed over his back, her touch both gentle and needy. His cock jumped when she shifted again, bringing their bodies tightly together. He ground his arousal against her and then moaned as her nails dug into his back. The woman was a temptress, a siren. And he was powerless against the yearning to have her.

Stefan bent her over his arm and kissed down her throat. He watched the way her chest heaved, the way her head lolled to the side to give him access. He heard her soft moans, saw her swollen lips still wet from his kisses.

He forgot everyone and everything except the woman in his arms. All that mattered was Morvan and the passion that raged between them.

He wouldn't be content until she was writhing beneath him, until she was so sated she couldn't move. Until he looked into her nutmeg brown eyes and saw her climax reflected there.

"Your wounds," Morvan said when her hand skimmed over one of his bandages.

Stefan took her mouth in another kiss. He didn't care about his injuries. He felt nothing but pleasure right now, and that's all he would feel.

He moved off the rock to kneel in the thick grass in front of her. Morvan's kisses were like a drug, and he never wanted it to end. A moan slipped from him. He had to feel her skin against his, to see her in all her glory. Stefan grabbed a handful of her skirts and pulled them upward.

A heartbeat later, she was helping him remove her gown. She toppled over as he finally got it off. Her laughter was the sweetest sound he had ever heard, and it brought a smile to his lips.

She looked up at him before she removed her boots. Stefan swallowed hard when he caught a glimpse of her bare thigh as she rolled down her stockings. Then all that remained was her thin shift.

Stefan held his breath, waiting for her to remove the last bit of her clothing. He had seen her naked, but he hadn't looked – much to his dismay. That's what his anger did to him.

But that rage was a world away at the moment. That's how he wanted it to stay.

He unpinned his kilt and let the material fall away. When he started to lean over her, she held up a hand.

"Wait," she said and sat up.

The way she looked at him, as if she didn't think he was real, perplexed him. There was no denying the awe in her gaze, and he didn't know what to do with it.

Out of his friends, he was the last of them that women

saw or even paid attention to. He wasn't sure how to react to the way Morvan reverently touched him, smoothing her hands over his chest while always being careful around his bandages.

Everywhere she touched, his skin burned for more. From his shoulders to his chest and down his abdomen she left a trail of fire. Not once did she recoil at his many scars. Not once did the light in her gaze dim.

"Magnificent." She lifted her brown eyes to his. "That's what you are."

"I'm a warrior, meant for battle and death. There's nothing good about me."

Her eyes crinkled at the corners as she rose up on her knees and cupped her hands around his face. "You are magnificent and beautiful and glorious."

Her eyes held nothing but honesty. No one had ever looked at him the way Morvan did now. Stefan slid a hand around her waist. With just a few words, her touch, and her direct gaze, she changed something within him. It didn't make sense, but nothing had since he'd encountered her.

"Are you real?" he whispered.

"Yes."

Their lips were close, the desire burning hot. Stefan took her mouth in a frantic kiss of need and...hope. He held out a hand to break their fall as he pushed her backward.

He covered her body with his, kissing her senseless while slowly working her shift up her thighs and over her hips. He'd never been so hard for a woman in his entire life.

Stefan yanked off her shift and then looked down at Morvan. He was enthralled by her curves, taken by her alluring body. Her breasts were plump, her nipples a dusky brown. His gaze stopped for a moment on the large bruise on her side that looked as if it were already healing. Her waist narrowed before her hips flared out enticingly.

Then his gaze settled on the black curls between her legs.

"By all that's holy you're a bonny sight," Stefan murmured as he cupped one of her breasts.

Morvan sucked in a breath and her eyes slid closed. Stefan massaged the globe before tweaking her nipple. She gasped, her fingers clutching his arms. He then bent and closed his lips around the turgid peak and sucked. Her hips bucked beneath him, grinding against him. Stefan moved to her other breast and flicked his tongue over the nipple.

Morvan was drowning in pleasure. Stefan was playing her body to perfection. She was lost, adrift in a sea of desire that besieged her. But she welcomed it, sought it.

As long as she was in Stefan's arms, she was safe. She couldn't explain it, nor did she want to. It was a fact, a simple truth that she knew to the very marrow of her bones.

She moaned as his continued assault on her body stirred long-buried hopes. His hands were everywhere, learning her, discovering her.

He kissed down her stomach to her sex. She lifted her head and met his gaze. There was a confident grin pulling at his lips as he parted her thighs and leaned down to kiss her where she needed him most.

Morvan dug her fingers in the grass and arched her back as the exquisite pleasure swarmed her. The intensity of it was too much, but she couldn't pull away with the way he gripped her hips. She was powerless to do anything but endure the relentless, decadent pleasure of his tongue.

She was mindless with need, her desire coiled tightly. Her body lay open for Stefan to do with as he saw fit. The carnality of his tongue as it teased her clit, the sensuality of his fingers holding her, took her to a place she had never been before. A place she hadn't known existed.

The orgasm came out of nowhere. She jerked, a scream locked in her throat as her body shook with the force of the climax. When the last tremor finally left her, she opened her eyes to see Stefan leaning over her.

His long, dark hair hung around his face, and his hazel eyes blazed with hunger. Morvan was captivated, fascinated.

Enchanted.

He reached for her, and she eagerly went to him. Sitting up, she wrapped her arms around his neck and her legs around his waist. He held her with ease, his large hands sensuously rubbing her buttocks.

There were no words between them. They didn't need any. Everything they felt and experienced was through their eyes and touch.

It was erotic, carnal. Wanton.

Morvan felt the head of his arousal at the entrance to her sex. She held her breath as Stefan slowly lowered her until she had taken all of him. Looking into his hazel eyes, she felt as if it were just the two of them in the whole world.

Then he began to move.

Stefan didn't know what heaven was, but with Morvan in his arms, he figured it was as close as he would ever get. He couldn't stop touching or kissing her. And the way she looked at him made him want to pluck the moon from the sky for her.

He groaned at the feel of her slick, tight sheath. She was all passion and curves, and she spurred his desire with just a touch.

He wanted – needed – to hear her cry out from the pleasure again. He yearned to see the bliss light her from the inside out. Never had he seen anything so beautiful.

His thrusts grew harder as he went deeper. Morvan's lips were parted, her skin flushed. With sweat slicking their bodies, Stefan drove them toward the pinnacle of ecstasy.

Stefan unwound Morvan's legs from his waist and flipped her onto her hands and knees. He came up on his knees behind her and ran his hand from her neck down her spine to her butt.

She looked over her shoulder at him, a gleam of excitement in her brown depths. He took his cock and guided it to her entrance. Then he entered her with one thrust. Morvan groaned and pushed back against him. Stefan grabbed her hips and began to drive into her. The louder she moaned, the harder he plunged.

He leaned over her and skated his hand along her neck to turn her face to the side so he could give her a hard kiss. When he pulled back, she met his gaze and licked her lips. He very nearly spilled his seed right then.

He sank deeper into her as she rocked back against him. He could feel his own climax building quickly, but he refused to give in.

He continued to pump his hips, driving into Morvan until he felt her sheath clamp down on him. Only then did he give in to his body and allow himself to climax. As he poured his seed inside her, experiencing more pleasure in that one moment than he had in his entire life, he realized two things.

He would do anything for Morvan, and she had taken a piece of his soul.

CHAPTER 6

Morvan lay nestled back against Stefan's chest. She couldn't remember ever feeling so happy. If she tried, she bet she could walk upon the clouds.

She took a deep breath, and it wasn't until she released it that she realized there was no pain.

"Why do you live alone?"

Stefan's question was spoken in a soft tone, but it startled her nonetheless. She shrugged. "It's how it has always been."

"Always? I find it hard to believe you've been by yourself since you were an infant."

Morvan turned to face him, tucking her arm beneath her head as she did. "I was found in the forest by an old woman named Maria. She didn't have any family of her own, so she kept me. My clan thinks I was left by the Fae."

"You never knew your parents?" he asked with a frown.

"Nay."

"Perhaps it's better that way."

Morvan guessed that he had no idea how telling his words were.

Stefan touched her cheek. "So, Maria raised you?"

"Until I was eight. We were out gathering wood after a heavy snowfall. Maria was old, and even though I could've gotten the wood myself, she insisted on coming. She slipped on the ice and fell. She never woke up."

His forehead furrowed deeply. "Surely one of your clansmen took you in after that?"

"They've always been afraid of me," she said with a smile. "It doesn't bother me."

"You've lived on your own this entire time?"

"I have." She smoothed a lock of hair back from his face. "What about you? Tell me of your family."

His gaze slid away. "There's no' much to tell. My mother died when I was ten and six."

"And your father?"

"Wouldna claim me."

Morvan covered his fist with her hand. "You obviously didn't let that stop you from becoming a warrior?"

"I was quickly becoming the monster you witnessed earlier after my mother died. The rage was steadily consuming me." His eyes returned to her. "Then I met my friends, Ronan, Daman, and Morcant. We were all from different clans, but somehow we became like brothers. They alone helped me remember who I was."

She had the distinct feeling that something bad had happened to them. "You speak as if they're dead."

"I doona know if they live or no'. I'm going to find out right after I find the old gypsy."

"You mentioned a gypsy before. What does she have to do with it?"

He skimmed a finger down her side to her hip. "She cursed us. Ronan and Morcant disappeared first, and then she looked at me. I heard her voice in my head, and then I was in a place as dark as the deepest night where no light found its way. There was only silence and darkness."

Morvan knew about the gypsies. Maria used to tell her to stay far away from them because they only brought trouble. And death.

"How did you get out of the darkness?"

Stefan shook his head and glanced at the rocks above them. "I'm unsure. One moment I was there, and the next I was on top of the cliff."

An uneasy feeling assaulted her. "And how long were you in the darkness?"

"I estimate a few years. I couldna judge the passing of time without any light. I concentrated on my hatred of Ilinca, and it fed the beast within me, growing my fury until it consumed me. Until you touched me."

Morvan tucked the stray hairs from her braid behind her ear to keep them from tickling her face. "What year was it when Ilinca cursed you?"

"1427."

Morvan rolled onto her back so Stefan wouldn't see her worry. Two hundred years. How could he have been locked away somewhere for two hundred years?

Her gaze snagged on the boulders high above them and the narrow, steep path she had climbed to the top of the cliff. Something had driven her there a few days ago, and she was beginning to suspect it all had to do with Stefan.

"What is it?" he asked.

"I never come onto Sinclair land. It is forbidden with the threat of war," she whispered. "Yet, I was drawn here yesterday. To the top of that cliff. I walked a maze of boulders that seemed to move on their own until I came to a wall of markings." She turned her head to look at him. "They were of Celtic design, and there was one I couldn't resist touching. The wolf."

Stefan blinked slowly. "My mother called me a wolf."

"It was after I touched the etching of the wolf that I saw you."

He inhaled deeply. "Everything I did brought me across your path. I found you last night unconscious outside your cottage and brought you inside."

No wonder she had a hole in her memories. She hadn't been awake for them. "It was you who took off my clothes."

"You were shivering," he said with a hint of a smile.

"And this morning? Was that you I felt watching me at the loch?"

He nodded.

Morvan laced her fingers with his. "You said that the year was 1427 when the gypsy cursed you. Stefan, it's been a lot longer than a few years since that happened."

"How long?"

"The year is 1609."

His entire demeanor changed. He rolled onto his back and stared at the stars.

Morvan wasn't sure if he wanted her near or not, but she recognized that he was hurting and she wanted to offer comfort. She scooted closer and rested her face against his shoulder. The sounds of the night filled the silence as he wrapped an arm around her.

Stefan was up and dressed by the time Morvan woke the next morning. He hadn't slept at all after she told him what the year was.

Before he'd had a mission – to kill Ilinca. Regardless that the gypsy had magic, there was no way she was still alive. Stefan wasn't sure what he was going to do now. Without Ilinca, he couldn't find his friends.

They could be anywhere, in any time.

He expected to feel only anger, but there was also sadness...and despair.

"I should look at your wounds," Morvan said.

Her voice pulled him from his thoughts. He looked over to find that she had dressed. Stefan returned to the same rock as the night before and sat. He looked over her head, thinking of the future and what he was going to do while her gentle hands moved from wound to wound.

"I don't understand."

Stefan looked down. "You doona understand what, lass?"

She sat back on her haunches and lifted her gaze to him. "Your injuries are all healed."

Confused, he looked down at his thigh and saw only a scar visible. He then inspected where one of the injuries had been on his arm, and another on his chest. Each one he looked at was the same – healed.

"How?" he asked as he looked at her.

She shook her head. "I'm not sure, but it explains why my ribs no longer hurt."

"Your bruise? Is it gone?"

Morvan slowly nodded. "There is barely any discoloration."

Stefan looked up at the cliff. "You were drawn here, and I appeared here. What is this place?"

"I don't know."

"Well, we can no' stay. I know where the castle is. We should go there."

"Nay," she said and scrambled to her feet. "I'm a child of the forest."

Stefan saw the fear on her face. He assumed it was the thought of going to a new clan. He stood and grasped her shoulders. "They doona know you, Morvan. You can no' return to your clan, so you must choose whether to go to another clan, or take your chances here and tell them all you know of the MacKays."

"I don't know anything."

"I guarantee you know more than they do."

She looked down and nodded. "What will you do?"

There was really only one choice for him. "I'm going to return to the place I was cursed and start looking for Ilinca or any gypsy who can help me find my friends."

"Good," she said, but her smile was forced and tight.

Stefan didn't want to leave her, but what kind of friend would he be if he didn't look for the men he considered his brothers?

"Which way to the castle?" she asked.

Stefan pointed and walked around her. "You could have a good life with the Sinclairs."

"I'm a child of the forest. It's where I belong. I never feel…right…unless I'm in the forest."

He glanced back at her, but she wouldn't meet his gaze. For all that she had done for him, he was shattering the glow from their night together.

A few moments later, she stopped and picked some berries. She handed a handful to him and picked some for herself. Stefan was starving. He hadn't had a good meal since he got out of the darkness, but then again, he was used to missing meals when needed. He should've realized Morvan needed to eat. What an idiot she must think he was to forget such a thing. So much for him taking care of her.

It just proved that he did need to leave her in more capable hands. No matter how much she calmed the monster inside him, no matter how she'd changed his life, he would only destroy her life.

They walked for another hour until Stefan saw the castle. He stopped on the rise of the next hill and waited for Morvan to draw even with him.

"You really think they'll take me in?" she asked. "What if they think I'm a spy?"

"I came here yesterday. The people," he started and saw an old gypsy woman standing off to his right. She was staring at him, her black eyes unblinking and her gray hair pulled away from her wrinkled face.

"The people what?" Morvan asked.

Stefan quickly glanced at Morvan, but then looked back off to his right. Only, when he looked for the gypsy again, she was gone. He cleared his throat as every instinct within him urged him to find the gypsy. "The people looked happy, if no' a little anxious, but that's understandable with the threat of battle."

"What's so important out there that you won't look away?"

He faced forward and shrugged. "Nothing. Shall we go to the castle?"

"Nay." Morvan faced him and smiled. "I'll be fine. Go find your friends, Stefan."

As he looked down at her, he realized he wasn't ready to part ways yet. Before he could put his thoughts into words, Morvan rose up on her toes and kissed him.

She put her cheek against his. "Be safe, my wolf."

Then she was gone. Stefan watched her walk away. He couldn't decide whether to go after her or Ilinca, and the longer he stood there, the harder it was for him to go after Morvan.

He didn't leave until he saw her reach the gates of the castle. What had he heard the people call it? Ravensclyde. It was a grand name for an impressive castle.

Stefan released a breath when Morvan was admitted into the bailey. Now that she was safe, he could focus on Ilinca. Stefan turned his back on the castle and walked to where he'd seen the gypsy.

Morvan touched her chest. There was an ache there that felt as if someone had yanked out her heart. Stefan had come into her life as quickly as he left it. She didn't regret a single minute she'd shared with him, but that didn't help the emptiness within her now.

She wasn't just empty without Stefan, she was lost without the forest. Morvan closed her eyes and pictured the tall pines, the thick birch, the sturdy oaks. She imagined ferns on the ground and the constant chirping of birds. The woods would help to heal her. If she could get back to them.

How, when she was homeless? She had nothing but the clothes on her back. The Sinclairs had welcomed her into Ravensclyde, but it wasn't her home.

"Morvan?"

Morvan opened her eyes to find herself meeting a gray gaze. The woman that addressed her was frowning, concern showing in her gray depths. Her red hair was pulled back in a loose bun. That's when Morvan remembered entering the bailey and introducing herself to two women.

"She doesn't look well at all," said a second voice.

Morvan shifted her gaze to the left and saw another woman with long brown hair and sky blue eyes. "I'm fine."

The redhead snorted. "You're as pale as death. Come inside so we can feed you," she said and took one of Morvan's arms.

The brunette took the other, nodding as she did. "Food, aye. That's what she needs."

Morvan let them lead her into the castle, but she wasn't seeing any of the people or the gray stones. All she could see was hazel eyes, long dark hair, and a breathtaking body.

"Eat," said the redhead as she shoved a trencher of food at Morvan.

When had they sat? Morvan glanced around nervously.

"It's not poisoned," said the brunette who reached over, pulled off a piece of meat and ate it. "I'm Leana."

"And I'm Meg. You told the guardsmen that you came to Ravensclyde from the MacKays."

Morvan nodded as she bit into the bread. Her stomach growled loudly as she chewed and swallowed. "I came to warn you that Donald MacKay is planning to attack."

"Again?" Leana asked worried, her gaze on Meg.

Meg's lips thinned. "He's already tried that once, and we defeated him."

Morvan hadn't known that.

"I saw Morvan's arrival, but not another attack," Leana said.

Morvan's gaze jerked to Leana. "You saw me?"

"I have...dreams," Leana explained. "I had a vision of you coming here to Ravensclyde two days ago."

Two days ago? That's when she was on Sinclair land and went to the cliffs. Stefan. Why did it feel as if all of this revolved around Stefan?

"Do you know why I'm here?" she asked Leana.

The brunette shook her head. "I see only glimpses. Did you just come to tell us of Donald?"

"Aye." They didn't need to know about Stefan. He was her secret, a stranger she'd conjured from the darkness and tamed – for a time anyway.

"Why?" asked a deep voice behind her.

Morvan turned around and saw two men standing with their arms crossed over their chests. They were imposing men, but after seeing Stefan fight, nothing could impress her anymore.

"Why?" the man with the pale green eyes and brown hair asked again.

Leana walked to the second man who had sandy blond hair and topaz eyes. "I told you about my vision. This is her."

The first man's gaze didn't waver from Morvan. She set aside the bread and said. "There was a stranger that came onto MacKay land. A small group of warriors came upon him and tried to kill him. He was...ferocious in his fighting and killed all but a few who ran back to Donald. I found the stranger after the fight and bound his wounds."

The man lifted a dark brow. "Then?"

"I left the stranger to go about his way. It isn't in my nature to leave an animal in pain unattended."

"He wasna an animal," stated the blond.

Morvan shrugged. "If you'd seen him fight, you would think otherwise."

The two men exchanged a glance. Then the dark-haired one asked, "I'm guessing Donald discovered you helped this stranger?"

"He did." Morvan swallowed, remembering how Stefan had so effortlessly saved her life. "Donald is...unforgiving. He threatened to burn me alive."

Meg touched her hand. "What happened to bring you to us?"

"The stranger," Morvan said. "He saved me."

The dark-headed man dropped his arms. "Where is this stranger? I'd like to talk to him."

"He's gone." Morvan felt the weight of the words, and they hurt far more than she'd expected – far worse than leaving the forest.

Stefan got as far as the stream before he came to a halt, unable to go any further. No matter how hard he tried, he couldn't take another step.

He couldn't stop thinking of Morvan, of how her nutmeg eyes held no anger or censor – just acceptance. She hadn't looked back when she'd walked to the castle. He knew because he had watched her every step of the way.

Without moving from the tree line, Stefan stared at the quick moving stream. It was the place where Morvan had changed his life. One touch had altered his entire course.

He looked to the sky to see night descending. Stefan turned on his heel and started back toward the castle.

Morvan rubbed her eyes and sat up from the comfort of the bed. She glanced out the narrow window of her room to see that the sun was high in the sky. It wasn't like her to sleep past dawn.

She rose and dressed, then brushed out her hair. She had embarrassed herself the night before, by falling asleep as Meg and Leana were talking to her.

Was it a dream, or had Meg introduced her husband as Ronan? It had to have been her thoughts of Stefan and her exhaustion mixing with her arrival at Ravensclyde. The more she thought about it, the more she couldn't clearly remember the name of Meg's or Leana's husband.

It was beyond rude to fall asleep on her hosts. But after the two women kindly brought her upstairs, Morvan had found a bath. It was all she could do to stay awake as she washed the day off her, but she managed it before climbing into bed.

She'd missed dinner, of that she was certain. And it was clearly a new day. How long had she slept?

Morvan tied off a strip of leather at the end of her braid and walked to the door of her chamber. She opened it and stepped into the corridor. It was the sounds of the hall that drew her in the direction of the stairs.

Those at Ravensclyde wanted Stefan's name, but she wouldn't give it. He had been detained long enough. He needed to find his friends. Morvan longed for the forest, to feel the bark of the trees against her palm and hear the wind moving through the leaves.

But the Sinclairs needed to know how dangerous Donald was.

Once she descended and stepped into the great hall, Morvan didn't know what to do. Neither Meg nor Leana was in sight. Morvan followed a delicious aroma to the kitchen and snagged some bread before she walked to the bailey. She stood against the castle wall and simply watched everyone.

It was odd for her to be in the company of so many and not have them look at her with scorn. Perhaps Stefan had been right and this was a new start for her. No one at Ravensclyde knew about her, and they didn't need to.

Morvan lifted her face to the sky and breathed in the air. She missed the forest, but she didn't expect to live her life in the castle. Until she was able to answer the questions Meg's and Leana's husband had of her, she would remain.

After that...she wasn't sure what she would do. Perhaps she would see if there was a vacant cottage in the forest. If not, maybe she would build herself something.

As she turned to go back inside the castle and look for Meg, there was a shout from near the gatehouse. Morvan looked and saw a horse rearing, its hooves pawing the air in a bid to get free.

The horse pulled free from the two men holding him and started running. Morvan looked behind her and saw a group of children frozen in fear as they watched the oncoming steed.

Morvan stepped in front of the white horse and began to hum even as she heard a shout from the castle steps. She ignored whoever was telling her to move away and hummed louder. The horse slid to a halt and reared again.

She shifted to keep from having a hoof hit her when the horse landed. Morvan put her hand on the steed's shoulder, rubbing his white hair. He jerked his head up and down twice, shaking his long dark gray mane before he blew out a breath and remained still.

His big black eyes closed when she ran her hand along his back. She saw the scars on the horse's mouth, legs, and back. He was abused. No wonder he was so wild.

"It's all right," she whispered as she rested her head on his neck. "I won't let anyone hurt you now."

"You either have a death wish or a gift," said a deep voice behind her. "Which is it, lass?"

Morvan glanced over her shoulder to see Meg's husband. So much for the people of Ravensclyde not knowing about her ability. "I'm sorry for falling asleep on you last night. I apologize, but I can't remember if we were introduced. I'm Morvan."

"I'm Ronan, and the halfwit with his mouth open in surprise behind me is Morcant."

Morcant grunted. "I'm no' a halfwit. She amazed me is all. Hell, Ronan, she shocked the entire bailey."

Morvan continued to rub the horse, the action calming her as much as the frightened animal. Morcant and Ronan. What were the odds of finding two men with the same names as the ones Stefan searched for? Was Daman around somewhere, as well?

She met Ronan's pale green gaze as he came to stand beside her and held out his hand for the horse to sniff. Ronan waited for the horse to accept him before he gently rubbed the steed's forehead. "You doona have to fear us here, Morvan. As Leana told you last night, she has visions. Whatever gift you have is welcome."

"Where is Daman?"

There was a flash of astonishment in Ronan's gaze before his face lost all emotion. "You've seen Daman?"

"Nay, but the fact you know the name means you also know the fourth one." She wasn't going to say Stefan's name on the off chance that it was all a coincidence.

Ronan looked at Morcant over his shoulder. A moment later, Morcant stood with them.

"Stefan," Morcant said. "The fourth's name is Stefan."

Morvan's knees buckled. She only managed to stay on her feet thanks to her hold on the horse's mane.

Ronan's brow furrowed as he leaned closer. "It was Stefan who helped you, was it no', Morvan?"

230 | DONNA GRANT

"Aye," she whispered. "He's the stranger I spoke of yesterday."

Morcant rested his hand on the hilt of his sword. "We need to go after him, Ronan."

Ronan nodded, but didn't take his gaze from Morvan. "Where did he go? Is he returning here?"

"He was on his way back to the place where it all began," she said.

Morcant let out a string of curses. "We can still catch him."

"Be careful," Morvan cautioned. "He can be a bit untamed."

Ronan's lips compressed. "We know firsthand."

She watched the two men stride off, hoping they were able to find Stefan quickly. Morvan walked the horse to the stables herself and fed him after putting him in his stall.

By the time she returned to the castle, she was exhausted. She was quickly surrounded by Meg and Leana who guided her to the solar.

"Is it true?" Leana asked her. "Is Stefan out there?"

Morvan nodded. "It is. The past few days have felt like someone aligned the stars to bring us together."

"How do you mean?" Meg asked.

Morvan told them the story of how she'd been brought to the cliffs by some unknown force, and how she and Stefan came to meet. She left out their night together, ending the tale with Stefan leaving her at the castle.

"He was here," Leana said with a shake of her head. "He was right here. If only he had come in with you."

Morvan picked at a sweetmeat. She had consumed four during her story. "He was so anxious to find his friends. All he wanted to do was get back to the place where it all began to see what he could find."

Meg leaned back in her chair, regarding her. "How much did Stefan tell you?"

"All that he knew. Was he right? Were they cursed?"

Leana sighed loudly. "They certainly were."

It took all Morvan could do to keep her eyes open as the two shared their stories of how Ronan and Morcant came to be at Ravensclyde.

"Is it fate that all three were brought to this clan?" Morvan asked.

Meg smiled. "It's magic."

Magic. Morvan wasn't sure if that was the correct word, but then again, she didn't know what to call whatever had compelled her to the cliffs to touch the etching of the wolf.

"Are you feeling well, Morvan?" Leana asked worriedly.

Morvan rubbed her hand along her forehead. "For some reason I can't shake the exhaustion."

"It's everything you've been through." Meg rose and helped Morvan to stand. "We'll let you rest in your chamber."

Leana smiled. "And we'll be sure to let you know as soon as Stefan arrives."

Stefan spent the entire day trying to make it across the stream. The farthest he got was half way before he got a bad feeling. As soon as his feet were back on Sinclair land, the feeling dimmed, but didn't go away.

He bedded for the night at the cliffs, but sleep eluded him. All he could see when he closed his eyes was Morvan as they'd made love beneath the stars in that exact spot.

Stefan was on his way back to the castle before the sun peaked over the mountains. He waited for a glance of

Morvan, because he knew she couldn't stay within the castle walls for long. She was a child of the forest, after all.

As the sun continued its ascent, there was no sign of her. Stefan decided to try a different route to leave. Surely this time he would make it back to the glen where he and his friends were cursed.

If he couldn't have Morvan, he could at least avenge his friends.

CHAPTER 8

For four days, Stefan tried to leave. He tried going different directions each time, but every dawn he found himself back at the castle hoping for a glimpse of Morvan.

He'd stayed at the castle longer than he should have, especially since there seemed to be someone following him. Stefan briefly contemplated waiting for whoever it was, but he didn't want to fight. He just wanted to see Morvan.

As the dawn of the fifth day came, Stefan walked from the trees across the open plain to stop a cart that had just come from the castle.

"Good morn," he called to the elder man, putting a smile on his face though he felt like anything but smiling.

The man nodded in return. "Good morn."

"There've been rumors around that someone from the MacKay clan has come to the castle. Is it true?"

The old man looked back at the castle for a moment. "Aye. It's a woman who came. It must be bad at the MacKay clan for their people to begin coming to Ravensclyde."

Stefan patted the horse pulling the cart. "What does the laird say?"

"The laird isna here yet, lad. He and his men will be here soon enough, I wager. If clan MacKay wants a war, they're going to get one."

Stefan had seen enough of death. He wanted to be as far from the battle as he could. Now he wondered if it had been a good idea to leave Morvan at Ravensclyde. "What have they done with the woman?"

"She's in the castle," the old man said and snapped the reins.

Stefan let him drive off. He walked back to the forest and circled the castle, his gaze on the battlements. The longer he went without seeing Morvan, the more worried he became.

Were they keeping her prisoner? Were they hurting her?

It was time he found out.

≈

"She's not waking," Meg said as she wiped a wet cloth across Morvan's forehead.

Leana stood beside the bed, her face pinched with frustration. "I've tried all the herbs I know. Nothing is working."

"We have to do something. If we don't, Morvan is going to die."

Leana looked at all of the herbs sitting around the chamber. "I don't know what else to do, Meg. She's pale as death already. And I don't know what's wrong with her."

"We've gotten some water down her. That's something at least, right?"

Leana licked her lips. "It's not going to be enough."

≈

Stefan was on his second round of the castle when he realized whoever had been following him had found him once more. If he took the time to confront them, it would be longer before he could get to Morvan.

He didn't understand the sudden urgency he had to reach her, but he wasn't going to waste another moment. It was essential that he get to Morvan immediately.

With his mind so focused on Morvan, he didn't realize how close his pursuer had gotten until the point of a sword pressed into the back of his neck.

"Slowly turn around."

Fury ripped through him. Who was this bastard that was going to keep him from Morvan. For five days, there hadn't been a seed of anger in him.

Until now.

Stefan spun around, ducking as he did. He came up and slammed his fist into the chest of his attacker, sending him flying backwards.

A second man stepped forward. Stefan threw his elbow back into the second assailant's throat. Then he fully faced his opponent and reared back his hand to punch him when the first man jumped on Stefan's back and held his arms so Stefan couldn't punch.

"Easy!" the man shouted.

Stefan, however, was long past the point of controlling his anger. The monster was back. He bared his teeth and lunged for the second man who was coughing. Then he thought of Morvan. He didn't want to be a monster anymore. He wanted to be a man worthy of her, one who could control all his emotions – especially his anger.

And just like that, his anger diminished.

Not that he was going to let the two men attacking him

win. Stefan got an arm loose and elbowed the man on his back.

"Stefan, please!"

It wasn't his name that got his attention, but the voice. There was something recognizable about it.

"Look at Ronan," the man said. "He willna be able to talk for a few days after that hit you landed in his throat."

Stefan shook his head. Ronan? He blinked several times.

"That's it, brother. Look at Ronan. Hear my voice. We didna let you succumb to your monster before. We willna let you now either."

"I'm in control," Stefan said calmly as he looked into the pale green eyes of Ronan. Despite his coughing, Ronan smiled. It *was* Ronan. It wasn't a dream, but the man himself. And the man on Stefan's back was none other than Morcant.

"Control, aye?" Morcant asked as he slid off Stefan's back. He came around to stand in front of Stefan, a bright smile on his face. "You *are* in control. We didna think we'd ever catch up with you. By the saints, it's good to see you again."

He allowed himself a few seconds as Morcant embraced him, pounding him on the back. Stefan then faced Ronan, helped him stand and motioned to his throat. "I'm sorry."

Ronan waved away his words and roughly pulled Stefan close so he could embrace him.

Steven couldn't believe he had his friends, his brothers back. He looked around, waiting for Daman.

"He's no' here," Morcant said. "Ronan was first, and I came a few months ago. Now it's you. All of us were drawn to Ravensclyde, so we're hoping Daman will be, as well."

Stefan faced the castle. "Morvan. I need to get to her."

Ronan slapped him on the arm and walked around him as he said in a hoarse voice, "Come."

"Nay. I need to be there now. Something is wrong," Stefan said glancing at the castle again.

Neither man questioned him. They raced to the castle. As soon as the guards saw Ronan and Morcant, they opened the gates to let them through.

Stefan followed his friends into the castle and up the stairs to a chamber. He threw open the door and felt as if someone had kicked him in the stomach when he saw Morvan lying so still upon the bed.

There were two women with her, but Stefan paid them no heed. He walked to the bed and tenderly lifted Morvan in his arms. "I shouldna have left you," he whispered.

"We're glad you're here," she said the brunette. "I'm Leana, and the one with Ronan is Meg."

"Thank you for looking after Morvan." Stefan turned to his friends. "She's a child of the forest. I need to get her there quickly."

"The forest is near," Meg said while standing next to Ronan.

Stefan noticed Leana stood with Morcant. Two of his friends had found women. He glanced down at Morvan. Somehow, he wasn't surprised. He had found much more than a beautiful woman. He'd found peace, and...love.

"I need to take her to the cliffs. The last time we were there, both of our injuries were healed. It's also the place where she pulled me from the darkness."

Morcant took his woman's hand and nodded to Stefan. "Lead the way. We'll do whatever you need."

Stefan walked out the castle doors and down the steps. There was a commotion near the gatehouse, and a horse came running out of the stables.

"No' again," Morcant said.

But Stefan wasn't concerned. "Morvan helped him."

"How did you know?" Leana asked.

Stefan waited for the horse to reach them. "Because the animals she helps never forget her."

He walked to the horse and smiled when the steed lowered himself into a bow so Stefan could climb upon his back with Morvan still in his arms.

Stefan grabbed the horse's mane in one hand. "We'll go to the cliffs."

He raced beneath the gatehouse and heard the sound of horses behind him. Stefan didn't need to look back to know it was Ronan and Morcant. Although he didn't realize until the horses drew even with him that Meg and Leana were on their own mounts.

The six of them entered the forest. Stefan saw the color begin to come back into Morvan's face, but it wasn't enough. She needed whatever magic was at the cliffs. For whatever reason, the cliffs were magical. They hadn't just compelled Morvan there, they had gotten her to release him from the darkness.

It felt as if an eternity had passed before he saw the cliffs. As soon as they reached them, he swung a leg over the horse's neck and slid to the ground. Stefan walked to where he and Morvan had made love, but nothing happened. He looked up at the cliffs.

"You'll never make it up there holding her," Ronan said.

Stefan looked at his friends. "I have to try."

"Then we'll help," Morcant replied.

Stefan was about to tell them he would do it himself, but then he remembered why he considered them his family. "All right."

Ronan and Morcant didn't even try to dissuade their women from accompanying them. Together, all four of them helped him get Morvan to the top.

He was sweating, his muscles fatigued by the time they reached the crest. Despite the fact he hadn't remained at the top long the first time, he recalled the tall boulders and the narrow passages.

Stefan led the way until he eventually found the wall Morvan had spoken of. He stood looking at all the carvings in the rock as the others fanned out around him.

"I doona know what this place is, but it led Morvan to me, and it has led me back to her." Stefan kissed her forehead and turned to lean against the wall.

Then he slowly lowered himself until he was sitting with Morvan in his arms. "With one touch she calmed the monster within me. I was in a fit of bloodlust and was after her. I was going to kill her because I couldn't control my anger. I grabbed her, and that's when the haze of fury cleared. I can't lose her."

Morcant squatted beside Stefan. "You said she's a child of the forest. You've brought her back. She'll be all right."

Stefan looked into Morcant's eyes before he turned to Ronan. "If she doesna live, you'll have to kill me. You both need to understand that. The grief mixed with my anger will be too much. I willna be able to be stopped."

Ronan put his hand on Stefan's shoulder. "We've no' let you down before. We willna this time either."

Stefan pulled Morvan closer. "You didna just give me peace, Morvan. You showed me gentleness and kindness. But your greatest gift was your love. Come back to me. I willna ever leave you again."

Hours faded with the daylight. With each passing hour where Morvan didn't wake, Stefan felt his anger try to stir. He refused to give in to it. He no longer cared about Ilinca and getting his revenge. All that mattered was Morvan and the new life he wanted with her.

Ronan and Morcant had found him, but more importantly, Stefan had found Morvan. For the first time in his life, he prayed. Long and hard.

The stars were bright overhead when Morvan finally shifted her head. Stefan's eyes snapped open. He held his breath, ignoring the four others sitting around the fire.

"Morvan," he whispered.

Her eyes slowly opened to meet his. "Stefan."

He couldn't contain his joy as he ran a hand down her face. "How do you feel?"

"Better. You came back?"

"Aye."

She nodded. "You figured out that Ronan and Morcant were here."

"I came back for you. I tried repeatedly to leave, but I could never get verra far. My mind was filled with you. It took me long enough, but I realized that I couldna leave you. You touched my soul, Morvan. You gave me a gift I thought I'd never have."

She was very still as she whispered, "What?"

"Love. I love you more than life itself. I know I'll have to earn your love, but I'm prepared to do whatever it takes."

She put her finger over his lips to stop him from talking. "You've already done all that you could. I saw you," she said, placing her hand over his heart. "I felt you. There is nothing else for you to do, Stefan Kennedy, because I already love you."

He couldn't believe fate had finally smiled upon him, but he wasn't going to question it. Stefan brought his head down to her lips and kissed her.

Morvan's arms wrapped around his neck and he deepened the kiss. Dimly, he heard the sound of four sets of footsteps leaving. Then he didn't care as the desire took them.

EPILOGUE

Morvan climbed down the cliffs with Stefan. They had passed the hours of the night with lovemaking, talking, and more lovemaking. She was pleasantly sore, and the look in Stefan's hazel eyes whenever his gaze met hers made her stomach flutter.

He had said she saved him, but in truth, she thought it was the other way around. She inwardly chuckled as she recalled him telling her that they had the rest of their lives to debate it.

As Stefan lifted her off the last boulder to the ground, Morvan faced Ronan and Meg and Morcant and Leana who had remained at the base of the cliff. They were all smiling.

Ronan cleared his throat. "At this point with Morcant, I asked him and Leana to come to the castle to help me fight the MacKays. I doona think that offer will be accepted by you."

"Nay," Stefan said and looked at Morvan as he tightened his grip on her hand. "Our place is in the forest."

"We'll help in the coming battle," Morvan said.

Stefan raised a brow. "You want me to fight?"

"They need you."

Morcant rocked back on his heels. "Are you no' afraid of his monster returning?"

Morvan cupped his face. "That's what I'm for."

"Then I guess we'd better get busy building you and Stefan a cottage," Meg said.

Ronan glanced up at the cliff. "As close to the castle as we can, right?"

They all laughed at the comment. Morvan looked up at Stefan as he pulled her against him. Fate had been leading her toward Stefan. For all those years she'd thought she would spend her life alone, it was all worth it to finally have the love of a man like Stefan.

"What of Ilinca?" she whispered.

Stefan shrugged. "I'd rather focus on you, and them," he said with a jerk of his chin to Morcant, Leana, Meg, and Ronan.

"And Daman."

Stefan nodded slowly. "And Daman. I'll find him."

Morvan didn't have any doubts. If all three of them had found their way to Ravensclyde, the odds were good that Daman would, as well. She couldn't wait until all four of them were back together again. Stefan was happy, but he wouldn't be complete until Daman was found.

The air stirred around her, and Morvan knew that the old gypsy wasn't finished with the four men yet.

~

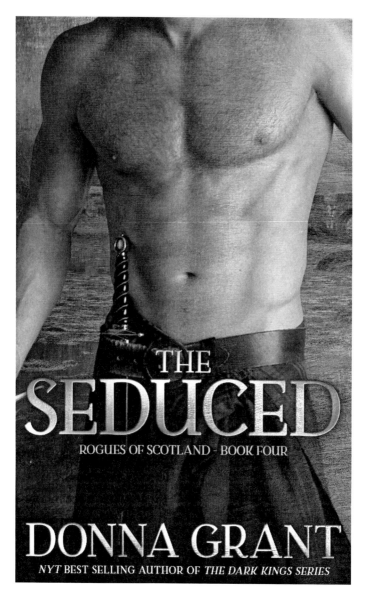

THE
SEDUCED

ROGUES OF SCOTLAND · BOOK FOUR

DONNA GRANT

NYT BEST SELLING AUTHOR OF *THE DARK KINGS SERIES*

PROLOGUE

Highlands of Scotland:
Summer, 1427

Daman Thacker sat atop his mount as silent as the rugged mountains around him. He looked over at the men he considered brothers – Morcant and Stefan.

As usual, the three waited on the fourth man of their group, Ronan. Ronan was the carefree one of them, the one who did what he wanted, dismissing the consequences. It was a hell of a way to live.

Oh, how Daman wished he could follow in Ronan's footsteps.

Stefan's horse snorted, shaking his great head, which caused Stefan to pat the steed's neck. The valley between the two mountains was wide. The summer sun was warm, with a breeze gently rushing past.

Above them, the shrill cry of a golden eagle broke the silence. Stefan glanced up, but Daman was scanning the ridge of the mountains. He smiled as he caught sight of Ronan.

Ronan's horse whinnied loudly, causing Stefan and Morcant to look toward the top of the mountain. Daman shared a smile with Morcant before Stefan glanced his way.

Ronan's horse pawed the ground, and a moment later, Ronan leaned forward. His horse raced down the mountain. Daman laughed along with Morcant. Ronan's wildness was just one of many reasons they had become friends, brothers.

It had begun a decade earlier when they happened to meet during a Highland Games. Their bond of friendship formed quickly and tightly during those few days, and not even the fact that they belonged to different clans kept them from meeting regularly.

As the years went by, their bond solidified into a brotherhood that nothing - and no one - could break.

Daman's mount danced sideways, eager to run, as Morcant finally got control of his horse and Ronan arrived.

"About time," Stefan grumbled.

Ronan raised his brow. "You might want to rein in that temper, my friend. We're going to be around beautiful women this night. Women require smiles and sweet words. No' furrowed brows."

Daman and Morcant's laughter didn't bother Stefan since he was used to such words from them. Still, Stefan shot Ronan a humorless look.

"Aye, we've heard enough about this Ana," Daman said as he turned his mount alongside Ronan's. "Take me to this gypsy beauty so I can see her for myself."

Ronan's lips compressed. "You think to take her from me?"

Daman and Ronan had played this game before. It wasn't in any of them to even think about trying to take away one of their women. But it was always a fun jest.

Daman's confident smile grew as his eyes twinkled in merriment. "Is she that beautiful?"

"Just you try," Ronan dared, only half jesting.

"Be cautious, Ronan. You wrong a gypsy and they'll curse you. No' sure we should be meddling with such people," Morcant said as he shoved his hair out of his eyes.

Morcant wasn't usually the voice of reason of the four, but his comment had Daman's smile fading. The gypsies weren't allowed to remain in one place for long. Many clans would prevent them from crossing onto their lands if they knew they were coming.

The gypsies might be beautiful, but they were dangerous, as well.

Ronan laughed at Morcant and reined in his mount. "Ah, but with such a willing body, how am I to refuse Ana? Come, my friends, and let us enjoy the bounty that awaits." He gave a short whistle and his horse surged forward in a run again.

Daman's steed blew out a breath, anxious to run, as well. The three remained behind for a moment while Ronan took the lead as he always did. Each had found their place within their small group that had formed so long ago during the Highland Games.

"I'm no' missing this," Morcant said and gave his stallion his head. The horse immediately took off.

Daman and Stefan shared a look, and as one, they nudged their mounts into a run. It wasn't long before they caught up with Morcant.

Ronan looked over his shoulder, a wide smile on his face. He spurred his mount faster. Morcant then leaned low over his stallion's neck until he pulled up alongside Ronan.

Daman watched as Stefan's horse closed the last bit of distance and came even with Ronan. Daman gave his mount his head and rode up beside Morcant.

A few moments later, Ronan sat up and gave a gentle tug

248 | DONNA GRANT

on the reins, easing his stallion into a canter. Daman and the others followed suit as they rode their horses four abreast.

Daman loved being with his friends, riding across their untamed homeland. Why then did he have a bad feeling about going to the gypsies?

There would be no stopping Ronan. Daman learned long ago that once Ronan had the bit in his mouth, he was going for what he wanted.

Then again, they all had their issues. Morcant's was women. He loved women – all women. That had gotten him into trouble more times than Daman could remember.

For Stefan, it was his anger. He oft times called it a monster, and when it took him, Stefan became someone else.

Daman had his own hindrance. It was his inability to ask for help – from anyone, even the men he thought of as brothers. It began when he was three and stealing food just to survive. He wanted more of a life for himself, and he wanted to do it all on his own.

It took years, but Daman was no longer homeless or starving. He was prized for his sword arm and often requested by his laird in times of need.

The four rode from one glen to another until Ronan finally slowed his horse further to a walk. They stopped atop the next hill and looked down at a circle of gypsy wagons hidden in the wooded vale below.

Daman looked at the caravan and the gypsies walking around. There was a large fire in the middle of the camp. Daman searched but saw no other Highlanders with the gypsies. His ominous feeling continued to grow, and he couldn't hold off letting the others know.

He shifted atop his mouth. "I've a bad feeling. We shouldna be here."

Morcant's horse flung up his head, and he brought his mount under control with soft words. "I've a need to sink my rod betwixt willing thighs. If you doona wish to partake, Daman, then doona, but you willna be stopping me."

"Nor me," Ronan said.

Daman waited for several moments as Stefan sat silently. Then, he gave Ronan a nod of agreement.

Daman wasn't surprised, but at least he'd told the others what he was feeling. Ronan was the first to ride down the hill to the camp, with Morcant right on his heels. Stefan galloped his horse down the hill as a young beauty with long, black hair came running out to greet Ronan in her brightly colored skirts.

Ronan pulled his horse to a halt and jumped off with a smile as Ana launched herself into his arms. Ronan caught her and brought his lips down to hers.

Stefan halted on Morcant's left side, and Daman rode up on Morcant's right. Daman glanced around, noting how the gypsies watched Ana with Ronan.

Ronan and Ana spoke quietly before Ronan turned her toward them. "Ana, these are my friends, Daman, Morcant, and Stefan," he said, pointing to each of them in turn.

Her smile was wide as she held her arm out to the circle of wagons. "Welcome to our camp."

Morcant quickly dismounted and dropped the reins to allow his horse to graze freely. He then walked between two wagons and into the center of the camp.

Stefan dismounted and patted his horse. "I'll be back," he mumbled and followed Morcant.

Indecision warred within Daman. The four of them were always fully invested in whatever they did, but for some reason, he couldn't walk into the camp. His gut churned with apprehension.

That's when he saw Morcant and Stefan exchange a look before they both glanced back at him. Daman slid from his horse and gathered the reins of all four mounts to tether them together.

"I'll keep watch," Daman said. He walked to an oak outside of the camp and sat.

Ronan wrapped an arm around Ana and walked away with her, saying, "Your loss."

Morcant gave a nod and continued to a woman sitting on the steps to her wagon, her bright turquoise and yellow skirts dipping between her legs while she braided a leather halter for a horse.

It was long moments before Stefan walked to the fire in the middle of camp and nodded to the three men sitting there.

Daman let out a sigh. Trouble was coming on swift wings. He knew it as certainly as he knew he would die in battle.

Daman scratched his jaw and ignored the thunder and lightning that had been on display over the mountains for the past half hour. The knot in his gut about the gypsy camp only intensified the longer he was there.

Something bad was going to happen. He knew it just as surely as he knew the storm coming in would last for an entire day. The sooner Ronan, Stefan, and Morcant were finished, the better.

Daman wouldn't make the mistake of returning with his friends again. And he would do his best to prevent them from coming back, as well. Perhaps a talk with the gypsies was in order. They were on his clan's land.

Three hours had already passed. It was time for him and his friends to leave. Daman rose and walked between the wagons to get their attention. Then he paused.

In the middle of the camp was a large fire, and many of the gypsies were sitting around it. Two were playing the violin, a hauntingly eerie song that somehow kept time with the thunder. Among the gypsies was Stefan, who stared into the fire as if searching for something. An old woman sat off by herself, her gaze on the wagon Ronan had entered hours ago.

Unease prickled Daman's skin.

He wanted to leave, but he wasn't going to go without his friends. Some unknown, unnamable emotion was coursing through him. Every instinct told him they needed to leave. Immediately.

Daman rose and walked to the edge of the camp. He looked at the ground, then up at the wagon where Ronan and Ana were. He could shout out Ronan's name, but his friend wouldn't answer even if he heard him.

Daman's gaze slid to Stefan. With Morcant busy, he could get Stefan's attention, but Stefan was talking to three gypsy males. Besides, Daman didn't need help. All he had to do was cross the boundary and get his friends.

He looked up at the sky and stared at the thousands of stars. The moon was only a sliver in the night, leaving the land cloaked in darkness. Daman ran a hand through his hair and returned to the tree where he'd been sitting. He'd wait for his friends as long as it took. Then he'd get them away.

No sooner had the thought crossed his mind, when the night was shattered by an anguished scream. It was filled with despair and fury dragged from the depths of Hell itself.

Daman's blood ran cold because he knew his apprehensions were becoming fact. He looked from Stefan at the fire to Ana's wagon where Ronan was exiting. Hand on the hilt of his sword, Ronan stood shirtless and looked at an old woman who stared at something in the grass.

Daman reached the edge of the camp when Morcant

exited a wagon still fastening his kilt. Something bad was coming for them.

Daman searched the ground where Ronan and the old woman were looking. The bright pink and blue skirts of Ana, Ronan's lover, were visible from the dim light of the fire. As was the dagger sticking out of Ana's stomach.

The odds of any of them getting out of the gypsy camp without a fight weren't in their favor. By the looks exchanged amongst the gypsies, they were prepared to die to avenge Ana – despite the fact Ronan hadn't killed her.

Daman looked to Morcant and Stefan and saw a slight nod of Stefan's head. Morcant slowly began to pull his sword from his scabbard as Ronan shook his head in denial.

"Ronan," Stefan said urgently as he palmed the hilt of his sword and waited.

There was a moment of silence, as if the world held its breath.

Then the old woman let loose a shriek and pointed her gnarled finger at Ronan. Ronan's eyes widened in confusion and anger.

Daman heard a gypsy near him whisper a name – Ilinca – as he stared at the old woman. Ilinca's face was contorted with grief and rage.

Words, hurried and unfamiliar, fell from Ilinca's lips. The language was Romany, and by the way Ilinca's dark eyes narrowed with contempt, it was a curse she was putting on Ronan.

Daman waited for Ronan to grab his sword and the battle to begin. When nothing happened, Daman looked harder and realized that Ronan was being held against his will. His pale green eyes were wide with confusion.

Daman opened his mouth to shout to the others, but Stefan drew his sword the same time Morcant rushed Ilinca. The old gypsy shifted her gaze to Morcant, and he halted awkwardly, her words seemingly freezing him in place.

Once it appeared Morcant was taken care of, her gaze returned to Ronan and she continued speaking in the strange language.

"Stefan!" Daman shouted.

But it was too late. Stefan's fury had been let loose, the monster was free. Stefan released a battle cry and leapt over the fire toward Ilinca. He hadn't gotten two steps before the old gypsy pinned him with a look that jerked him to a halt instantly.

Then the old woman's gaze turned to Daman. He sighed and thought of his friends. There was one rule between the four of them – they lived or died together. Daman stepped over the boundary and a cold tremor rushed down his spine at Ilinca's triumphant smile.

He was immediately surrounded by men. Undeterred, Daman left his sword in the scabbard and used his dirk and his hands to slice, stab, punch, and kick anyone stupid enough to get close.

Five men fell – two dead. He put another three on the ground before he found his limbs immobilized. No matter how hard he tried to move his body, he couldn't.

The men parted, and Ilinca walked to him. Daman looked around, but Ronan, Morcant, and Stefan were gone – vanished as if they were never there.

He glared down at the old woman. He desperately wanted to tell her how he was going to kill every last gypsy he came across as punishment for what she had done to his friends, but the words wouldn't come. Ilinca controlled every bit of him.

"Why didn't you enter the camp with your friends?" Ilinca asked him.

His eyes narrowed as he realized she had allowed him the

ability to speak. She wanted answers, but he wasn't going to give them to her. His lip curved in a sneer.

"I shouldn't expect you would answer. Even if I would help you, you wouldn't ask for it, would you? Too proud, like so many others. Your friends have been cursed, but you probably already knew that." Ilinca drew in a breath and looked him over closely. "Why did you have to come into camp? You were wise enough to keep out earlier."

Daman saw her hands shaking. Her eyes were bright with unshed tears. She was upset by Ana's death, but he was desperate to find his friends. Even if it meant talking to her. "Where are the others?"

"Someplace they can't hurt anyone or themselves."

"Ronan didna kill Ana."

Ilinca lifted her chin. "He may not have stuck the blade in her, but he's still responsible. Just as Morcant is responsible for bedding an innocent and ruining the chance to align our people."

Daman tried to move his arms, but she still held him in place. "And Stefan?"

"You know the answer to that better than anyone else here. That one's rage is what got him cursed."

"What are you going to do with me?"

The old woman stepped closer and the gypsies closed in around her. "I had a vision a week ago of this very night, though I didn't see my granddaughter's death. I knew the four of you would have something important to do."

"Do? I'm no' important."

"I can only repeat what I know. What I saw." Her shoulders drooped. "My magic will ensure each of you reach your destination. What you do there is up to you. You can be freed. Or you can spend eternity in your prison. The choice is yours, and your actions will determine the outcome."

"I'm going to find my friends," he stated.

Illinca's lips pressed together briefly. She held up an amulet. "The next time you see this, your destiny will be before you. The path you choose will seal your fate."

Daman got that bad feeling again as Ilinca placed her hand on his forehead. He wanted to jerk away, but she still held him frozen. His eyes grew heavy, and the more he fought to keep them open, the more tired he became.

"Don't fight it," Ilinca's voice whispered in his head.

It was in his nature to fight. He fought as hard as he could against whatever she was doing to him, but it was too much. The world went black in an instant, like the snap of someone's fingers.

Ilinca sighed as she dropped her hands and took a step back from Daman. Then she nodded, and the men carried him to her wagon and brought him inside. Grief rose up in her like a tidal wave. She would tend to Daman later. Right now, she needed to bury her granddaughter.

Once that was done, she had a destination to reach.

"Grandmother?"

Ilinca held out her arms for Ana's younger sister. When Amalia wrapped her arms around her, Ilinca held her tight. "It's almost over, my sweet."

"You didn't say Ana would die."

"I didn't know." Ilinca didn't stop the tears from falling. "Ana was impetuous and kind, but she wasn't as strong as you are."

Amalia looked up at her. "Where did you send those men?"

"Far away."

"And the fourth? Why didn't you send him, too?"

Ilinca glanced at her wagon. "Because he's the key to all of it."

CHAPTER 1

MacKay Clan

Innes stood in the great hall of the castle staring at their dwindling clan. Every day more and more people left. Not that she blamed them. People were starving, and with most of the warriors dead, their clan was weak.

She fingered the amulet hidden beneath her gown. It had been placed around her neck when she was just seven summers. Her mother had told her to never take it off. It had been passed down through their family for over two hundred years.

"You may need it one day, Innes," her mother said.

"Need it how? It's just a pendant."

"It's not just any piece of jewelry, sweetling. It possesses magic. There is a warrior hidden on this land. He's sleeping, waiting for the time when we need him most."

Innes had thought her mother was making it all up until she was shown the sleeping warrior the next day. From that moment on, rarely a week passed when she didn't go see him.

Her brother's voice boomed through the hall as he tried

to quiet everyone. Innes knew they were in trouble. There had been an attack in their forest by a lone man who had killed several of their men, as well as the defection of another clan member to their enemy, the Sinclairs.

"Enough!" Alistair shouted. He ran a hand through his dark hair, his nostrils flaring. "We will survive. We were a great clan once, and we will be again."

"What of Donald?" someone shouted.

Innes watched her brother's hands fist at his sides. It infuriated him that Donald was making more trouble for the clan instead of helping. Then again, their brother wanted to lead. Donald's pride was hurt from not winning the clan's support to become laird.

Alistair met her gaze, and she gave him a nod. She normally didn't take sides with her brothers, but in this, she wholeheartedly agreed with Alistair.

"My brother will be brought to heel," Alistair said, his words ringing clear and loud through the great hall. "Family or not, he is destroying this clan. I vowed to rebuild us, and I'll no' stop until I do."

The talk then turned to the stores of food for winter. Innes turned and walked from the castle. She made her way down the castle steps to the bailey, which was so quiet it was eerie.

It used to be one of her favorite places. All the noise, all the people. It was a central place for the clan. Now, it was a reminder of all they had lost.

Innes walked through a hidden postern door and out of the safety of the castle. They had only one man standing watch at the gatehouse, but she didn't want anyone to know where she was going.

A cool wind whipped around her as she walked across the land, reminding her in not so subtle a fashion that winter would soon be upon them. Their food stores were alarmingly low. The men who would be out hunting were now dead thanks to her youngest brother.

Donald had always been impetuous. He'd always been jealous of Alistair as well, but he seemed to realize that Alistair would be the one to lead. Over the past few months, however, Donald had become increasingly argumentative. He questioned Alistair's every decision and command.

Then, to her horror, he began to sway some of the remaining younger men to his side, claiming he would set things right one way or another. Donald's idea of *setting things right* was to attack the Sinclairs. Unfortunately, that idea turned into action.

It was a stupid, thoughtless move. The Sinclair clan wasn't only large, they were powerful. Their laird had several castles on his land being held by commanding, formidable men.

Donald thought he could attack Ravensclyde to see how strong their new lord – Ronan Galt – was, but he and his men had been put in their place quick enough.

How she wished that had been the end of it. Donald and his remaining men returned to the castle to heal and lick their wounds, and her brother swore to both her and Alistair that he would never attempt to oust Alistair again.

Yet, three days ago, he'd done just that.

Innes continued over the rocky landscape and up a steep hill. She had to lift her heavy skirts on the way up. Thunder rumbled as dark clouds rolled in. The air was heavy with the scent of rain.

She hurried down the opposite side of the slope hoping to beat the rain. Half way down, the sky opened up and drenched her. Innes didn't slow as she reached the valley and took a quick left into a grove of trees where the cave was hidden.

Once inside the cave, she stopped to catch her breath.

Innes wiped away the wet strands of dark hair sticking to her face.

Just yesterday, she had been to see the warrior as she had every day since Donald had begun to push against Alistair's rule. But last night, she found no rest as her thoughts jumbled into what was happening and the possible outcomes.

She didn't need a torch to see the way. She knew where every stone was, where every hole lay. Her heart began to pound and her stomach twisted into knots when she walked down the narrow, twisting tunnel that eventually opened up to a small cavern.

A slab of stone sat in the middle of the cavern, and upon that slab slept the warrior. Magic had kept him ageless and sleeping for two hundred years, just as magic kept the torches spaced evenly along the walls lit.

She didn't know what had happened to put him in such a situation. Her mother hadn't known either. The truth of that part of the story was forgotten long ago– or never stated.

Innes walked around the man. He looked so peaceful, so content. Through the years, she had come to him often and spoke of her worries and her dreams. Without realizing it, he had helped her get through some of the worst times in her life.

She had always thought him handsome with his long, wavy mane of golden hair and his rippling muscles. But a few years ago, she began to...long to touch him.

The first time, she barely laid a finger on him before she snatched her hand back. Eventually, she came to need to feel his skin beneath hers, no matter how innocent the touch.

Innes walked to him and rested her hands upon his upper arm, feeling the strength, the hard muscle beneath her palms. Feeling his warmth.

She took a deep breath and slowly released it as she let

her gaze wander over his face. Unable to stop herself, Innes caressed her finger over his wide forehead and down the slope of his nose. She brushed across his square chin and along the hard angles of his jaw up to his sharp cheekbones. She traced the blond brows that slashed over his eyes.

Her gaze lowered to his mouth. She leaned closer, rested her hand on the side of his face and outlined the shape of his wide lips with the pad of her thumb.

"I think I've come to need you," she said into the quiet. "That's not good. If everything goes according to Alistair's plans, I'll be married after the first of the year. I'm sure my new husband won't approve of the time I spend with you, talking and...touching."

She glanced down at his chest. His saffron shirt used to be closed, but she had parted it the year before to see more of his impressive chest.

"I'm your guardian," she continued. "And yet, I feel as if you're the one who has been watching over me." She dropped her forehead onto his chest and squeezed her eyes closed. "Donald did it again. He took some of his men out into the woods to attack the people of Ravensclyde, but he stumbled across a man that nearly wiped them out. Donald has gone out for a second attack, and I fear if Alistair doesn't do something soon, Donald will be the ruin of us."

She paused and raised her head to look at him again. Innes straightened and took his large hand in hers. "My mother says you're a great warrior. That one day you'll be the answer to our prayers."

Her heart knocked against her ribs at what she was contemplating doing. With her chest heaving and her blood running cold through her veins, Innes squeezed his hand between hers.

"I was told that I should only think of waking you under the direst of circumstances. Our clan is starving, and our numbers are rapidly shrinking. Other clans are eyeing our lands because we don't have enough warriors to fight. I think that's pretty dire."

She wiped at her eyes with the back of her hand. Once she revived him, there was no sending him back to sleep. He would be awake, his will once more his own. His life had been paused while he slept, and when he woke, he would once again begin to age like everyone else.

"I pray this is the right thing to do. Alistair is doing everything he can, so now it's my turn." She pulled the amulet from beneath her gown and then over her head. Innes looked at the silver piece, the markings faded from being held so many times. "Alistair is a good man, but he needs help. Please be that help for us."

Innes held the amulet for a few moments longer, debating on whether to leave without waking him, but the fate of her clan was at stake.

"Please be the answer we need," she whispered and gently placed her lips over his.

Innes set the amulet in his palm and closed his fingers over it just as her mother had instructed. She leaned back and waited, hoping he would wake immediately, but as the minutes passed without movement, she began to doubt.

She removed the amulet and put it in his other hand. Still nothing happened.

"Of course," she said and shook her head ruefully. "It would've been too easy to be able to wake you and have you save the day. Keep the amulet. I don't know why my family was bade to watch over you, or why you're in this cave, but I hope someday you get to wake."

Innes jumped when thunder boomed so close that the ground shook. Pebbles and dirt rained down from the ceiling of the cave. She glanced at the man to see him still asleep.

Utterly defeated, she turned and ran out of the cave and back to the castle.

The sweet voice was back. Daman drifted upon nothingness, but every once in awhile he heard a woman's voice. He hadn't been able to hear the words at first. It was just sound, a calming, reassuring sound that he sought. Then the words became clear, as if she were right next to him.

It felt like an eternity in-between the times he heard her. Immeasurable time stretched endlessly before him. He didn't know her name, didn't know her face or why she was with him, but he felt...comforted whenever she was near.

It wasn't just her voice that affected him. It was her touch, as well. How he longed for more, craved more of her soft caresses.

She only ever touched his arms, face, and chest. Yet he yearned for her to go lower, to take his cock in hand. But she never did.

The sadness in her voice this time gave him pause. As did the part where she'd said he was supposed to help her. Help her how? He didn't even know who he was or why he couldn't seem to wake from the endless sleep.

He suddenly needed to know why her family kept watch over him, and why she thought putting something in his hand would wake him.

She'd mentioned marriage. He didn't want her to marry and never touch him again. He needed to see her face, to know her name.

To run his hands over her skin as she had done to his countless times.

He wanted to know the color of her hair and eyes, to see

her smile. Most importantly, he wanted to be the one who saved her clan.

For the first time, he really fought against the strain of sleep. The warm metal in his hand heated, and his fingers gripped it tighter.

It felt as if he were swimming in a sea of tar. Every time he tried to surface, it yanked him back. But he kept swimming, kept struggling.

He kept her voice running through his head. His skin tingled from the memory of her touch.

Then, he saw the faintest pinprick of light. He fought even harder against the tide pulling him under, keeping him asleep. The more he struggled, the more the light grew.

Suddenly, his eyes snapped open and he sucked in a mouthful of air. He sat up, looking around for the woman. But his eyes only found an empty cavern, dimly lit from torches along the walls.

He looked down at his hand and opened his fingers. The moment his gaze locked on the amulet, he recognized it.

"The next time you see this, your destiny will be before you. The path you choose will seal your fate."

The old woman's voice was loud in his mind as her words replayed. What path did she mean? To him he had but one – to help the woman who came to him.

The question was: who was the woman, and where did he find her?

Innes had changed her gown and was drying her hair with a cloth when there was a knock at her chamber door followed by Alistair's voice saying her name.

"Come in," she bade and turned to face the door.

He took in her appearance and raised a brow. "You disappeared again."

"You had things under control."

Alistair looked at her with the dark eyes of their ancestry and sank into the chair next to the hearth. "I already have one sibling against me. It looks good to have you there. Shows your support."

"I was there," she argued. "Everyone saw me."

"Where did you go?"

He had asked so many times, and despite the fact she had never told him, he kept asking. "I needed to collect my thoughts," she answered.

"And what if Donald was out there?"

Innes spread the cloth next to the fire so it would dry and gave her eldest brother a droll look. "Donald wouldn't hurt me."

"Just as I thought he'd never go against me." Alistair propped his elbow on the arm of the chair and leaned his face against his fist. "He's no' returned, Innes."

She sat at his feet, tucking her legs beneath her. "And you're afraid if you send a party out looking for him that they'll either end up dead by Donald's hand or the men from Ravensclyde."

"Aye." He sighed heavily, his shoulders drooping. "Why did Da try to steal the sheep back with just a handful of men? Why didna he take me or Donald with him? Maybe then he wouldna be dead."

"You can't think that way. Da went without you because he knew it would be dangerous. He was trying to protect you. And he knew you would lead the clan if anything were to happen to him."

Alistair spread his arms around him. "Clan? Have you seen the people? More leave each day. I'm surprised another clan hasna come to take our lands by now. The only thing keeping them away is the threat of Ravensclyde descending upon us."

"So what do we do? Do we hand over our lands?"

Alistair cut her a look. "Of course no'."

"Then quit complaining and start figuring out a way out of this."

"I have."

The way he said those two words, with determination and regret, brought chills of foreboding to Innes. She knew exactly what Alistair was referring to. Marriage.

Everyone in their family sacrificed for the clan. She was just one of many, so there was no need to rant or cry about it. Especially if it saved the clan.

"Who will I marry?"

Alistair moved to sit beside her on the floor. He took her

hand in his, while his dark eyes searched hers. "I doona want to do this."

"I know. You must do what you can for our people."

"If there were another way-"

"It's all right," she interrupted him. "I've known my fate for some months now. You're laird. As a woman of this family, I'm used as a way to negotiate peace through marriage."

Alistair tugged on her black hair. "I wanted you to be happy. I wanted you to have the kind of marriage our parents had."

"What about you? Don't you want that kind of marriage?"

He shrugged absently. "I doona believe I'll have that luxury. I'll broker my own marriage to another, stronger clan. But first, I must bring Donald to heel."

"If the men of Ravensclyde haven't already done it for you."

"Part of me prays they have," Alistair said in a low voice. "I doona relish fighting my own brother."

Both of them knew Donald wouldn't back down without a fight, and for Donald, who wanted to be laird, that meant to the death.

Innes knew the strength of both her brothers. Donald was good, but he often let his emotions get the better of him. Alistair was calm and cool during battle. He would win, but it would kill a piece of his soul in the process.

"We'll survive this," she stated.

Alistair gave her a crooked smile. "I'm going to ensure that you do."

≈

He was famished. His stomach rumbled with the need for food as he inspected the cavern. As he thought, there was nothing but rock and torches. No water, no food. And no female.

At least he thought there was nothing until he spotted a sword leaning against the wall near the entrance. He smiled as he recognized his weapon.

He strode to it and wrapped his hand around the pommel. Then he grasped the sheath with his other hand and slowly pulled the sword free. A quick inspection showed that the blade was as sharp as he wanted it.

How could he remember the sword, but not recall how he came to be in the cavern?

The more he thought about it, the more his memories seemed to vanish before he could begin to grab them. He gave a shake of his head and sheathed his sword before he strapped it around his waist. It was time to go hunting for food.

He followed the only opening out of the cavern. He had to duck beneath the arch, and the tunnel was only marginally taller. Bent over, he had to navigate the winding and incredibly narrow passageway. Thunder continued to boom, and the rain grew louder the farther he walked.

Finally, he came to the end and was able to stand straight as he stood in a cave that opened out to the world beyond.

It was all gray, the rain blocking his sight of anything farther than ten feet ahead. So much for hunting. Food would have to wait. Water, however, wouldn't.

He walked out of the cave and lifted his head, eyes closed and mouth open to catch the rainfall. With every mouthful, the taste of the water was like heaven. He had no idea his throat was so parched, or that he ached to taste something so refreshing.

When his thirst was quenched, he lowered his head and returned to the cave. He paced, energy to get out and discover where he was coursing through him. He had to be in Scotland. The fates wouldn't be so cruel as to take him away from his beloved land.

The rain prevented him from seeing any landmarks with the rate in which it fell. The thick clouds stopped any shred of light from filtering through. And then night fell.

He sat in the middle of the cave staring out, watching the lightning zigzag between clouds in violent outbursts.

There was something he needed to do, people he needed to find, but he couldn't remember. All he knew was that he had to get out of the cave.

≈

The castle was quiet in the pre-dawn hours. Only a few women were in the kitchen preparing the morning meal. Innes was on her way there when someone grabbed her from behind and clamped a hand over her mouth.

She struggled, kicking to no avail.

"Enough," a deep voice grated in her ear.

Donald. She stilled, anger filling her. How dare he treat her so roughly? And what was he doing back at the castle without Alistair's knowledge?

Donald was as tall as Alistair, but he had the barrel chest of their father. It was an easy feat for him to carry her up the stairs and down the hallway to the master chamber.

"Knock," he ordered her. "It's time we three had a talk."

If Donald had wanted to kill Alistair, he'd have already been upstairs and done the deed. That was the only reason Innes lifted a shaky hand and pounded on the wooden door.

A moment later, Alistair opened the door. His smile

vanished when he took in Donald holding Innes. "What the bloody hell?"

Donald pushed his way inside. Only then did he release Innes. She hurried away, turning her gaze on Donald so he knew how furious she was.

"What is the meaning of this, Donald?" Alistair demanded.

Their brother closed the door and leaned back against it, his arms crossed over his chest. His kilt was dirty and his shirt was torn. His short hair was at odds with his dark bushy beard. "Did I hear right, Alistair? Are you going to reprimand me for doing what you should be doing, brother?"

"We have enough trouble. The last thing we need is to be at war with the Sinclairs, as well. Think!" Alistair said and pointed to his head.

Donald snorted. "I am thinking. Raiding is what we do in the Highlands. We need food."

Innes had heard enough. She stepped between her brothers and looked at Donald. "Going against Alistair so publicly is turning people against him – which is exactly what you want. We should be united to save our clan."

"I'm the answer to the clan," Donald said and swung his gaze to Alistair. "And he knows it."

Alistair's gaze narrowed. "This again? You willna be happy until you're laird."

"You doona see the bigger picture."

"And father did?" Innes asked angrily. "Is that why he snuck off in the middle of the night with only five men to take back our sheep?"

"Da led this clan with strength," Donald stated.

Innes nodded. "Aye, he did. He was also impulsive and rash, just like you, Donald."

Donald lifted his lip in a sneer. "You have the same blood running in your veins, sister."

"I do, but I learned patience from Mum." She swallowed and looked between her brothers. "I also learned that there is someone else who could be the answer to saving the clan."

Donald snickered and shook his head. "You're no' talking about that fool hidden away in the cave, are you?"

She blinked, blindsided that Donald knew about the man. Innes swiveled her head to Alistair to see his calm gaze on her. "You both knew? I thought I was the only one."

"Nay," Alistair said. "We've always known."

"Then why haven't you woken him?" she implored.

Donald waved away her words. "There's nothing he can do."

Innes was tired of the bickering between her brothers. It had begun the moment their father's body was returned to the castle. She crossed her arms over her chest and took a few steps back so she could see them both. "We'll see about that."

Donald's face mottled with rage. "I'll be the savior of our clan."

Innes could only gape when Donald threw open the door and stalked away. She glanced at Alistair, and then both of them hurried after their brother.

As Innes lifted her skirts and ran down the stairs, she glanced back to see Alistair strapping on his sword. She didn't have to ask to know that Donald was planning to kill her warrior.

The battle between brothers might very well come sooner than she wanted. That was if Alistair intended to stop Donald from killing the man their family had protected for generations.

She wasn't sure of Alistair's intentions, and there wasn't time to ask. All she could do was hope that the amulet had woken her warrior as her mother told her it would.

CHAPTER 3

He was thankful that the rain stopped by morning. For a moment, he thought it might continue on for another day. The storm had been fierce.

But as the sun peeked over the mountains, he stepped from the cave and smiled. Scotland. The mountains rose toward the sky, the bright green grass covering every inch. A ray of sunlight shone on the mountain so blindingly that he had to shield his eyes to be able to take in the view.

And what a view it was. Half the mountain was bathed in golden light, giving the grass a vibrant look that almost seemed unreal.

This was his home. The weather was unpredictable at best, and the same mountains looked different every day depending on the conditions.

He breathed easier knowing he was in Scotland. Now, he needed to find some food.

Innes caught up with Donald after they walked out of the castle, but her words were falling on deaf ears. Nothing she said halted him.

"You can't do this," she repeated when they reached the cave.

Donald chuckled, the sound devoid of humor. He didn't slow as he ducked and walked into the tunnel. "You'll realize you need to put your faith in me as soon as you stop thinking some dead man held in magic will help us."

"Never," Innes stated.

The tunnel was too narrow for Donald to turn around, but she knew anything could happen once they reached the cavern.

Except Donald stood still as stone when he reached it. Innes had to walk around him to see what had made him pause. When her gaze took in the empty slab, she could only stare in shock.

It worked! She had woken the warrior.

"Where is he?" Donald demanded as he swung his head to her.

Innes shrugged in bewilderment. "I've no idea."

Alistair's gaze lowered to her neck, and Innes knew the minute he noticed that her necklace was gone.

"You should've let me kill him here," Donald said. "Now, I'll have to hunt him down."

Donald roughly pushed past her to retrace his steps out. She walked to the empty slab and placed her hands on it. If only she had waited a little longer, she might have been there when he woke.

"I wish you'd told me you were going to wake him," Alistair said from behind her.

Innes turned and lifted her gaze to him. "I didn't know

that either of you knew about him. Mum told me to keep it secret."

Alistair shrugged. "It doesna matter now. We need to focus on stopping Donald."

Once more, Innes was running after Donald. This time she followed Alistair, who tracked their brother. When they came upon him, Donald was sitting on a fallen tree, his sword out with the tip in the ground as he braced both hands on it.

Innes was instantly on guard. So was Alistair, if the way he slowly circled Donald were any indication.

"You woke him, did you no'?" Donald asked in a soft voice.

Innes wasn't fooled. That tone of voice meant he was furious. She now wished she had gone back to the castle. How many times had she and Alistair chased after Donald when they were growing up? Sometimes they were able to talk him out of doing something foolish before he did it, but most times, they chased after him to get him out of trouble after the deed had been done.

Not until their father died did she see the real Donald, the man he kept hidden all those years. In his eyes, she saw that he would say anything, do anything to get what he wanted. Nothing and no one would stand in his way.

For the first time in her life, she truly feared Donald.

Donald got to his feet, his gaze never wavering from her. "Why did you have to do something so stupid?"

"It's done, Donald," Alistair said. "Leave it alone."

"I doona take orders from you," Donald said, briefly looking at Alistair. "Anyone who isna with me is against me. And our little sister just proved she was against me."

Alistair took Innes's hand and tugged her away. "Get to the castle."

She didn't want to leave her brothers. One of them was going to die that day, and she feared it just might be Alistair.

Innes turned to start running back to the castle when Alistair shouted her name. Out of the corner of her eye there was a blur of movement and then a grunt.

She slid to a stop and looked back to find that her warrior had effortlessly flipped Donald over onto his back. The warrior had his knee in Donald's neck and a dagger pointed between two ribs.

She met the warrior's gaze and marveled at eyes that were as blue as the sky. They stared at each other for long, silent moments until Donald began to struggle.

The warrior slammed a fist into Donald's jaw and knocked him unconscious.

≈

He couldn't believe his luck when he heard the woman's voice. The rabbit he was hunting quickly forgotten, he followed the voices that led him to the cave. The woman wasn't alone though. Two men were with her, and by their looks, they were related.

Not wanting to be cornered in the cave, he decided to wait for their return. It didn't take them long. The first to exit was the burly man with the short hair and bushy beard. It wasn't long before the second man and the woman followed.

He followed them until they found the first man again. He'd known before anyone spoke that the bearded one was going to attack. At first he thought the man's assault might be against the other man, but when he realized his focus was on the woman, he refused to sit by and let it happen.

The moment the bearded man went after the woman, he jumped from his hiding place and took him down. He ignored the second man, his eyes locked on the dark-haired beauty with her olive skin and black eyes.

There was something about her coloring that triggered an emotion inside him. He felt as if he was supposed to be wary of it, but for the life of him, he couldn't remember why.

He had no idea how long he and the burly man stared at each other before he finally had to knock the man out.

"Daman."

He jerked his head to the other man, a frown forming. Was that his name? How did he not know his own name?

"I'm Alistair," the man said. "Laird of the MacKays, and the man you took down is my brother, Donald. Thank you for that. I wouldna have gotten to Innes quick enough."

Innes. He found his gaze back on her.

Alistair cleared his throat. "I'm sure you have questions, Daman. Let's get back to the castle first."

He looked down at the man he had knocked out and slowly got to his feet. Innes had woken him, and Donald had been about to kill her because of it. Daman couldn't believe a brother would do that to a sister.

Daman could feel her closeness. He ached for her touch, but somehow he managed to keep his hands off her.

"Daman," she whispered. "I never knew your name."

He looked at her, drowning in the dark depths of her eyes. She was exquisite. Her black hair was thick and straight, the silky length hanging down her back. How he wanted to run his hands through it and have the strands drape around him as she leaned over him.

Daman took in her oval face, the clear complexion. Her lips were full and parted. Her eyes were wide and turned up seductively at the corners, giving her an exotic look.

Black brows arched elegantly over eyes that watched him. Unable to help himself, he reached up and gently traced a

277 | THE SEDUCED ←

brow, just as she had done to him on many occasions as he slept.

Her eyes widened as her breath left her in a rush.

"We can no' tarry," Alistair said. "We need to get Donald to the castle and in the dungeon."

"How did you know Daman's name?" Innes asked Alistair.

Alistair glanced at Daman. "Mum told me."

It took both Daman and Alistair to lift Donald and half-carry, half-drag him to the castle. Daman had a difficult time concentrating on anything other than the woman walking in front of him.

Innes intrigued him, fascinated him. Captivated him.

With his gaze on her, he never saw the root. Daman tried to catch himself, but with the added weight of Donald he knew he was going to fall. He tried to call out and warn Alistair, but no sound passed his lips.

Daman fell hard to his knees, struggling to keep his hold on Donald and not let him fall. Daman tried to say Alistair's name again. Then he tried Innes's, but once again there was no sound.

His voice had been taken from him. He had memories of talking, so he knew at one time he could. Why had that changed?

"Daman?" Alistair asked. "Are you all right?"

Daman nodded and got to his feet. He lifted his eyes and saw Innes staring at him, her brow furrowed.

By the time they reached the castle, men were there to take Donald from him and Alistair. Daman gathered his breath as he looked around the bailey – a bailey that was nearly empty.

"Most of our people are gone," Alistair said sadly. "I'm losing my clan."

Daman looked into Alistair's dark eyes and shook his head as he frowned.

"It began a year ago when our feud with the Blair clan escalated to another battle. We faced a bitter loss that day with over half of our warriors dead or dying. While we made the trek home with our wounded, the Blairs raided the castle and took all our sheep."

Daman glanced at Innes to see her giving instructions to a couple of women.

"It didna take long for our food stores to run low," Alistair continued. "Soon, people began to leave. My father took a handful of men and tried to take our sheep back. He was killed in the process."

Daman took in the account and began to piece things together. Obviously, Donald wanted to be laird, but that was Alistair's role. How far would Donald go to get the title himself? Daman suspected he would do anything.

"Our clan chose Alistair as laird over Donald," Innes said as she walked up, confirming Daman's suspicions. "Donald hasn't forgiven Alistair for that. Or me for siding with Alistair."

Alistair wrapped an arm around Innes. "We've lost a lot of our clan because I'm unable to feed them. Donald gathered a following of men and took them to another rival clan, the Sinclairs, to raid them. In the process, many of those warriors died."

Innes leaned against Alistair's chest. "Donald has made an enemy of the Sinclairs that we don't need."

"War is coming," Alistair said. "And I doona have men to fight with me. I doona wish to battle the Sinclairs, especially when I know the Blairs are looking to take our lands. I need allies, no' enemies."

"That's where you come in," Innes said.

Daman's frown grew. Him? What was he supposed to do?

Sure, he was a good fighter, one of the best actually. Was he meant to ride into battle with Alistair? If that was what Innes wanted him to do, then he would do it.

But they would fail.

It didn't matter how good a man was if he didn't have the forces behind him.

Alistair waved his arm around. "You're welcome here, Daman. I didna want my sister to wake you, but perhaps it was what we needed."

Daman followed them into the castle wondering just how much he would be willing to do for the lovely Innes. Then he knew the answer – anything.

CHAPTER 4

Innes couldn't stop looking at Daman. He was quiet, his bearing commanding even without speaking a single word. Without meaning to, he drew everyone's gaze.

She swallowed hard when he came to stand beside her in the great hall, his hand brushing hers. A spark zipped through her, primal and...erotic.

Then he looked at her.

His blue eyes were intense as they searched hers. Chills still raced over her skin from when he had traced her eyebrow. She wanted to ask him if he knew she had done that to him countless times, but she didn't have the nerve.

"You must be hungry," Alistair said. "We doona have much, but we'll gladly share what we do have."

Innes felt lost when Daman's gaze slid from her and moved to Alistair. He touched her brother's arm to get his attention. Once Alistair turned to him, Daman pointed to a bow and a quiver of arrows propped near the hearth.

Alistair frowned as he looked at the weapons then back at Daman. "You want to use them?"

Daman nodded and then walked to the hearth. He slung

the quiver over his head, settling the strap across his chest. He lifted the bow and tested it by pulling the string back and looking along the sights. He lowered the weapon and caught Innes's gaze once again.

Innes realized then why Daman was so quiet. "You can't speak, can you?"

Daman's gaze briefly lowered to the ground before he shook his head.

Alistair asked, "Have you always been mute?"

Again Daman shook his head.

Innes wasn't sure she would be so calm if she woke after two hundred years without the ability to speak. Yet, Daman seemed entirely composed.

Daman pointed to Alistair and then the bow before he opened the castle door.

"You want to hunt," Alistair said, a slow grin forming.

Her brother hesitated, and Innes hurried to say, "I'll be fine. Donald is locked away, and we'll close the gates."

Alistair pulled on the end of her hair and strode away to get his bow and quiver. Innes looked back at Daman to find him watching her closely.

She noticed the silver chain around his neck that disappeared beneath his saffron shirt. Her necklace. The thought of it touching his skin made her stomach flutter in excitement.

If only she had been there when he woke. She would've had him all to herself for a time.

"We willna be far," Alistair said, breaking into her thoughts.

Innes jumped and jerked to her brother. "Of course. Be careful. Both of you," she said and looked at Daman.

Alistair exited the castle first. Daman hesitated before he gifted her with a smile and followed her brother. Innes walked to the doorway to watch them.

Her brother barked orders to the men standing guard at the gatehouse and those along the battlements. Alistair spoke while Daman nodded or pointed to something. It continued for a bit at the gate before they walked beneath the gatehouse. Alistair turned right, and Daman turned left.

Innes's heart jumped when Daman glanced back at her before disappearing beyond the gate. Only after the gate was closed and bolted did she shut the castle door and face the hall.

∽

D aman returned to the castle with a deer and four hares. He would've hunted longer, but he couldn't shake the overwhelming need to get back to Innes.

The black-haired beauty was an enigma. All those times she had visited him, spoke to him...touched him. Her caresses had heated his blood, singed his skin. With the barest of touches, she made him crave more.

Now that he was awake, he wanted to yank her against him and taste her lips as he'd longed to do while he slept. She had no idea what her nearness did to him. She tied him in knots, and at the same time, she calmed a raging storm inside him that he hadn't yet figured out.

Right at the tip of his memory was the knowledge of something he was supposed to do, but every time he got close to figuring it out, it slipped further away.

The castle gates opened and Daman discovered Innes there to greet him. Her eyes lit up at the sight of the meat. It almost made him want to go back out and get more.

She took the hares from him as she said, "Alistair isn't back yet. You've made everyone very happy."

It was her bright smile that caused something in his chest to expand. Things were bad off at the MacKays. He wasn't sure what he was supposed to do, but he knew he would help in whatever manner asked of him.

As soon as he and Innes walked around the side of the castle to the kitchen, Daman saw the women. They were standing around, waiting for him. He shrugged the deer off his shoulder and laid it on the ground. Then he stepped back and let the women take over.

"Follow me," Innes said.

As if Daman would refuse. They passed through the kitchens and then up the stairs. He watched the sway of her hips and his cock hardened.

A memory flashed of brightly colored skirts. Then, just like that, it was gone again as if it never were.

Innes didn't halt until she reached the door to a chamber. She put her hand on the latch and waited for him. Her dark eyes held a hint of shyness, but there was curiosity and awareness, as well.

"You have no idea how much you've helped us today. Donald would've tried to kill Alistair, and though Alistair knows Donald needed to be brought to heel, he's still family. You saved Alistair that trouble and stopped Donald's attempt to take over the clan."

Daman didn't know what to say. He had only done what he thought needed to be done.

"Then there is the hunting. Alistair has put it off to search for Donald, but there is only so much one man can do. Thank you."

He didn't want her thanks. He wanted...her.

"Do you remember anything before you awoke?" she asked.

Daman nodded slowly.

"You remember why you were in that cavern?" she asked hopefully.

He hated to disappoint her, but he couldn't lie. Daman

gave a swift shake of his head. How could he explain that he remembered instinctive things, but didn't know his name? It didn't make sense, even to him.

He knew he was formidable in battle and could wield a bow or spear as well as a sword. He knew he could ride a horse, steering the steed with nothing but his legs while charging into a fight so he could use his weapons.

Beyond that, there was nothing.

He wanted to ask her to help him figure it all out, but the words wouldn't come. Somehow, he knew that he'd never asked anyone for anything.

"There's a bath waiting," Innes said into the silence. "And food. It's the least I could do."

She started to walk past him, and he grabbed her hand. Her head jerked to him, her eyes wide. He placed his other hand over his heart and bowed his head.

Her smile was slow and sweet. "You're welcome."

He knew he should release her hand, but the feel of her soft skin was his undoing. His thumb grazed the top of her hand in slow circles.

When her lips parted and he noted the wild beat of her pulse in her neck, all he could think about was kissing her, of pulling her against him and feeling the warmth of her body as he held her.

He gently tugged her closer, his thumb still caressing her hand. She leaned toward him. Daman lowered his gaze to her mouth as he ducked his head.

He hesitated for just a moment, giving her time to pull away. When she didn't, he touched his lips to hers.

The low moan that rose from within her had his body demanding more. He turned them both, pressing her back against the wall.

He kissed her again, adding more pressure. As soon as her lips parted, he slipped his tongue between them. Their tongues touched and danced while her arms wound around his neck and her fingers slid into his hair.

Daman deepened the kiss. The more he sought, the more she gave. Her kisses were seductive and innocent, enticing and wanton.

This was the woman who had awakened him, who wanted him to help her clan. The last thing he should be doing is assaulting her. Besides, it would not be good to have Alistair discover them like this after having been taken into their home. Daman needed to stop.

If he didn't stop now, he wasn't sure he would be able to later. His desire for Innes was that great.

He ended the kiss and pulled back. The sight of her kiss-swollen lips made him groan, but no sound could be heard.

Her eyes opened, blinking up at him dazedly. She touched her lips with her fingertips. "I have no words for how amazing that felt."

Satisfaction filled him. If only she knew how close he was to kissing her again.

He cupped his hands around her face and looked deep into her black eyes. Such beautiful eyes. They were so dark and deep that he could feel himself falling into them.

She lifted her lips to him, silently asking him to continue kissing her. Just as he began to lower his head, he heard Alistair's voice below.

Daman gave her a quick kiss and stepped away. When she didn't move, he turned her toward the stairs and gave her a gentle shove. Only when she began to walk did he go into his chamber and shut the door.

He sighed heavily. The kiss had been beyond his expectations. Innes was captivating, and she must have worked some kind of spell on him because he was bewitched.

A warning zipped through his mind, cautioning him to

be wary. But as he tried to search the dark corners of his mind for why, he once more came up empty.

Daman removed his sword, boots, kilt, and shirt to walk naked - except for the necklace he still wore - to a wooden tub filled with water. It was still relatively warm. He scrubbed himself twice before he rose and dried off.

He touched the amulet around his neck. It was the same one he'd found in his hand when he regained consciousness in the cavern. If Innes was the one to wake him, did that mean this was hers? He knew it didn't belong to him.

Daman put his clothes back on and walked to the small round table and chair in his chamber. He sat and poured ale into a tankard as he looked at the trencher of food before him.

After the first bite of cold meat, he realized how famished he was. It didn't take long for him to clean the trencher of every morsel.

He sat back to finish his ale as he looked around his quarters. It was a medium sized room. The bed sat against the far wall with bed curtains that were dark blue velvet. They were a little frayed, having seen better days.

It was more visible evidence that the MacKays were in trouble. Daman wasn't sure how they had lasted as long as they had.

With little food, very few men to hold the castle, and fighting within the family, they were ripe to be taken over.

Daman tried not to think of Innes, but he couldn't seem to help himself. That kiss had set him ablaze. The fire within for her had already flamed hot. Now, he burned.

Did she know how she made his blood heat? How he yearned to have her near? How he longed to hold her?

He thought she had been with him for decades, because that's what it felt like. But it was more like years. Just how long had he been in that cave?

Why was he put there? Innes and Alistair must know the answers. If only he could ask them. But that was rather hard without his voice.

He rose and began to pace the room. There were no memories. He responded to his name, he knew he could fight, and he knew he could hunt. Other than that, his mind was blank.

Except for the clawing feeling that he was supposed to be doing something.

Looking.

He latched onto the word. Looking. He was supposed to be looking. But for what? For who?

Daman squeezed his eyes closed and gripped his head. A dull ache had begun, settling in at the base of his skull. The pain grew until his entire head pounded.

It took him a moment to realize there was a second pounding – that of a fist against his door.

CHAPTER 5

I nnes shifted in her seat in Alistair's chamber. She couldn't get comfortable. Ever since that scorching kiss with Daman, she'd been unable to think of anything other than him.

All through the evening meal she'd kept hoping he would come down, but Alistair had wanted to give him time. After the meal, however, Alistair waited until the hall cleared and then went after Daman.

Since neither she nor Alistair was sure of how many more of their people sided with Donald, they decided to keep their conversation private. There was nowhere more private than the master chamber.

Innes jumped when the door opened and Alistair filled the space. He gave her a frown and stepped aside. Then her gaze landed on Daman. Their eyes locked, held. It was a good thing she was sitting down because she was certain her legs wouldn't have held her after she saw the desire reflected in Daman's blue gaze.

"Thank you again for helping me hunt," Alistair said as he stopped at the hearth and turned to Daman.

Daman glanced down the hall before he closed the door behind him. He bowed his head and crossed his arms over his thick chest as he leaned against the wall.

Alistair clasped his hands behind his back as the fire popped behind him. "I wish things were no' so dire for us. I was none too pleased that Innes woke you, but now I think she did the right thing."

Innes saw Daman's slight frown, his hesitation, as if he were trying to figure things out. There was something about the way the lines bracketed his mouth that made her think he was in pain.

She held up a hand to stop Alistair before he continued. "Daman, do you know why you were in the cave?"

He shook his head slowly.

Innes frowned. "That part of the story was lost to us. I was hoping you would remember. All we've been told was that you would one day save our clan."

Daman held her gaze for a moment before his blue eyes slid to Alistair and he shrugged.

"Aye, I didna think you would know that either," Alistair said with a sigh. "The truth is, you doona have to do anything. Our family has kept watch over you for two hundred years."

Was it Innes's imagination, or had Daman jerked at the mention of the time that had passed?

Alistair continued, saying, "Now that you're awake, you can do whatever you wish. Nothing holds you here."

Daman pointed to Alistair and then to Innes.

Innes glanced at her brother. "Daman, you don't owe us anything."

"She's right. You doona," Alistair said. "But I'm asking if you'll stay and help us fight if needed. Now that Donald is no longer a worry, I must turn my attention to the Sinclairs. They want a meeting."

Innes swiveled her head to Alistair, shocked. This was the first she had heard of it. "What?"

Her brother pulled out a rolled missive from the sleeve of his shirt. "This arrived before the evening meal. David, the laird of the Sinclairs, wants to meet at our border. He is bringing the Lord of Ravensclyde with him."

"And his army, no doubt," Innes said tightly. "The Sinclair doesn't want to talk. He wants to fight."

Alistair tucked the missive back up the sleeve on his left arm. "David is an honorable man, Innes. I believe him. I was hoping Daman would accompany me."

Daman was nodding even as Innes asked, "When is this meeting?"

"In the morn."

She closed her eyes in despair. Her world was truly crumbling around her. If only Donald had stood with Alistair instead of against him.

"I would like you there as well, sister."

Innes's gaze snapped open to look at her brother. If he wanted her with him, that could only mean one thing – a marriage proposal.

She couldn't pull a breath into her lungs. They were frozen with dread. How could she possibly go to another after having Daman with her?

After his kiss?

She was being selfish, but that didn't stop the feeling from continuing. The lives of her brother and her clan rested with her. She could broker peace if she were willing to be the bride of the Sinclairs' laird.

Innes had known her fate for years, even if she hadn't known which man she would marry. Why was she rebelling now?

"I sent a missive to The Sinclair two days ago," Alistair said into the quiet, as if reading Innes's thoughts. "He was willing to meet, but now that Donald has attacked, I doona know where we stand."

She tried to swallow, but her mouth was too dry. "Give him Donald. Let the Sinclairs exact their justice."

"I'm sure they will want that, but Donald is family. I'll punish him myself."

Daman shook his head and looked pointedly at Innes.

She shivered, remembering the fury she'd witnessed in Donald's gaze before Daman intervened. Donald would've killed her.

"Hmm," Alistair said. "Good point, Daman. But Donald willna be leaving the dungeon so he can no' hurt Innes." Alistair walked to the round table near the hearth and motioned Daman over. "I've made a map of our land, as well as where we border with the Sinclairs and the Blairs."

Innes watched as Daman strode to the table and braced his hands on the wood as he let his gaze wander the map. Occasionally, he would point to something. Alistair would then explain the area in detail.

While the men studied the map, Innes kept thinking of marriage. She touched her lips, her stomach fluttering as he recalled how Daman had turned and trapped her between him and the wall.

Chills raced along her skin as she remembered the feel of his lips – firm and eager – and the way he'd held her.

As if there were no tomorrow.

In some ways, there wasn't. Not for them.

Innes waited until both men were too engrossed in the map and their planning – Alistair talking and Daman either nodding or shaking his head – to notice her before she got up and quietly exited the chamber.

She made her way back downstairs to the kitchen. Innes pushed up her sleeves and began helping a few others clean up from the meal. More and more people left the clan every day. Pretty soon, it would only be her and Alistair.

She stopped washing dishes as it hit her. No, she wouldn't be with Alistair, she would be with her new husband far away from here. Her marriage would foster peace between the Sinclairs and MacKays. That also meant that Alistair would have the backing of the Sinclairs.

It would be enough to keep the Blairs away. The Sinclair clan was the strongest around. No one went against them. The support of the Sinclair clan would allow Alistair to find himself a wife and procure another ally. Hopefully their people would return by then.

It was the only way to survive.

Why then did it feel as if she were doing the wrong thing? Why did it feel as if her place was to remain right where she was?

Innes was so conflicted. She wanted to help save her clan, but she also wanted Daman. The way he looked at her, it was as if he knew her. Which was silly, since they'd just met. She had been visiting him every day for years, but he didn't know that.

Did he?

Innes finished the washing and dried her hands. She walked from the kitchen as Daman was coming out of the solar, his head swiveling as if he were looking for something.

As soon as he spotted her, he walked to her and took her hand. Excitement coursed through her when he laced his fingers with hers. She lifted her skirts with her free hand and followed him up the stairs all the way to the battlements. She sucked in a breath when the cold air hit her.

Daman turned to face her as he pulled her against him. His heat enveloped her, wrapping them in a cocoon of warmth. He gently touched her face with first one hand, then the other. One hand slid into her hair and around to the back of her head. His gaze was intense, the desire palpable.

There were no words needed between them. The passion was too great, the need too forceful.

She rested her hands on his chest and wished that there were no clothes between them. She ached to be pressed skin against skin. Everything she thought, everything she *was* centered upon Daman.

His eyes lowered to her mouth a heartbeat before he kissed her.

Innes wrapped her arms around his neck and melted into him. It wasn't a soft, learning kiss like the one from before. This one was full of fire and heat and longing. And her body responded instantly.

He deepened the kiss before she could right herself, sending desire pooling in her belly. Before Innes knew it, she was pressed against the battlement wall by Daman's hard body.

She ran her hands over him, touching every part that she could. There wasn't a part of him that was soft. Just steely muscle beneath her palms.

Her head dropped back as he kissed down her throat. Innes didn't know such passion existed, but now that she did, there was no way she could marry another.

Cool air hit her legs a moment before Daman's large hand hooked beneath her knee and yanked her leg up. Innes gasped at the feel of his hard arousal pressed against her.

In the next instant, she was holding air. She grasped the battlement and lifted her head to search for Daman. He was standing against the back battlement wall, his face contorted with regret and need.

Innes knew she couldn't go to her groom anything but an innocent, but it wasn't him she was thinking about. It was

Daman and how she felt in his arms. Nothing mattered but this moment.

She held out her hand to him, but Daman gave a rough shake of his head and drew in a shaky breath.

"I don't care what Alistair has planned," she said. "I don't want this to stop."

Daman's blue eyes flared with desire. He slowly looked her up and down, his intent clear. If he kissed her again, there wouldn't be any stopping him.

Innes crossed the distance until she stood in front of him. "I don't want you to stop. Ever."

He cupped her face and stared at her as if his world had just been ripped to pieces.

"I've waited years to have you open your eyes and see me," she said. "I've tasted your kisses, felt your desire. Don't take that away."

He jerked his head behind him, indicating the castle and clan.

Innes licked her lips and shrugged. "Everything I have ever done has been for the clan. I'm not thinking of anyone or anything other than me and you right now."

Daman looked as if he wanted to argue the point more. Then, he released a deep breath as his frown disappeared. He gave a nod. Once more, he slipped his hand in hers. Together, they faced the battlement door and walked back into the castle to his chamber.

As soon as the door closed behind them, Innes was once more yanked against him in a fierce kiss that took her breath away.

CHAPTER 6

D aman was shaken, staggered.
          Stunned.
          With every kiss, every touch, Innes sank deeper into his soul. He knew he shouldn't be with her since she was promised to another, but he couldn't walk away. He had to hold her, just as he had to take his next breath.

She had become the center of his world.

He didn't wonder why or worry. He simply accepted the fact.

Innes grounded him in a way he couldn't understand. Even the knowledge that he had been asleep for two hundred years wasn't enough to send him away. Because without her, without her soft voice and beautiful, dark eyes, he knew he would go mad.

She was the only one who spoke to him while he was in the cave.

She was the only one who touched him as he lay sleeping.

She was the only one who penetrated the darkness, giving him...hope.

She was the one who awakened him.

Daman ended the kiss and leaned back to look at her. He wished he could tell her how she gave him a reason to live. He wanted to tell her that her beauty left him breathless.

More than that, he desperately wanted to tell her that she healed the raw, aching wounds deep inside him with only a smile.

He didn't know what plagued him, what made him think he had something to look for. Only that he instinctively knew that he did. It ate at him constantly. But Innes eased his soul, soothed his heart.

She didn't make him forget what gnawed at him. Instead, she made him believe that he would eventually do all that was needed of him.

"No one has ever looked at me like that," Innes whispered. "You make me want to blush and believe I can fly all at the same time."

He could make her feel like that just by looking at her? Daman had never experienced anything like it before. If only he could speak. Then he would tell her of all the feelings inside him. The biggest one? Hope.

Daman didn't know why that one stood out. Was hope absent before? As soon as he began to search his mind for memories, the headache returned.

Innes immediately frowned and smoothed her hands over his face. "I don't know what's troubling you, but don't think of it now."

Nay, now wasn't the time for it, not when he had Innes in his arms. Daman dropped his hands to her hips and began to gather her skirts. There was a shyness and innocence about her that made him feel protective – and strong.

He pulled her dress over her head, but before he could reach for her shift, she dropped to her knees and pulled off his boots one at a time. When the second one hit the floor,

Daman pulled her up and backed her to the bed. He couldn't help but grin when he saw the desire in her gaze.

He gently pushed her down so she sat on the bed, then it was his turn to take off her boots. After he'd removed them, he placed his hands on one slender ankle and slowly ran his hands up her calves to her thighs.

Her chest rose and fell rapidly, her lips parted. She braced her hands behind her on the bed, leaning back just enough. She had no idea how difficult it was to clamp down on his control and not cover her body with his right then.

Daman began to roll down her stocking. He hadn't realized until that moment how sexy a stocking could be, but being able to caress her skin as he rolled them down made his cock ache with need. Her second leg was just as erotic. By the time he finished, they were both panting and needy.

Daman stood and unpinned his kilt. It fell to the floor at his feet. Innes sat up and slid her hands beneath his saffron shirt.

Innes sucked in a breath at the feel of his skin beneath her palms. It was great to touch but she wanted to see, as well. She shoved the shirt up. Daman jerked it off and tossed it aside, leaving her gaping at the specimen before her.

He was simply...glorious.

Every inch of him was honed with muscle. She took in the sight of his wide chest, the rippling sinew of his stomach, and his thick arms.

Then she looked down at his arousal jutting out between them, thick and hard.

He placed his finger beneath her chin and lifted her gaze to his face. She stared into his blue eyes for several moments before he bent and kissed her.

In an instant, she was flat on her back, his delicious weight covering her. The world blurred and faded as she lost herself in the kiss – in Daman.

He rolled onto his back, taking her with him. She was so lost in the kiss that she didn't realize he was taking off her shift until he briefly ended the kiss to pull the garment over her head.

His hands were everywhere, stroking, learning, caressing. It felt...right.

She was surprised when he pulled her knees up so that she straddled him. Then he sat her up. Innes gazed down at him, her hands braced on his chest.

Daman took in the sight of her, wondering if she knew just how stunning she was with her dark hair falling around her in disarray, her lips swollen, and desire in her gaze.

His cock jumped, his balls tightened.

His heart clenched.

How could he have such a woman in his arms and let her go on the morrow? He couldn't. He knew it in his bones. Innes was his. If he had to fight a hundred armies, he would. Just to have her as his.

Daman cupped her breasts and ran his thumbs over her nipples. Her eyes slid closed as a sigh left her lips. He rolled her nipples between his fingers as her head dropped back, causing her long hair to brush his thighs and cock.

He teased her nipples mercilessly until soft cries left her lips. Her hips began to rock as she dug her nails into his chest. When Daman could take it no more, he sat up and latched his lips around one turgid peak.

Her hands grasped his head as she moaned low in her throat. Daman suckled first one breast and then the other as their bodies rocked against each other.

He could feel her arousal, and it drove him mad with need. In a blink, he flipped her onto her back and slid a hand between their bodies to the dark curls that hid her sex.

Daman gritted his teeth when he felt how wet she was.

He gently slipped a finger inside her. Her legs parted as her hips rose up to meet his hand.

He removed his finger and began to slowly, lightly circle it around her clit. Daman inwardly smiled when he heard her breath catch and felt her body melt into the bed. Her chest heaved as her cries grew louder, her moans longer. He alternated between teasing the swollen nub and thrusting a finger inside her.

She was shaking, her body close to release. But he wasn't finished with her yet.

Daman scooted down her body until he was nestled between her legs. Then he placed his lips on her.

She whispered his name, her hands fisting in the blanket. Daman watched her as he licked and laved her clit, ruthless in his desire to give her pleasure.

Never had he felt such need to sink into a woman, to claim her. He couldn't wait to fill her and have her legs wrap around him.

The only thing that dulled the moment was the reminder that she wasn't his. Alistair intended her for another. Daman briefly wondered if he should refrain from claiming her as he yearned to do and simply give her pleasure.

Then she climaxed and coherent thought left him.

Daman watched the ecstasy cross her face, felt her body shake with the force of the orgasm. He rose over her, his cock poised at her entrance.

Innes opened her eyes as the amazing bliss began to recede. Her body still pulsed. She blinked up at Daman, only belatedly realizing that he was no longer touching her.

His jaw was clenched, and there was a question in his eyes.

There was only one answer for her. Innes wrapped her hand around his arousal, amazed at how hard it felt, yet at the same time, the skin was as soft as velvet.

She brought him to her entrance. There was a moment where surprise flickered in his eyes, then he slowly entered her.

The feel of his thickness stretching her while he gradually thrust deeper and deeper inside was exquisite. Their gazes were locked as their bodies joined again and again until he met her maidenhead.

She clung to his shoulders, unsure of what came next, but ready all the same. He pulled out of her until just the tip of him remained, then he tugged her knees up and plunged inside her.

Innes gasped at the pain when he breached her innocence. She squeezed her eyes closed, surprised that he remained still until the worst of the pain was over.

She once more opened her eyes to find him watching her. He gently touched her face, as if asking if she were all right. It amazed her that Daman could be so powerful and strong, yet gentle at the same time.

A smile pulled at her lips as she nodded. The corners of his mouth tilted in a grin. Then he began to move again.

Innes was swarmed with pleasure. It consumed her, overwhelmed her, and she welcomed it because it was Daman who brought it out in her.

His hips began to move faster, driving him deeper, harder. She was swept along, her body eager for more. Sweat slickened their bodies as she wrapped her legs around him and locked her ankles.

She began to lift her hips to meet his thrusts. He might not be able to talk, but his face conveyed his pleasure better than words ever could.

All too soon, he grunted and pulled out of her. She held him tightly as his body jerked. It wasn't until she felt something on her stomach that she realized he hadn't spilled his seed inside her.

They remained there for a long time before Daman rose and found a cloth. He wet it with a pitcher of water and then returned to the bed, cleaning off his seed and then the blood of her innocence from between her legs.

Innes couldn't remember the last time someone had taken care of her like Daman did. It just proved how different he was, and why she didn't want anyone but him.

She watched as he cleaned himself. When he finished, he dropped the cloth, pulled back the blankets and raised a blond brow. He wanted her to stay. It made her heart want to leap from her chest with joy.

Innes got beneath the blanket and then found herself pulled back against his chest as he reclined against the headboard, his arms around her.

They sat in silence for long moments, but she hated that she couldn't see his face to see what he was thinking. She held no regrets. She hoped he didn't either.

Regardless of what was to come, this night was hers. She'd made the decision to be with Daman and have some joy when no other decision had been hers to make. No one and nothing could take that away from her.

Just as no one could take Daman from her.

Daman was wondering how in the world he would be able to watch Innes leave with David Sinclair? He wasn't sure he could.

Nay. He knew he couldn't.

He was prepared to fight Alistair and the Sinclairs for her. That's how much she meant to him, even before he had marked her as his.

"I don't regret this," her sweet voice broke the silence. She turned to face him, her brow furrowed slightly. "I don't want you to either."

He shook his head as he smiled.

Innes chuckled as her shoulders drooped. "Good."

Daman tugged at the ends of her hair, amazed at the thickness and how it felt like silk in his fingers.

"When you first saw me, you looked as though you knew me."

He nodded and touched her lips.

"You heard me talking to you?" she asked in surprise, her dark eyes wide.

His smile grew as he gave another nod.

"Did you hear others before me?"

He'd only ever heard her. Daman shook his head, his smile dying.

"I knew when Mum showed me to the cave and I saw you that you would change my life," Innes said. "I just didn't realize how much."

He laced their fingers together, grateful that he couldn't talk because he had no words. She claimed that he had changed her life, when in fact it was the opposite. Innes had given his life back to him, and in the process, had given him something to fight for – her.

Daman placed her hand over his heart. He didn't fully understand the feelings churning inside him, but he recognized that he hadn't felt them for another woman. Regardless of the life he'd once had, he knew there hadn't been a woman before Innes.

Nor would there be one after her.

She blinked rapidly and lowered her gaze. "For all eternity, you will be in my heart, Daman," she whispered.

He pulled her back against his chest and wrapped his arms around her. Long after Innes had fallen asleep, Daman's mind went over every scenario in which he was allowed to keep her. And every one of them ended in battle.

The hours ticked by steadily, as if fate were set against him. He watched the sky lighten through the slit in the shutters.

An hour before dawn, Daman looked down at Innes sleeping in his arms and felt his heart tighten in fear. He couldn't lose her. Without her, he would be lost.

He touched her face, letting the pad of his finger skate down her cheek. She woke gradually and finally her eyes opened. Her smile was radiant when she looked at him.

Up until she saw the sky.

"You shouldn't have let me sleep. I wanted more time with you," she said, her voice laced with regret.

Daman stopped her when she started to rise. He had no way of asking her if she would consider remaining with him. He could only hold her, hoping she saw the need in his gaze, felt the longing in his embrace.

"I must get to my chamber before Alistair finds me gone," she whispered and gave him a lingering kiss.

She was out of his arms in the next instant, her dress hastily thrown on as she gathered the rest of her things and reached for the door. She paused and looked over her shoulder at him.

Then she was gone.

Daman wanted to hit something, to scream his fury. If only he had friends he could seek out. It would be the first time he asked for help, but he was willing to do anything for Innes.

Innes stood in the bailey stroking her horse's forehead when she heard the voices from within the castle. Alistair was bellowing, and suddenly, everyone was rushing about.

She looked to the castle entrance as the door was thrown open and Alistair emerged followed by Daman. Her heart dropped to her stomach like a stone. Had Alistair discovered that she had given her innocence to Daman?

Daman's gaze was a mixture worry and anger as he looked at her, his hand resting on the hilt of his sword. But that fury wasn't directed at Alistair.

"Someone released Donald," Alistair told her in a tight voice as he walked down the castle steps.

Innes looked around at the faces of her clan. Those who

remained had left the village and taken shelter at the castle. One of them was responsible.

"Who did this?" she asked them as she came around her horse. "Do you want to see another clan take over the castle? Because that's what is going to happen. Who would dare to go against your laird and free Donald?"

No one bothered to respond, and it infuriated her.

"Do you have any idea what Alistair and I have done for you? Do you even care? Perhaps we should let the Sinclairs take over," she said, her voice failing at the end.

She had been willing to give herself to the Sinclair laird for peace, but her clan didn't want peace. Why should she wreck her life for people who didn't care?

Innes felt a presence beside her and knew it was Daman. He turned her away to lead her back to her mare. His strong hands wrapped around her waist, and she looked into his eyes.

His long hair was tied back in a queue, giving his stark features more of a dangerous look. His blue gaze sought hers. Then he gave her a slight nod.

Innes took a deep breath. "I'm all right."

At that, he lifted her onto her horse and walked to his own. Innes didn't look back as she and Daman left the castle with Alistair.

They hadn't gone far from the gatehouse before she said, "Perhaps we should just keep riding and forget the clan."

"Nay," Alistair said. "They're my responsibility."

"They freed Donald," she stated. "I think that says everything."

"We doona know who freed our brother, but it wasna the entire clan," Alistair argued.

Innes snorted. "The fact is, someone did. Someone went against you and released him. We don't know who supports you and who supports Donald. I fear we won't know that until Donald challenges you again."

Daman was riding ahead of them, his gaze sharp. Innes thought of the previous night and waking up in his arms. If only every day could be like that. Was it too much to ask that she be allowed to be happy? That she be able to choose a husband for herself?

"Do you love him?"

She was pulled out of her musing by Alistair's question. Her eyes swung to him. "What?"

"I'm no' blind, Innes. I see how you look at him. More importantly, I see how protective he is of you."

"I woke him."

"Aye. But I think there's more you're no' telling me. I want things to go smoothly today. In all ways."

She looked forward, her gaze landing on Daman. "You mean you want to know if I'll refuse to go with the Sinclairs."

"That's exactly what I mean."

"Have I given you any reason to doubt me?"

Alistair was quiet for a long time before he said, "No' until now. Our clan needs peace, Innes."

"Then give them Donald," she argued. "They know he's the culprit."

Alistair blew out a breath. "We must all make sacrifices for the clan."

Innes felt tears threaten. She was a laird's daughter. She knew better than to cry over things out of her control. It didn't make it any easier to swallow, however.

∼

Ravensclyde Castle

Stefan sat atop his horse outside the gatehouse looking toward the border between the MacKay and Sinclair lands. The missive from Alistair MacKay had been a surprise, but a smart one, nonetheless.

A horse and rider sidled up next to Stefan. He didn't need to look over to know it was Morcant. He, Morcant, and Ronan had been up since before dawn scouting the castle for signs of another attack.

David believed the MacKay laird, but the three of them were not so inclined.

"What are you thinking?" Morcant asked.

Stefan looked over at his friend and rubbed his jaw. He didn't want to be meeting with a laird. He wanted to be out looking for Daman. The four of them had been cursed by a gypsy two hundred years earlier. Ronan had been the first out of his dark prison, with Morcant second out of his. Stefan had arrived just a few days ago.

All three of them had been drawn to Ravensclyde. They refused to believe it was coincidence, which is what gave them hope that Daman would be found soon.

"Stefan?" Morcant asked with a frown.

"I'm thinking of Daman."

Morcant nodded. "I had hoped Leana would have a vision about him."

It wasn't only Morcant's wife that had special abilities. Morvan was a child of the forest, able to help animals in a way no other could – and she was all Stefan's.

"We only got to visit a few places on Sinclair land before we were called back to Ravensclyde," Stefan said. "He could be out there waiting for us."

Morcant shifted atop his horse. "I doona expect our meeting with The MacKay will take long. Once everything is sorted as David wants, we can get back to our hunt."

"It was three months between Ronan getting out of his prison and your arrival."

"We'll find him, Stefan."

None of them ever talked about the possibility that Daman hadn't been cursed with them. Daman hadn't gone into the gypsy camp with them initially, and he didn't have the flaws the rest of them had. The only thing Daman had a problem with was asking for help.

The sound of horses approaching from behind alerted Stefan that it was time. Ronan and David drew even with them, and the four of them headed out to the border.

By marrying Meg Alpin, the cousin of Laird David Sinclair, Ronan had become Lord of Ravensclyde. It still boggled Stefan's mind how he, Ronan, and Morcant had made a life for themselves after being cursed.

"We willna be going to war, lads," David said.

Morcant glanced at him. "I'll be prepared either way."

"David believes Alistair MacKay," Ronan repeated Morcant's earlier words. "The marriage will bring peace."

Stefan frowned as he glanced at the young laird. Without the two hundred year difference in their ages, David would be around their age. He was intelligent, brawny, and fierce as only a Highlander could be. "Nay. Only Donald MacKay locked in our dungeon will bring peace."

"If Donald acted alone," Morcant added.

David might believe the MacKay laird, but by Ronan's tight lips, he was prepared for war, as well.

"I doona make agreements lightly," David said and pinned Stefan with a look, his dark gray eyes intense. "I learned the truth of the MacKays. Donald is trying to oust his brother for control. Alistair is doing what any good laird would do. He's saving his clan."

"And you're willing to take a bride you've never met?" Ronan asked.

David smiled, though it was forced. "I doona have the same luxury as you three to marry someone I love. I'm laird. I marry for alliances."

"I wouldna think the MacKays are much of an alliance," Stefan said.

"Their land borders mine," David said. "If the Blairs decide they want the MacKay lands and holdings, I'll have to prepare to go to war with them. The Blairs take whatever they want, and I'll no' have my people put through that. Most of the MacKay clan has come to us. Once they realize the MacKays are allied with the Sinclairs, and Alistair has ensured Donald can no' cause any more trouble, the people will return to the MacKays."

Morcant nodded and said, "Alistair will once again have soldiers to hold off the Blairs."

"As well as my men," David added. "I'll be married to his sister."

CHAPTER 8

Daman wanted to pretend he couldn't hear the conversation between Alistair and Innes, but it was impossible. He felt her pain and it infuriated him that he couldn't help her as she needed. All Daman could do was fight and kill. He was damn good at it, too.

If he couldn't stop Alistair from handing his sister over to the laird of the Sinclairs, then all Daman could focus on was watching out for Donald.

The middle MacKay wasn't just loud and abrasive. He was obvious. Daman hadn't bothered to mention that Donald would show up at the meeting because Alistair already knew, and there was no sense in putting an added worry on Innes.

Daman may not have been part of a family, but even he knew that to go against a brother as Donald had Alistair was beyond terrible.

Donald had put everyone at the castle at risk, and he didn't seem to care. All Donald wanted was power. He was an idiot. It took more than brawn to lead a clan.

Daman had learned that from...

His thoughts went blank and his head began to throb dully. He ground his teeth together against the pain as the realization hit that he had almost remembered something. But what?

And who was he thinking about?

Need to be looking.

Daman gave a shake of his head. His thoughts were jumbled, his mind swimming with an urgency he couldn't elude. He was supposed to be looking for something.

Or was it someone?

He glanced over his shoulder at Innes. He had already found her, so she couldn't be it. Was it Donald? Nay, he was just a troublemaker. Besides, Daman didn't know of him until he woke.

Whatever pushed Daman had been with him for a long time – possibly as long as he had been asleep.

"We're no' far," Alistair said.

Daman licked his lips, wishing he could ask Innes specific details. If he could only talk, he might find out what he was supposed to be searching for. She might even know more details of his past.

A warning tickle pulled him out of his thoughts and focused him once more on his surroundings. They came to a river, and Daman waited for Alistair and Innes to cross before he followed.

He glanced behind him as the hairs on the back of his neck rose. Someone was watching them. Donald most likely, but how many men had Donald brought with him?

Once across the river, Daman nudged his horse into a gallop and caught up with Alistair. He motioned with his head behind him as Alistair's gaze landed on him.

The laird of the MacKays frowned. "Donald?" he whispered.

Daman lifted one shoulder in a shrug as he set his hand

atop the hilt of his sword. Alistair then moved his horse over and motioned Innes forward.

Finally, they reached the border between the MacKay and Sinclair lands. Daman saw a man sitting atop a large gray stallion. The man had light brown hair hanging to his shoulders and a full beard. His gaze was focused on them, looking each of them over. With the way he sat confidently and with a commanding presence atop his mount, he was obviously the Sinclair laird.

They came to a stop with ten feet separating the groups. Daman then let his gaze move to the rider next to the laird. The man's horse pranced in agitation. Daman looked into the man's face to find the Highlander staring at him intently.

Daman frowned as the man refused to look away. He watched Daman as if he knew him, which was impossible. The man couldn't know Daman, he had just been awakened after two hundred years of sleeping in a cave.

Daman inwardly snorted. Two hundred years. The passage of time was mindboggling, but it was the knowledge that someone had put him there that really caused anxiety. He had no recollection of anyone or anything that would explain that, and neither did he have time to think on it at the moment.

"David," Alistair said. "Thank you for meeting with us."

David bowed his head. "Attacking your clan didna seem right after so many have left."

"My brother will be punished," Alistair promised.

David glanced at Innes. "Where is Donald?"

Daman once again narrowed his gaze on the man next to David. It was obvious he was a warrior, a man trained with a sword. No wonder the Sinclair laird had brought him along.

If Daman were David, he would have brought more warriors. Daman had wanted Alistair to bring more men. The problem was, there weren't enough left.

"As of last night, he was in our dungeon." Alistair sighed. "Unfortunately, someone released him."

"Does he know of this meeting?" the man next to David asked.

David motioned to him. "Alistair, this is Ronan Galt, Lord of Ravensclyde. He is married to my cousin, Meg."

Alistair nodded to Ronan in greeting. "No doubt Donald knows of this meeting. It's why I've brought Daman along as extra protection for my sister."

"Where did Daman come from?" Ronan asked.

Daman tensed. Why would he ask such a question? Wouldn't anyone assume Daman was part of the MacKay clan?

"He has always been with our clan," Innes stated in a clear voice.

Her leg brushed Daman's as her horse shifted, and it was all Daman could do not to reach over and take her hand, to pull her onto his horse and claim her lips.

Ronan looked from Daman to Innes and back to Daman. There was something about the way Ronan stared that agitated Daman. If he could talk, he would demand that Ronan state whatever bothered him.

"You look like a capable warrior, Daman," David said.

Daman glanced at the laird.

"He is," Alistair answered. "He's already taken Donald down once."

"Why can he no' tell us this himself?" Ronan asked.

Innes pinned him with a scathing look. "If you must know, he can't talk."

"He can no' speak?" Ronan repeated with a deep frown furrowing his forehead.

"I didna think we were here to talk of Daman," Alistair said. "I thought we met to talk of peace."

David nodded slowly. "That we did, Laird. Innes, did your brother tell you the terms?"

"He did."

Her voice wobbled, causing anger to rise up within Daman. She shouldn't have to make such a sacrifice because of Donald's mistakes. Daman's grip on his sword tightened.

"Are you in agreement?" David asked her.

Innes hesitated. Daman could feel her gaze land on him briefly. "I've always been willing to do what was needed for my people."

"But?" Ronan pressed.

"She has nothing else to add," Alistair stated with a meaningful glare directed at Innes.

Tension filled the area as David and Alistair watched Innes while she looked at the ground. Daman and Ronan were once more locked in a stare.

"Well now, is this no' cozy," Donald said as he walked out of the brush behind them, the blade of his sword resting against his shoulder.

Daman whirled his mount around, unsheathing his sword. He was about to charge Donald when Alistair said his name. Daman looked at the laird, waiting.

"What are you doing here?" Alistair demanded of his brother.

Donald chuckled. "You know why I'm here."

"You can't win against the Sinclairs," Innes said. "Why would you want them as an enemy?"

Donald merely smiled. "I never said I wanted them as an enemy. What I wanted was for our clan to see how weak Alistair is. I needed our people to see that I'm the only one who can protect them?"

Daman lifted his lip in contempt. *Protect*. Donald didn't know the meaning of the word.

"That's why you tried to kill Innes?" Alistair demanded,

his voice lowering in his anger. "We had enough trouble with the Blairs, Donald. If you had stood beside me, we could've stolen our sheep back and fed our people. Your so-called plan sent our people away and gained us a potential enemy in the Sinclairs."

Donald lowered his sword until the point was in the ground and set both of his hands on the hilt. "I've got my men with me, Alistair. Who do you have? One man who is supposed to save our clan? He willna last against my men."

Daman swung a leg over his mount's head and slid to the ground. He gently shoved the horse away.

"Nay, Daman," Alistair said. "This is my fight."

Innes tried to dismount, but Daman was too quick. He kept her atop the horse and gathered the horse's reins beneath its chin. He then turned the horse toward the Sinclairs.

"Daman," Innes whispered.

He looked up into her dark eyes. Gypsy eyes. Why hadn't he noticed that before? She had the same coloring as a gypsy. It was exotic and beautiful.

And deadly.

Where had that thought come from? Daman shoved it aside and drank in her features. She had to be kept safe. There was about to be a bloodbath, and the only ones who could keep her out of it were the Sinclairs.

Daman turned to David and raised a brow in question. David nodded once. Daman walked Innes and her horse over the border and handed the reins to Ronan.

"Daman," Innes said again, louder this time.

He turned his back to her and returned to MacKay land. Alistair and Donald were already circling each other, their swords drawn and at the ready.

Donald was the first to attack. The clang of swords was loud in the quiet. Alistair easily blocked the swing and sidestepped, knocking his shoulder into Donald. Donald stumbled backward, his lips twisted in rage.

Alistair was quick, his attacks calm and on target. Donald let his emotions rule him, causing him to miss Alistair several times. Daman began to relax when it became apparent Alistair would win. Donald cut Alistair's arm, but Alistair turned away before it could go too deep.

Donald attacked again. Alistair didn't turn away this time. He met his brother's attack and used Donald's force to turn him slightly so that Donald fell on his back.

Alistair put the point of his blade at Donald's throat. "Call your men out here."

"Nay."

"It's over, brother," he said and kicked the sword out of Donald's hand. "I've defeated you, and since I can no' trust our people no' to release you again, I'm going to hand you over to The Sinclair."

Donald's dark eyes blazed with hatred. "You'll have to kill me."

Alistair lowered his sword and took a step back. "I'm no' spilling the blood of my brother. Everyone here saw your defeat."

Daman couldn't be happier. Alistair's actions proved he was meant to be laird. The best thing to do would be to kill Donald, but Daman understood why Alistair hadn't been able to.

Daman was walking toward them when Donald reached for his boot. Daman opened his mouth to call out to Alistair, but there was no sound. Daman rushed to Donald, but Donald had already risen to his feet and plunged a dagger into Alistair's back by the time Daman reached him. Daman could hear Innes screaming.

Daman slammed into Donald, sending him crashing to

the ground. Daman knelt beside Alistair and cradled his head as he looked into the dying man's eyes.

"Doona let him rule," Alistair said. "Doona let him hurt Innes." Then he issued his last breath, his eyes closing.

Daman gently laid Alistair down and gathered his sword as he stood. He pointed to Donald's sword with his own, waiting for Donald to pick up the weapon and face him.

As soon as he did, Daman attacked. He swung his sword in wide arcs as metal met metal time and again. Donald was taller by a few inches, but he didn't have the skill Daman did.

Daman blocked Donald's sword countless times. He kicked Donald and slammed his elbow into his face, which only caused Donald to become angrier. His swings went wide as his emotions took over.

He waited for Donald to get close and then plunged his sword into the man, feeling it sink deep into Donald's body. Surprise showed on Donald's face, as if he couldn't believe he was dying. Daman then shoved Donald off his blade and turned around.

"Daman!" Innes shouted as she came running at him.

CHAPTER 9

Daman gathered Innes in his arms and held tight, turning his face against her neck. She had lost both brothers that day. Daman should have paid closer attention. He might have been able to save Alistair.

"It's not your fault," she whispered, her hands stroking his head. "Alistair should never have turned his back on Donald."

Daman opened his eyes to find Ronan and David watching them. A moment later, two more men rode up beside Ronan. Daman released Innes and pushed her behind him as he glanced over his shoulder to see if any of Donald's men would attack. There were just two men who walked out from behind trees to stand over Donald and Alistair's dead bodies.

There was no doubt Daman could take Ronan and the others. He would rather do it after Innes was back at the castle, but he doubted David would allow her to leave.

David's lips compressed for a moment. "What a waste," he said. "Alistair was a good man. That was quick thinking, Daman."

Innes stood behind him, her hands gripping his tartan. Daman gave her a push. But just as he thought, she wouldn't leave.

"Daman has always been quick," Ronan said.

David grunted. "So you told me."

Daman looked between the two before his gaze shifted to the newcomers. One man had sandy blond hair and yellow-brown eyes while the other had light brown hair and hazel eyes. Their gazes were a mixture of shock, surprise, and happiness.

"Daman," said the man with the blond hair. "You know us."

He snorted and shook his head. He didn't know these men.

"He doesna recognize us, Morcant," said the second man.

Daman took a step back. He needed to get Innes to safety. There was no way he was turning her over to David Sinclair. Not now. Not after she had lost her family.

"Where have you been?" Ronan asked. He nudged his horse and guided it across the border onto MacKay land. He drew up before getting too close. "We've been looking for you. It's been a long time since the gypsy camp."

A flash of brightly colored skirts in the grass flashed in Daman's mind a heartbeat before an old gypsy woman's face, her dark eyes filled with anguish and fury.

Ilinca.

The name sprang into his mind, but Daman knew that was the old woman's name. She was a witch. A gypsy witch. She was the one responsible for putting him in the cave and having him sleep for two hundred years.

He hated gypsies for what she had done.

Daman jerked his head to Innes to see her dark coloring. Gypsy. He squeezed his eyes closed and turned his head back to Ronan.

Ronan slowly dismounted from his horse and dropped the reins. It made Daman frown because he had seen Ronan do that action before, he just didn't know how or when. Somehow, Daman also knew that he had picked up the reins from Ronan afterwards.

"It was my fault," Ronan said. He ran a hand down his face. "I can admit that now. I should never have gone to see Ana those times. I was the one who urged the three of you to accompany me," he said, motioning from Daman to the other two men.

Ronan cleared his throat. "You were the smart one. You remained outside the camp."

Daman closed his eyes as his head felt like it was splitting open. He grabbed it, doubling over from the agony. As if from a great distance, he could hear Innes calling his name. It took Daman a moment to realize he had fallen to his knees.

More flashes of faces and events filled his mind in rapid succession. He opened his mouth and tried to bellow, to ask someone for help, but there was only silence and the roar of pain.

Three pairs of large hands gripped him, steadying him. Daman kept his eyes closed for fear of letting in any light that might make the throbbing worse.

He saw Ronan, laughing as he put his arm around a dark-haired woman with bright skirts. Those same skirts he had seen lying in the grass. With blood.

Ana.

Daman felt something tighten around his chest, cutting off his air. He fought to fill his lungs with air even as an image of Morcant held immobile by Illinca filled his mind.

Then there was Stefan. The rage he dealt with constantly taking him over. In a blink, all three of his friends – his brothers – were gone. Illinca had used her magic to curse them.

All of his memories returned in a tidal wave, drowning him in sorrow, happiness, anger, and hope. And just like that, the pounding in his head stopped and the constriction around his chest eased. Daman remained still for a moment.

"He's no' rocking anymore," Morcant said.

So the three of them were holding him. Daman lifted his head, intending to talk to them. But all he saw was David holding Innes who had tears coursing down her face as she shouted his name over and over.

Daman threw off his friends' hold and jumped to his feet. How he wanted to demand that David release Innes. No sooner had the thought entered his head, than the words left his mouth.

Everyone stilled.

Innes blinked at him. She shrugged out of David's hold and took a step toward him. "You spoke."

Daman reached out and pulled her against him. "Aye. I can speak again."

"What happened to you?" she asked with a sniff.

Daman leaned back. He gazed into her dark eyes before he looked over her head to David. Then he turned his head to the side to where Ronan, Morcant, and Stefan stood.

How many times had his friends told him that asking for help wasn't a sign of weakness? To him, however, it was. Illinca had taught him the importance of asking for help by taking away his voice.

"I remember. Everything." He drew in a deep breath. It felt great to be able to speak again. It felt even better to see his friends.

Now he knew why he'd had that unshakable feeling of needing to search for something. He was meant to look for Morcant, Ronan, and Stefan.

Instead, they had found him.

"Everything?" Stefan asked.

Daman nodded. "I saw her curse each of you. I saw each of you disappear. I crossed into the camp, and she used her magic to keep me still. She said she'd had a vision, knew we would be there, but she hadn't seen Ana's death."

"I still say Illinca needs to die," Morcant mumbled.

Innes's head jerked toward Morcant. "Did you say Illinca?"

"What of her?" Ronan asked.

"She's the grandmother of one of my ancestors, Amalia. Amalia brought Daman to our land and married the MacKay laird."

Stefan scowled. "Are you telling me that you were no' in a dark prison, Daman?"

"I was asleep," he answered. "I woke in a cave. It was Innes who pulled me out of my sleep."

Innes touched his cheek. "It was foretold that he would save our clan."

"So he has," David said. "Alistair couldna kill his own brother, but Donald didna have such morals. With Donald dead, the MacKays will need a new laird. I think you've found him, Innes."

Daman saw her smile as she looked at him. He shook his head. "I'm no' a leader."

"You always have been," Ronan said. "You just didna want to take the role."

Daman faced his friends. "I couldna remember any of you. I knew I was missing something, but I couldna figure out what it was."

Morcant was the first to enfold him in a hug and pound on his back. Daman was smiling when Morcant stepped away, his head down as he brushed something from his cheek.

"Leana is making him soft," Stefan said right before he

pulled Daman in for a hug. "It's good to have us all together again."

Then it was Ronan's turn. Daman couldn't be happier. Until he saw David. His smile vanished as he faced the laird.

"I know you and Alistair had an agreement," Daman began.

David held up his hand and grinned. "I doona have to ask Innes what she wants. I saw it in the way she couldna get to you fast enough. I wouldna dream of coming between the two of you."

"I'm sure you've heard things you didna understand today," Daman said.

David laughed and mounted his horse. "I know all about Ilinca's curse and the four Highlanders she bound. It's been a story told for generations in my family. Why do you think we had the mirror Ronan was trapped in?" he asked before he turned his horse around and rode away.

"Will you help me with Alistair's body?" Daman asked his friends.

The four draped Alistair across his horse. Daman wasn't surprised to see Donald's two men cart Donald's body off into the forest. He knew their faces, and he wasn't sure he would allow them back onto MacKay land.

That's when he stopped his train of thought. It wasn't his land.

"What next?" Innes asked him.

He looked down at her. Her eyes were still red from her tears. He wanted to ask her to be his, but it wasn't the right time. She needed to bury her brothers.

"We bring Alistair back home."

Innes nodded and turned to Ronan, Morcant, and Stefan. "You are welcome to come with us."

Us. Daman wrapped an arm around her, feeling more

free than he ever thought possible. The only way things could get any better was if Innes agreed to be his wife.

He inwardly smiled. Wife. It was something he hadn't ever considered, and yet as soon as he had woken, that's all he had thought about. Well, not so much making her his wife but remaining with her. It was all the same in the end.

Three months later…

Innes was holding her cheeks, they hurt from laughing so hard. It was only a few months since Alistair's death, but Daman had helped her heal in ways he would never know.

Donald's body had never been recovered. Neither were the two men who freed him from the prison, which was fine with her.

Just as she'd assumed, the clan eagerly accepted Daman as their laird. Whether he knew it or not, he had the commanding presence, intellect, and warrior mentality that made a great laird. People recognized that.

In the months he had been laird, there wasn't just peace with the Sinclairs. He, Ronan, Stefan, and Morcant, along with a handful of MacKay men, stole back the sheep the Blairs had taken.

The Blairs tried to steal them again, but Daman had been prepared for them. The Blairs now knew that the MacKays weren't a clan to be messed with. Retribution would be swift if they did.

Daman's laughter rang out in the hall as Meg elbowed Ronan in the stomach. Innes had heard each of their stories of how the men were cursed and how they came to be in this time. Their stories of finding love were even more interesting.

Innes had slept in Daman's bed every night since returning to the castle. She wondered how much longer he would take before he asked her to be his. She was growing tired of waiting.

"I hated Ilinca," Stefan said. "My first thought was to kill her when I realized I was out of the darkness. I still hate her. Some," he added as he looked at Morvan. "She did bring me to my woman."

Morcant lifted his goblet. "To our women. Even I'll thank Ilinca for that."

Innes watched as Daman smiled and lifted his goblet with the others, but he was restless. "What is it?" she leaned over and asked.

He shook his head.

Innes knew him well enough to know the look pinching his lips. He was worrying over something.

She rose and sat on his lap. When his gaze met hers, she touched his face. "I wonder, Daman, if you know that I love you."

"Aye, lass. I know," he said, his face softening. "Just as you know I love you."

It was the first time he had said the words. She did know it by the way he touched her, treated her, and the way he spoke to her. But a woman needed to hear it all the same.

"Then when are you going to ask me to be yours?"

He tugged at her long, dark hair. She had left it free because he had asked her to. "I wanted to give you time. You lost both of your brothers in one day."

"All I ever need is you."

Daman set his goblet down on the table and cupped her face with his hands. "Innes MacKay, yours was the only voice I heard in my sleep. Yours was the only touch I felt. As soon as I woke, all I wanted was to find you. Even without my voice, we were able to communicate. With a voice or without, I'm no' me without you.

"I wasna going to let David have you that day. I didna care if I had to fight thousands of armies. I was willing to do it to have you by my side, to have you as mine. From the first moment you spoke, from the first time you touched me, I've been yours."

Innes felt the tears spill down her face. Daman's face swam in her vision as she listened to his words.

"Be mine. For now and always. Will you consent to be my wife and rule this clan beside me?"

Her throat was clogged with emotion. All she could do was nod, and then he was kissing her.

Gypsies, magic, curses, and love. Innes didn't know how Ilinca knew the four Highlanders would bring about such change in the clans, and it didn't matter. The men were there, and the women who fell in love with them were willing to stand with them no matter what the future held.

Daman had saved the MacKay clan. He had also saved her. That last bit might not have been in the prophecy, but Innes didn't care. She knew the truth in her gypsy heart.

"Marry me. Right now," Daman said between kisses. "I've had the priest waiting for weeks."

Innes laughed as she jumped up and started running out of the castle toward the chapel. She didn't get very far before Daman grabbed her hand.

Then they were in the chapel, surrounded by friends – family, really – as they became husband and wife.

"My wife," Daman said with a smile.

"My rogue."

AFTERWORD

Thank you for reading **Rogues of Scotland Box Set**. I hope you enjoyed the stories! If you liked this book – or any of my other releases – please consider rating the book at the online retailer of your choice. Your ratings and reviews help other readers find new favorites, and of course there is no better or more appreciated support for an author than word of mouth recommendations from happy readers. Thanks again for your interest in my books!

To live in the light, they hunt in the dark…turn the page to get a sneak peek of EVERSONG, the first book in the popular The Kindred series.

EXCERPT OF EVERSONG

THE KINDRED SERIES, BOOK ONE

West Morland, England
September 1349

It was a good day for hunting witches. Then again, Leoma believed every day was a good day to hunt.

She kept the hood of her cloak pulled forward to conceal her face as she meandered through the crowd. The few days of fair weather they'd enjoyed, allowed the soggy ground a chance to dry so that mud no longer squished beneath her shoes. The market was filled with people, and while she detested the crush of bodies, it gave her cover.

Chickens squawked, men yelled, women haggled, and even a dog or two barked. The smell of freshly baked bread and raw fish, along with rank body odor, clung to everything. Leoma ignored all of it, including the children that ran through the market without a care or worry—picking pockets when they could.

With her pace unhurried, it was easy to blend in with the crowd while her gaze was focused on her quarry—Brigitta.

The witch was easy to pick out with her flagrant beauty that she happily showed off.

Leoma battled the rising hatred within her. Edra, her mentor, warned her about letting anger rule. But it was becoming more and more difficult to keep it at bay.

While Leoma had begun learning to battle witches the day Edra and Radnar found her starving on the streets, it hadn't been until Brigitta cruelly and viciously killed Leoma's closest friend that she truly understood vengeance.

"Ease your mind."

Leoma inhaled deeply as Edra's words came back to her. While releasing her breath, Leoma centered herself. It had been six weeks since she left the safe haven of the abbey ruins Edra and Radnar had made into a home.

All those years of training with various weapons and learning how to fight against witches were being put to the test. This wasn't the first time Leoma had gone hunting, but it was her first time alone.

For weeks, she had been steadily closing in on Brigitta. Two days ago, Leoma finally found her. It was obvious by the way the witch traveled with determination that she had a specific destination in mind.

It was really too bad she would never make it.

Leoma smiled, her hand on the hilt of her sword hidden beneath her black cloak. She couldn't wait to sink the blade into the witch's heart. Or better yet, slice off her head.

Meg's face popped into her mind. Leoma had to close her eyes against the assaulting image of her best friend's decapitated body.

If only Leoma hadn't insisted they split up in order to corner the witch. If only she'd realized that Meg was terrified. If only….

There were so many regrets that haunted her, and Leoma was sure they would remain until her dying day.

She touched the inside of her left forearm. Before she left her family, another tattoo had been added to her body. The Vegvisir.

The Icelandic word meant signpost, but the magical stave was much more than that. It helped the bearer find their way and never become lost. The Vegvisir would not only help Leoma track Brigitta, but it would also bring Leoma back to her family.

She dropped her arm and moved away from a cart to continue following the witch. It was only Brigitta's habit of remaining right in the mix of people that kept Leoma from attacking. Because Leoma wouldn't have the weight of any more innocent deaths on her conscience.

If she had to track the witch for a year in order to get her alone, then that's what Leoma would do.

Brigitta suddenly halted and looked over her shoulder. Leoma ducked behind a building. She peered around the corner, her gaze taking in Brigitta's stunning face with her long, black hair up in braids, and bright blue eyes that seemed to hold everyone entranced—everyone except Leoma.

A few moments later, the witch continued on. Crowds parted without Brigitta ever saying a word. It was as if others recognized the power within her without understanding what they felt.

While men stared after Brigitta in a lust-filled haze, none were brave enough to approach. It sickened Leoma that so many were so easily manipulated by a beautiful face. Couldn't they tell the witch could end them with a thought? Did they even care?

To Leoma's surprise, Brigitta stopped again and simply looked around as if searching for something.

Or someone.

Leoma remained hidden, wondering just what the witch

was up to. Had it not been for Edra, Leoma would never know that there was magic in the world, or that there was a Coven who recruited the most powerful witches in order to grow.

For what exactly, no one knew. Yet.

But that knowledge was something Leoma hoped to bring back to the abbey.

The Coven once sought Edra. They had hunted her for seven years until Edra took a stand. With the love of her life, Radnar, by her side, Edra defeated the witches sent to either bring her into the fold or kill her. That's when Edra decided to create her own coven—a Hunter's Coven.

Leoma was the first of the homeless, abandoned, and starving children that Radnar and Edra found. Some trained like Leoma, and others, like Meg, found different duties at the abbey.

No one was forced to do anything they didn't want to do, but everyone pulled their weight. It allowed Radnar and Edra to supply a safe place for anyone who wanted or needed it.

Leoma couldn't imagine growing up any other way. While Radnar had been her first teacher, he hadn't been her only or her last. Other knights and warriors found their way to Radnar and helped train those wanting to be a part of the Hunter's Coven.

The sword Leoma carried had been designed by Radnar and created by Berlag, their master blacksmith. And then Edra had filled it with magic so Leoma could kill witches.

Because a witch could survive a normal blade. It took something special to make sure a sorceress remained dead. And Leoma would make damn sure Brigitta never hurt anyone again. It might very well cost Leoma her life, and she accepted that.

As soon as she saw the witch move, Leoma scanned the crowd, looking for anyone who could be meeting up with

Brigitta. Leoma might get lucky and find a second witch. It wouldn't be the first time she fought multiples.

She had the scars—and the tattoos—to prove it.

Leoma counted to twenty before she slid from her hiding spot to follow Brigitta. To her surprise, the witch walked into the Three Moons. Leoma flattened her lips as she eyed the tavern.

It wasn't that she minded going into such establishments, it was just that she spent most of her time fending off advances from drunken idiots who thought that anyone with breasts was fair game for a tumble into bed.

But she wasn't going to let that stop her from discovering all she could about Brigitta, just in case Leoma did survive the battle and made it back to the abbey. Any information— no matter how inconsequential—was needed.

She made her way around the building made up of small stones and wooden pillars to make sure the witch didn't sneak out the back. Then Leoma waited until she found a group of men walking into the pub. She snuck behind them and went unseen by most.

The tavern was packed. Loud, boisterous groups singing and laughing occupied several long tables. Those enjoying food and drink took other, smaller tables.

Leoma noted the hearth and roaring fire, as well as the shadowed parts of the interior. She quickly found a smaller table with an elderly couple who didn't bat an eye when she sat with them. Leoma gave the woman a nod and set a few coins on the table before sliding them toward her.

The woman took the money and didn't look at Leoma again. That allowed Leoma to let her gaze wander the tavern as she inhaled the delicious aroma of food, which was prob- ably why the place was so popular.

With little effort, Leoma picked out the men she knew could be trouble. Danger filled the air around them like a dark cloud despite their laughter and noise—or perhaps because of it. They drank too much and made sure everyone could hear their boasting. But so far, the men were content to focus on imbibing instead of fighting.

Just before her gaze moved away, she spied someone she had somehow previously overlooked—twice. He sat motionless in a shadowed corner with a mug of ale before him and his gaze directed toward the stairs.

She eyed him, wondering how she could have missed him in her perusal of the occupants. She put his face to memory. Dark hair, thick with just a hint of wave, that fell loose to his shoulders. A lean, rugged face that had sharp cheekbones and a square jaw with a slight indent in his chin ensnared all her senses.

His lips were wide and sinfully full. Thick brows slashed over piercing eyes a deep color she couldn't quite discern from the distance.

Leoma couldn't remember ever encountering a man with such a striking face before, and the fact that she didn't want to look away disturbed her greatly.

But it wasn't just his features that captured her attention. There was an air about him that declared he and battle were well acquainted. If he were a knight, his plain brown cloak and leather jerkin beneath hid the chainmail. He reclined in the chair as if he didn't have a care in the world, and yet his expression told a different story. He was intent on something.

Perhaps he was hunting, as well.

She regretted that she wouldn't find out for sure because she was intrigued. And she almost felt sorry for whoever the man was after. He seemed the type who would not give up until he ran his target to ground.

Leoma pulled her gaze away and looked at the table. This would be the time when Meg told her to flirt. Meg had always pushed Leoma to do the things she watched others do. Her friend made her a part of the world instead of just someone observing it.

But Leoma was better at watching. The few times she tried to do as others did, it hadn't turned out well. It's why Leoma was so suited to witch hunting. It was a solitary business. And she was damn good at it.

She began to wonder how long she would have to wait for some sign of Brigitta when the witch walked down the stairs with a young woman. Their heads were close together as they whispered.

Leoma saw Brigitta pass a small bag to the woman before they reached the bottom step. The woman hugged Brigitta and hurried to the back of the tavern with a bright smile in place as silence fell over the occupants.

Brigitta's grin was coy and sly when she caught men staring. She gave them a little wave before walking out. Leoma glanced at the back of the tavern. A part of her knew she needed to see what the witch had given the woman, but Leoma didn't want to lose Brigitta.

Yet, if Leoma found her once, she could again. Leoma waited until the conversation in the taproom resumed, and then she discreetly rose and made her way to the back.

"I got it," came a feminine voice.

Leoma leaned around the corner to find the woman showing the bag to a man.

"We can have a child now," the woman said excitedly.

The man eyed the bag. "I'm not sure about such methods."

Leoma knew the risks involved with using magic for such things. The couple would be indebted to Brigitta forever. And the witch wouldn't hesitate to take what she wanted from them—most likely their firstborn child. There was no way Leoma could allow that to happen.

She put a smile on her face and walked toward the

couple. "My apologies. I don't mean to interrupt, but I think I'm lost."

The woman set the bag on a table near the hearth as she turned to Leoma. "It sometimes happens. Would you like something to eat?"

The tavern owner hurried out to the customers when someone shouted for more ale, leaving Leoma with his wife. The first thing Leoma had learned in her training was to be swift of hand.

She walked closer while the woman spoke. "This is a wonderful place. I'm glad I stopped in."

"That pleases me greatly to hear," the woman beamed.

When the wife glanced out the doorway, Leoma swiped the bag. "Can you show me the way out, so I do not get lost again?"

The woman's smile grew tight, most likely irritated at being interrupted, but she replied, "Of course."

Just before Leoma followed the woman out, she tossed the bag into the fire.

Leoma began searching for Brigitta as soon as she was out of the tavern. She caught a glimpse of the witch heading west and made to follow when the same gorgeous man from the tavern snared her attention. She allowed herself a moment to stare while he saddled a horse. But it was the way his gaze kept returning to Brigitta that made her frown.

Leoma hoped the man wouldn't interfere. She'd hate to have to put him on his arse, but she'd do it in a heartbeat. The witch was her prize.

≈

Read more from EVERSONG
available now at www.DonnaGrant.com

ABOUT THE AUTHOR

 *New York Times* and *USA Today* bestselling author Donna Grant has been praised for her "totally addictive" and "unique and sensual" stories. She's written more than one hundred novels spanning multiple genres of romance including the *New York Times* bestselling *Dark Kings* series featuring immortal Highlander shape shifting dragons who are daring, untamed, and seductive. She lives with her two children, two dogs, and four cats in Texas.

www.DonnaGrant.com
www.MotherofDragonsBooks.com

facebook.com/AuthorDonnaGrant

instagram.com/dgauthor

bookbub.com/authors/donna-grant

amazon.com/Donna-Grant

goodreads.com/Donna_Grant

pinterest.com/donnagrant1

NEVER MISS A NEW BOOK

FROM DONNA GRANT!

Be the first to get notified of new releases and be eligible for special subscribers-only exclusive content and giveaways. Sign up today!

∾

Sign up for Donna's email newsletter at
www.DonnaGrant.com

Made in United States
North Haven, CT
28 January 2024

48034220R00212